Arcane Felonies

Ava L. Bishop & Auburn Tempest

Copyright © 2023 Dauntless Publishing Inc

All rights reserved. No part of this publication may be reproduced, distributed or transmitted in any form or by any means, without prior written permission.

Cover Design: BookCoversbyMelody

Note: The moral right of the author has been asserted.

This is a work of fiction. Names, characters, places and incidents either are the product of the author's imagination or are used fictitiously, and any resemblance to actual persons, living or dead, business establishments, events, or locales is entirely coincidental.

No part of this publication may be reproduced, stored in a retrieval system or transmitted, in any form or by any means without the prior written permission of the author, nor be otherwise circulated in any form of binding or cover other than that in which it is published and without a similar condition being imposed on the subsequent buyer.

The scanning, uploading, and distribution of this book via the Internet or via any other means without the permission of the author is illegal and punishable by law. Please purchase only authorized electronic editions, and do not participate in or encourage electronic piracy of copyrighted materials.

Your support of the author's rights is appreciated.

Dauntless Publishing Inc — 1st ed.

ISBN: 978-1-990853-78-4

CHAPTER ONE

*T*here was no magic in the world that could keep me from tossing my cookies within ten minutes of setting foot on a boat—or any watercraft, really. It had been the same since I was eight and made my family's trip to Disney World disgustingly memorable. I closed down Splash Mountain for an entire afternoon, not to mention the disaster at the lazy river ride. Even my sister, Lindsey, had pinky sworn to never speak of it again.

The icy gray waves of the Atlantic Ocean slapped against the hull of the boat, spraying salt water into my face. I groaned and clung to the railing, praying for the sweet mercy of shore. I had pulled my hair back into a tight knot, but the shrieking wind tore some sad little coppery strands loose to lash at my face. If there was any mercy in the world, I wouldn't puke into my hair, because that would be the absolute topper to the day.

The captain of the charter boat gave me a look that I could only describe as concern mixed with a healthy dash of condescension for the landlubber. "Miss, we're not even out of the harbor yet."

I wanted to say something snotty, but the boat heaved again, and my stomach tried to do the same. Gritted teeth and every ounce of will in my body was all that kept me from being sick. Instead, I ended up sweating and draped over the railing like a painting of some sad Victorian maiden.

The captain shook his head, clearly fighting back a smile at my absolute misery. "We mostly get people looking to fish this late in the season. Bluefin tuna are biting this time of year. Not many, uh… sight seekers. The water's a bit rough."

A bit rough? That's what he called screaming winds colder than the freaking arctic circle, and waves that bounced the boat up and down like a trampoline park? If I could focus enough to do math, I could've calculated how much energy I'd need to suck out of the Boston harbor to freeze the whole thing. Then I could've *walked* to where I needed to go.

It was almost December. That could've worked. Probably.

A broad hand touched my back, and when I didn't kick up a fuss, it stroked my spine. I could barely feel it through the sweater and puffy coat I wore, but it was still a welcome gesture.

Another chunk of my hair broke free, snapping around my face like Medusa's snakes. Bastian leaned forward and dutifully smoothed it back. I could have kissed him—if I wasn't afraid I would puke on him—but instead, I forgave him for being all calm and untouched by the boat's horrible rolling.

"Anything I can do?" His low voice was a rumble, but he was pressed close enough that I could hear him over the roar of the engine.

Another wave slapped the boat, spraying salt water into my clammy face. "Can you open a Void space in my stomach and disintegrate everything in there before it comes back up?"

Bastian hummed and finished tying back the beast that was my hair. "I think that might actually make you implode."

I swallowed the saliva pooling in my mouth and tried to

focus on the horizon like the captain told me—it didn't help. "Fine. We'll call that Plan B, then."

Bastian chuckled at my side. While normally I would be happy to have coaxed it out of him, I was too sunk in my misery, clinging to the side of the ship so tightly they would need a crowbar to get me off at the end of this hell ride.

He leaned against the railing, looking completely at ease, his shaggy dark hair ruffling slightly in the wind. I took back my forgiveness. What the hell was that? Even the captain and his assistant had to brace themselves when the boat did a particularly nauseating roll. I had no idea how anyone could look that much like a fallen angel while wearing lime green sneakers and a life jacket so eye-searingly yellow it could probably be seen from space.

He squinted against the glare of the early morning sun reflecting off the waves. "Where are we headed?"

"The last sighting was just past Spectacle Island," I gritted out, my teeth locked together in a death rictus. "A cargo ship thought it was a basking whale shark. A fisherman reported it as a clump of garbage caught in the tide. It seems to stay in one area, so the tear must be around there."

There had been days since the Aether Storm tore its way across the world and ripped holes in the Akasha when I thought things would never calm down. The magical barrier was supposed to keep reality from ending up like an Escher picture, but since the failed ritual, raw creation had poured into the world, bringing people's random thoughts to life.

Normally, it took years to spawn something. There had to be a force of collective belief driving the Aether forward.

People just had to believe the lore hard enough to give it life.

But with the Akasha looking more like a sieve than a wall, random crap kept getting conjured. It had slowed down a lot from those first weeks after the storm, but now I was dealing with the harder to find tears in reality, which is why I had to charter a boat to take me out into Boston harbor in late November. The captain and his assistant were nice enough people, but between the sub-arctic cold and feeling like I might barf until I turned inside out, I couldn't recommend the trip.

Zero out of ten.

It didn't help that I didn't know what I was looking for. Magical creatures—or Aether-born—had an aura of disbelief surrounding them. It wasn't that people didn't see them... it was that the human brain ignored them or made them appear like something a mundane person could more easily understand.

A swarm of pixies might look like wasps. A zombie might look like a staggering transient. Unfortunately, that didn't keep the zombie Aether-born from eating passersby. The polite ignoring only went in one direction.

Whatever people had seen out in the water hadn't been a basking shark, or a pile of garbage—because trash didn't try to bite ships that got too close. And since my fellow Magi didn't have any interest in coming to Boston to clean up the little burps in reality, that meant that it was on me.

I couldn't blame them. They had their own cities to take care of. It was just... with Boston being ground zero for the whole disaster, things were more hectic in my stomping grounds.

At least I wasn't totally on my own.

"You know, I was a little disappointed when I first found out people don't actually turn green," Bastian said, holding out a bottle of water. "They just go pale. And you didn't have a lot of room to travel there to begin with."

"Sorry to let you down." I glanced at the bottle and shook my head. "It'll just be ammunition at this point."

I could have explained how it was the byproduct of dead white blood cells that made the skin color most people thought of as illness 'green', but by that point stubbornness—and maybe magic—were the only things keeping my extremely light break-fast down.

Seaton University might have kicked me out of my PhD program, but they couldn't do anything about the geekiness. That was terminal.

Bastian gave me another sympathetic pat on the back.

I appreciated him coming with me for moral support, at least. Of course, there was also the fact that he had been spawned from the Void—the most destructive force in the known universe—and that made him hell on wheels when it came to back up in a fight.

The other Magi and the Aether-born reacted to Bastian somewhere between disgust and pants-wetting terror. Assuming they hadn't fled when they felt his particular brand of black-hole nothingness strolling toward them. They all seemed weirdly hung up on the idea of the Void being bad or evil, which was dumb.

Entropy wasn't evil. It simply *was*.

And sure, Bastian could be a little uncanny valley at times, but he was also curious, intelligent, and went out of his way to help people, assuming they stayed still long enough for him to try.

He was also gorgeous... with chiseled cheekbones and a jaw that could cut glass, amazingly full lips, and eyes the color of the space between stars. He also kissed like he was starving for it, but I was trying not to think about that while losing the battle to keep down my coffee and a single piece of dry toast.

The captain was doing his best as a tour guide, thinking we were a happy couple out for a day of sightseeing on the water. He was straight up shouting by that point to be heard over the wind and the scream of seagulls overhead. Still, he tried to give us a brief rundown about Castle Island, and eventually resorted to waving his arms and pointing.

The pedantic part of my brain was hung up on the fact that Castle Island was actually a peninsula, but I did my best to cram that snotty little voice back into the closet.

5

The boat slid sideways over a wave that sprayed fishy, seaweed-scented water at me, and then the inevitable happened. Leaning over the rail… I chummed the water like a boss.

I had held out for nine minutes and thirty-seven seconds, and then all bets were off.

Bastian made sure I didn't plummet into the unforgiving sea, and then silently handed me the water bottle so I could rinse my mouth.

"How do I feel worse? What the hell?"

It was a curse. It had to be. Dark sorcery was at play here.

It was a good thing I first met Bastian when I was panicked, covered in road rash, and fleeing from monsters trying to eat me, because if I had any delusions about him thinking I was a calm, collected Magi about town, the past ten minutes would've smashed that image.

I took a sip of the water, and my stomach rolled. It didn't openly revolt, so it was something. "Thank you for the water. And sorry about all… this." I waved a hand, taking in the boat, the cloudy gray sky, and me.

Bastian leaned forward, bracing his forearms on the railing. "I was happy to come. I've never been on a boat like this before."

That made me pause, the water bottle halfway to my mouth. "But you've been on a boat, right? You would've had to have been at some point, right?"

"Oh, sure." The wind blew his inky hair across his brow. "I came to this country in a huge, three-masted frigate… but nothing like this."

It was easy to forget how old Bastian was. He didn't seem to know the exact year himself, but from the tidbits he dropped, I strongly suspected it was a length of time that would be measured in eras, not decades.

Normally, he acted like any other person, right until he did something like bite into a raw reaper pepper and chew like he was eating a carrot stick with no reaction. Or when I glimpsed him out of the corner of my eye, and he looked like he was way too big for the body he was wearing, like he should have existed in more dimensions than the four I was familiar with.

It was trippy.

But he was easygoing, didn't get grossed out, and—as mentioned—ridiculously hot.

The ship skipped a wave, and my stomach did a sympathetic backflip. "I should have brought an ice pack or something."

A broad, cool hand pressed against my forehead, and I almost groaned at how good it felt against my sweaty, flushed face. I made myself keep hanging onto the bottle and the railing, because pressing Bastian's hand to my face like a cat was a level of no chill I wasn't ready to drop to just yet.

"You're the best," I mumbled, closing my eyes. Bastian had always run cool—probably because he was a living embodiment of the infinite Void—but he wasn't as close to icy as he'd been when we first met.

Ever since we'd diverted the effects of the Aether Storm, Bastian had been changing. Not in any way that I noticed, other than him maybe being a bit more expressive. But Bastian— who'd been exactly the same since being created by a bunch of power-mad idiots trying to craft the world's greatest weapon— had sure noticed.

His hair was growing... for one thing.

I didn't say they were *huge* things.

I'd done that to him. I knew I had. I wasn't sure if I regretted it or felt guilty. I guess that would depend on if Bastian liked the changes or not. He seemed to like them. He enjoyed feeling things more, at least. Maybe it had been stupid, giving him that bit of Aether when we'd been merged to reroute the storm.

It had been so small... just a tiny seed of life.

Of course, magic wasn't any different from any other part of life—for every action, there was an equal and opposite reaction.

I shared the power of creation with Bastian, but only by taking in a little piece of the Void.

And even standing there, on the deck of a ship that was doing its best to make me barf up what I'd eaten for Christmas last year, I could feel it. The Void sat like a sliver of ice in my belly, the kind of cold no number of blankets or hot drinks could ever touch.

Bastian had gone still, even for him, and I pried my eyes open to find that he was staring at me, his face blank. It took me a second to rewind and go back over what I'd said... I told him he was the best. Was that wrong? "Sorry, did me complimenting you make it weird?"

Bastian smiled, his face relaxing, making him look like a person and not something carved out of marble. "No. It just isn't something I hear often."

Well, great. Now I was sad *and* seasick.

It just sucked. Bastian was a nice person—way nicer than I was, hands down. But people avoided him, even when they didn't know exactly how he'd come into the world. The magical community, if I could call it that, treated him like he had the radioactive plague.

Maybe it was because he came into my life while saving me, but he'd never felt threatening to me. I bumped my shoulder against his, still too worried about last night's dinner making a reappearance for anything closer. "I like that you're quiet inside."

His grin stretched into something blinding. He reached up and tweaked one of the strands of bright red hair that had weaseled its way free. "I like that you're vibrant."

Heat crept up into my face, and I couldn't keep a dumb grin from joining it. Was that how he saw me? Vibrant? "I think that's the nicest thing anyone's ever said to me."

He moved closer, and my breath caught in my throat. The sound of the motor fell away, even the wind died down to a gentle murmur. Warmth that had nothing to do with magic slipped through my veins like molten honey, and I braced myself against the railing to keep from pitching forward into those night-dark eyes.

Something slammed the bottom of the boat, rocking us into the air for a heart-stopping moment. The only thing that kept me from pitching overboard was Bastian yanking me forward into his chest. His arms felt like carved marble around me, locking me into place as he grabbed the railing with his free hand.

"Man, I cannot catch a break," I muttered into the nylon of his life jacket. My pulse was a thick beat at the side of my throat. Adrenaline prickled over my skin at the near fall.

"Sorry about that, folks," the captain called as the sound of the engine died. "Must've hit some underwater debris. Everyone okay? Still with us?"

"Yeah, we're good." It came out muffled, since my face was pressed against Bastian's chest. That seemed to remind him that he was squishing me, and he took a half step back, so I wasn't wedged between him and the railing anymore.

"What are the chances that it was actually debris?" he asked.

The sigh that came out of me felt like it had been dragged up from my toes. "With me on board? Almost nil."

While the captain and his helper fussed around checking for damage on the boat and ensured the propeller hadn't hit anything, I stared out over the choppy gray waters.

I'd made a lot of progress with magic since my first days as an apprentice Magi, when I mostly struggled not to set everything around me on fire any time I got agitated. A lot of that had to do with my mentor packaging up decades of his own experience and dropping it into my brain like a zip file before he went missing during a ritual backlash.

Still, I'd put a ton of work into my magic, trying to adapt it to how I viewed the world, and it had been going pretty well.

One thing I still super-duper sucked at, though, was reaching outside myself to 'sense' things going on in the world around me. Even thinking the word made me feel like I was meditating under a crystal pyramid, but the fact was, energies connected and bumped against each other, and it was possible for a Magi to read those currents.

I didn't want to because—as previously stated—I sucked at it, and we were standing on top of a chunk of highly flammable boat floating on the ocean. But the waters of the Atlantic were dark enough that there was no way to see anything over two inches below the surface. Something nasty could be hiding in the fathomless depths beneath my feet.

And with that cheerful thought...

"I'm going to take a look," I told Bastian. "Can you keep me from falling off the boat?"

His lips curled with amusement. "I think I can manage."

I took a deep breath as my eyes slipped closed. It didn't help, but it seemed like the thing to do. Reaching outside of myself was still weird as hell. I felt my body, but it was like my skin was too thin, or my senses were dialed up to twenty-seven, and also like none of those things.

This was the problem with magic. How the heck was I supposed to take notes for research if what I learned didn't make any sense?

Even with my eyes closed, the world exploded into a brilliant kaleidoscope of colors, the chaos of it igniting against the darkness of my eyelids. The ocean was every shade of blue and green, rushing currents flowing into and around each other like a twelve-dimension highway.

Hydrogen and oxygen atoms pulled and pushed in long chains.

There were so many little lives flowing with the currents. Some were so small a thousand of them fit into a drop of water

—others were almost bigger than I could wrap my brain around.

Golden and glowing, they moved like fireflies in the dark.

I tried to drown out the hum of the boat, the carefully contained explosions of the internal combustion engine. Bastian helped with that, his cool sinkhole presence at my back. The silence of him was echoing, slowing the stately dance of the world simply by existing in it.

Everything was connected in their strange ways. All things moved in the same patterns; different footwork, but the same dance. The world hummed the tune, and everything followed along, connected by tiny, thrumming threads of power.

I could've fallen into that pattern face first, lost myself in it, sunk down right to the bottom of the ocean, where the world ran thick and dark with a terrible gravity. But Bastian's hands on my hips were my anchor. He kept me aware enough of my body to not go flying off into the turning of the world.

I almost missed it, the tear in the world's wall. It was a huge, gaping thing just below us, but the ocean was enormous, so I figured it was an honest miss. Once I brushed against it, I knew it was what I was searching for. It felt like a wound in the pattern of the world, sluggishly bleeding pure creation into the depths of the ocean.

Not good.

Still, I didn't rush to yank it closed. If something came through—and all signs pointed to yes on that one—then sending that something back through the rip was the much easier path to getting rid of both.

All I had to do was branch out to find whatever Aether-born creature slipped through into the world, return it, seal up the tear, and then I could get off the boat and back onto sweet, sweet land.

I reached out and down, straining the edge of my awareness. Bastian's arm slipped around me, heavy and solid and grounding. The Atlantic was so freaking big. A lot of nautical miles to cover. Even outside of myself as I was, I felt the icy sweat beading along the edge of my hairline. Maybe I should've tried to use sonar. Did magical creatures show up with sonar? I wished there was someone I could've asked.

Something rushed through the water, sliding through the patterns of wave and current like a silver needle. It was big. It was fast. And it was hungry.

My eyes snapped open, and I grabbed Bastian's arm while the sudden shift back to myself left me staggering.

I hadn't needed to find it after all.

It found me.

CHAPTER TWO

The Aether-born creature slammed against the bottom of the boat, and I felt the resulting shockwave all the way through my sternum. The boat jolted into the air, tilting sickeningly while the captain and his crewman shouted and ran. I could barely make out the words through the roaring of my pulse in my ears. Water erupted around us as we slapped back down.

Bastian was like a rock the entire time. He didn't stagger, he didn't jump. He just stood there rooted, like even if the whole boat broke apart, he could just stay right there with his feet braced on the ocean.

I didn't want to test that, though, and not just because I suspected he'd sink like a rock.

I gripped the railing, the water I'd sipped sloshing around in my stomach. "Found it."

Bastian snorted.

And then the Aether-born breached, and any urge to laugh died in my throat.

It rose up and up and up, its shadow falling over the boat.

Waves slapped against heavy, sinuous coils as the sea serpent tipped its head to peer down at us.

My mouth went dry, my eyes so wide they felt like they might pop right out of my skull.

Big. It was really big… and right there, in my face. And in a weird, horrifyingly destructive way, it was almost beautiful.

Holy heck, that was way too many teeth.

Its scales were a dark, murky grayish-blue, but running along the length of its body were lines of bright red bioluminescence, highlighting heavy muscle and picking out the underside of scales like lines of trailing blood. Its head was long and tapered, more like a dragon than a snake, and oh man, I hoped it couldn't breathe fire or acid or anything like that.

It looked like the kind of creatures explorers used to draw at the edge of maps to warn people that travelling past that point was cloudy with a high chance of death.

Red bioluminescence—that was rare.

Blue was way more common, so that was what most deep-sea creatures could see. Red was the opposite end of the visible light spectrum, which meant the behemoth would be effectively invisible down in the abyssal depths of the ocean.

Bastian's arm flexed around my waist, dragging me back to myself.

Right—survive now, admire later.

After the alarming heave into the air, the captain and the crewman were checking the engine and the side of the ship. The general aura of non-belief that protected people from seeing Aether-born meant they hadn't noticed the enormous snake monster about to take a chunk out of us.

Too bad not seeing monsters didn't keep them from eating people.

It also meant they weren't going to help me by getting out of the way. So, when the serpent opened its mouth opened wide—

and boy was there a lot of teeth crammed in that mouth—and darted forward, I grabbed for the Aether.

Always hovering at the edge of reality, golden and glowing and exploding with potential, the magical energy encircling worlds rushed eagerly into my hands.

Kinetic force was the force of motion, and I needed us to move—like yesterday.

A twist and some creative work with a couple of laws of thermodynamics, and I *shoved* at the water. The ship surged forward so fast that the bow lifted into the air. The captain staggered, and might have fallen right off the back if his buddy hadn't grabbed him.

The serpent hit the spot where the boat had sat a couple seconds before, water fountaining up into the sky, and the mini tidal wave pushed us further out of range.

Stupid maritime traditions. Stupid local legends.

Sea serpents were a pretty staple myth among coastal communities, and that meant the full force of the Aether, backed by people's beliefs, would be behind the monster. Never mind taking a bite out of things, it was only a matter of time before it started sinking ships.

Okay, so it had to go. I was pretty laid back with Aether-born, especially compared to my fellow Magi. They tended toward the 'banish on sight, no thank you' method. I normally left them alone to live their lives—assuming living their lives didn't involve mass destruction and eating people.

Of course, that left me with the question of how the hell I was going to catch the damn thing when it had the entire freaking Atlantic Ocean to hide in.

This was why I hated boats and water. For millions of years, creatures had evolved to survive in the pitch-black, crushing depths below us, which meant that every single one of them was automatically better in it than me.

The easiest way would be to convince the sea serpent to go

back through the torn spot in the Akasha, and then patch the hole behind it. But something told me it wasn't in much of a listening mood.

"I don't think I'll be much help," Bastian said, sounding way too calm and vaguely apologetic. "If I let loose enough Void to dust it, I'm probably going to take the boat, too."

The thought of suddenly finding myself treading water a mile out to sea had a shudder ripping down my spine. Hard pass.

"Yeah, let's not disintegrate our host's boat." My stomach twisted as I scanned the water. I couldn't see a thing. Every ripple of the waves could be an enormous shape rising out of the depths to take us out, and I didn't want to reach out again to find it because I might be too slow to react if it tried to eat us.

Breathe, Aisling.

I pulled in a shaky breath. Okay. I needed to think and plan it out. I wanted the sea serpent to go back through the Akasha where it would be the Aether's problem again. I didn't have anything to bribe it with, and somehow doubted it would go if I asked nicely.

I didn't want to *kill* the beast—it was basically an animal doing its thing and living its life—but having it kill *us* wasn't an option either.

So, full-on assault was the only course of action.

No matter how deep into the woo-woo my life had plunged, I couldn't wrap my head around a lot of the things my fellow Magi believed. No candles, or chanting, or crystals for me. And the whole 'earth is one of the four elements' bullshit didn't work either.

Dirt was comprised of forty different elements on its own.

No. I had spent years slogging my way through academia, working toward my PhD in physics, and that was still very much how I saw the world.

Everything was made up of molecules, even big scary sea

monsters that could have destroyed our boat at any second. And molecules could be manipulated, especially when I had the full power of the Aether behind me, letting me directly manipulate on the macro level.

I couldn't outmuscle the behemoth. When you can't go big, go small.

I reached for the power again, filling myself with the feeling of warm sunlight on the inside of my skull, and twisting it into a familiar shape. There were reasons people used harpoons at sea, and it wasn't for aesthetic. Why fix what isn't broken?

The worst part was waiting. The slap of water against the boat was too loud. The wind was too strong, too abrasive, numbing my skin. Every part of me was tense, standing there in Bastian's arms like a statue.

The current below us stirred, and the boat jostled.

I tensed... my breath stuck in my throat like a rock.

It came from beneath us, a huge maw opened to bite the boat in half. I launched the energy in my hands, and it flew through the air, right into the monster's throat.

There was no blood. It wasn't a *real* harpoon, after all. That was just the easiest way for me to picture it. No, I wasn't trying to kill the thing. I had something very different in mind.

Quantum entanglement: when different molecules work together and form a system that can no longer be seen as separate from each other. The power I launched roared through the sea serpent, uniting it as one with my will.

Too bad I hadn't thought about the momentum.

I had a single moment, standing there holding my rope of light energy like a dope, thinking, *oh shit*. The serpent's mouth kept coming toward us, backed by some serious tonnage of muscle.

Then Bastian lunged forward and grabbed hold of the line. With a twist of his hips, he heaved with his arms, whipping the line up and over the boat.

And the entire freaking sea serpent followed the arc. Heavy coils and scales blocked out the sun overhead as it whipped by in an arch. The boat lurched down, water cascading over the railing. I was pretty sure I heard something crack, and the captain shouted, but I couldn't make out the words because I was too busy standing there with my mouth slack.

At least I kept it together enough to hang onto the line after Bastian let go.

Hot damn, arm strength.

I shook it off, my fingers convulsing over the line of power in my hands. It took some mental footwork, but I sent my will down the line, taking control.

It was a bit like puppeteering a marionette. If the marionette was three thousand pounds and really wanted to eat your face. The serpent was fighting me. It was hungry, angry, a little freaked out at being flung like a guppy, too. But I didn't care about controlling it for long. I twitched my will along the line of entangled molecules and used the line like reins.

Sweat beaded along the back of my neck as my pulse thudded. The wind howled, dragging the breath from my mouth, and I grit my teeth and bore down on the line between the serpent and me.

With a wrench and a yank, that huge body sailed right through the tear in the Akasha, and the second the last few feet of tail vanished through the veil between worlds, I slammed it closed.

I slapped Aether over the hole in the worst spackle job in history. Piled heaps of it, smoothing more and more into position until I was worried it might cause problems in other places. Only then did I sag forward against the railing, my breath coming in short, sharp bursts.

Bastian folded his arms on the rail and leaned down beside me. "Are you okay?"

I opened my mouth to answer, and the boat pitched again. I

had to slam my teeth together as my stomach turned over, and for one terrifying, mortifying second, I thought I was going to throw up on Bastian.

The moment passed, and I let my head hang over the rail, watching the gray-green waters ripple. "Please just tell them to get us back to shore."

With a chuckle and a light pat on my back, Bastian moved to talk to the captain.

He'd just suplexed a sea monster for me, so I wouldn't get pissy about his obvious amusement. The boat rolled again, and the smell of seaweed and fish and salt had my stomach sloshing and me praying for a merciful death.

If the monsters didn't get me, the waves would.

CHAPTER THREE

$\mathcal{A}$fter groaning goodbye to Bastian, I staggered home to take a long, hot shower. I chugged down a cup of tea while doing my best not to taste it, and I almost felt human again.

The sun was setting, painting the sky in plum and indigo. I had a great view of it through the enormous window that dominated the far wall of the apartment. I snuggled down on the couch and tossed a blanket over my legs as I dragged out my notes and the files on my laptop.

After years of student housing and roommates of varying terribleness, I hadn't even known Boston had apartments that nice. It was a little old-fashioned, and the elevator was more decoration than anything else, but it was an amazing, open concept loft—built in the days before people knew about open concept lofts.

It was also rent controlled... and had come furnished— except for my bedroom.

Of course, it did have a couple drawbacks.

The bedroom door opposite mine cracked open, and one

brilliant, citron-colored eye peeked out. I stared, my mug halfway to my mouth. "What are you doing?"

When nothing jumped out at him, Stefan cracked the door open a little further and stuck his head out. "I'm checking to see if your terrifying boyfriend is here."

That set off a weird mix of feelings. A little thrill ran through me, followed by something close to exasperation, which tended to be my default emotion when I was dealing with my roommate.

My notes dropped into my lap, and I twisted on the couch so I could see him easier. "First of all, Bastian isn't my boyfriend." Unfortunately. I mean, we shared a frankly incredible kiss, but it was a 'save the world' moment, and then he disappeared for a while and we never talked about it. Ever. But we spent a lot of time together, and he volunteered to come along with me if I was doing something potentially dangerous, so I knew he at least liked me a little.

I just didn't know how much. Besides, 'boyfriend' felt juvenile for a person who might have been over a millennium old. He was a bit shaky on the passage of time.

All of that was so freaking junior high it made me roll my eyes at myself.

"Second, I don't get why you're scared of him. He came with me to rescue your pasty butt when you got kidnapped, remember? Why would he put in that kind of effort if he wanted to turn you into a fine powder? And third, what the hell, Stefan? You're a *vampire*."

"So?" he demanded. He stopped hiding in his room, stepping out to lean his shoulder against the doorframe. He crossed his arms over his chest, almost cradling the curves of his pectorals left visible by his artfully unbuttoned shirt. It had to be on purpose. "That doesn't mean what it used to."

Once upon a time, in the bad old days of the dark ages, Stefan had spawned into existence straight out of a Slavic nightmare. A 'vampir', which was basically a half a step up from what we called zombies today. Gross, shambling, searching the night for blood with little in the way of cognitive thought. But, as the years passed and mankind's collective belief of what exactly a vampire was changed, the Aether updated Stefan accordingly.

From a blood-swollen corpse to a swooshy-haired teen heartthrob with prominent cheekbones, a sulky mouth, and a jaw line I could have whittled a stake with. He once told me if he ever started to sparkle again, he would throw himself into the sunlight and end it all.

Still, Stefan was a top tier predator with superpowers, while Bastian was a laid-back guy who loved puzzles and black and white movies who, admittedly, contained the power of all destruction and entropy within him. But it wasn't like he went around murdering people willy-nilly. I didn't understand why so many people were ready to wet themselves at the sight of him.

Of course, I'd seen him dunk chicken nuggets into a chocolate milkshake, so there were the occasional horrors.

Stefan made his way toward the couch, but when he reached out to touch some of my papers, I gave him a glare that was a solid seven on my personal scale. It was my heated scowl that had almost reduced undergrads to tears occasionally.

He snorted and perched on the opposite arm instead.

"Bastian isn't scary."

He peered at me like he was waiting for a punchline. When one didn't emerge, he shuddered. "Maybe you feel something else when he's around. But trust me, he's plenty scary."

It wasn't a fight I was going to win, so I didn't bother. Instead, I grabbed a few more scraps of notes and put them into a better order. Compiling everything into a single file was the better way to go, but somehow writing things down long-hand made them stick better in my brain, so I always ended up with a pile of scrap paper, napkins from various restaurants, and on one memorable occasion, an eighth of a roll of toilet paper.

Stefan frowned down at the pile of clutter in resignation. He'd seen my bouts of work before, so he was familiar with the chaotic burst of mess that spread over the living room. I never left it for more than a couple of hours, so he didn't comment, and I used the time to shuffle my papers into something resembling an order to give him a good look over.

Ever since Stefan was kidnapped by a cult of wannabe Magi who tried to harvest him for energy, I'd been worried about him. Not that I could let on that I was concerned. Stefan reacted to people caring for him like cats did to being dunked in cold water. That had probably been the closest to death he'd been in over five hundred years.

But he hadn't been going out as much as he used to, and even weirder, he hadn't been bringing home his usual parade of nighttime guests. There was a time when I bought a sleeve of takeout cups so his partners could have a coffee on their way out the door, and they were now gathering dust in the cupboard.

He felt safer at the apartment, especially with the wards and protections I set in place, but I didn't know how else to help him. I couldn't just *ask*, because both of us would rather chew glass than have a talk about feelings of any kind.

Still... as much as I hated it... I was worried.

Stefan was a horndog and drank blood, but he wasn't even in the bottom five of roommates I'd had, and I hated seeing him nervy.

He picked up a couple of sheets of paper with equations scrawled across them, ignoring my warning glare. His head tipped to one side, and he flipped the paper upside down, like that would help him read it. "What are these for? They look like hieroglyphics."

"I'm... looking for something." Some*one*, really. I worried my

23

lower lip between my teeth, looking over my work. I hadn't made much in the way of progress, but I also couldn't sit around and do nothing.

Giving up wasn't my style.

When I was first tossed headlong into a world of ghoulies, ghosties, and all the things that went bump in the night—and sometimes at four in the afternoon—I survived because of Cornelius Abernathy.

He was pompous, high-handed, and at times downright infuriating, but he also took me under his wing and showed me the ropes. I only knew how to manipulate the Aether because of him. Heck, if he hadn't shown up, I would've been eaten by a metal praying mantis monster the first night I touched magic.

And then, in the middle of a sabotaged ritual to shore up the weakening Akasha, he disappeared along with the entire Senior Council of Magi. One minute, almost thirty of the most powerful people in the world were united to save humanity. The next, a handful of terrified apprentices were alone and trying to survive a horrific magical storm that tore across the world.

It'd been months since that night, and I was still mopping up the aftereffects—like the sea serpent in the bay—but I hadn't seen a single sign of Cornelius.

The man could turn dirt into diamonds and make a portal that took him from Cambridge to Marblehead in a fraction of a second. I couldn't picture anywhere he could've gotten blasted where he couldn't jump right back, polishing his glasses in annoyance.

Unless he couldn't.

That had to be the reason. It was the only reason that I'd accept.

"Why don't you use the spell that helped you track me down when I got pinched?" Stefan twisted the page again, scowling in a way people usually reserved for baby puke, and I snatched the paper out of his hands.

"It's not that simple." Sure, that spell worked. I used a bit of Stefan's 'energy', to follow him to a crappy cult leader's layer in time to save him. But Stefan had been in SoWa, which, while an annoying drive, was still in Boston, and in the same realm of existence. "I'm pretty sure what I'm trying to find is in the Akasha."

When Cornelius introduced me to magical nonsense 101, the way he described the Akasha was a barrier between worlds. It was what kept the raw force of the Aether from crashing into the world and the Void. Reality kind of hung in a perpetual stalemate between creation and destruction.

It was probably poetic in some light.

But over the course of trying to track down some missing Aether-born and dealing with a bunch of angry Magi who hadn't been super happy with the whole Aether Storm situation, I found that it might be more than a magical wall.

The Akasha was a *realm*. A place, not a thing.

Similar to how marshlands act as a buffer between water and dry ground, the Akasha buffered realms. And if my hypothesis was correct, that was where I'd find the Senior Council. Calculating where an object might end up based on the movement of the tide, or the wind, or the gravitational pull of the earth, was doable.

Trying to calculate where someone might disappear to when I didn't even know how many dimensions might be involved? That was a fast track to nowhere.

Not that I hadn't broken my brain trying to do it, anyway.

Stefan gave a low whistle. "You don't make your life easy, do you? How will you find it?"

Wasn't that the ten-million-dollar question? Sure, I knew I could tear the Akasha. Normally, my problem was trying to magically spackle the holes over and keep every random passing fancy from popping into reality. But then what? I had absolutely no idea what was on the other side, how to navigate it, or how to track someone down once I was there.

I flopped back against the couch cushions like my bones had vanished. "I have no fricking idea. I don't know enough about it, but anytime I ask the other Magi, they all look at me like my head has spun around, and I've started speaking in tongues. I get the impression there are capital R 'rules' about that kind of thing, but that is extremely not helpful."

Stefan's nose wrinkled, and he pushed a takeout menu covered in formulas away from him like it was some kind of arcane script that might blow up in his face. "So, ask someone else."

I gave him the look the comment deserved. "Wow, they weren't kidding when they said with age comes wisdom. The problem is, the one person who I know understands the Akasha and claims to have real estate there, scares the pee out of me."

The Dragon was one of the most powerful Magi in the entire world. He would have to be to have the moniker 'The Dragon' and no one making fun of him for it. And to be fair, he'd been nothing but an attentive host when I was summoned by a bunch of really scary people angry at the Council. He did his best to put me at ease, but it was hard to relax when sitting in a room with people when I could *feel* the power inside of them.

It was like having a tea party while surrounded by half a dozen active nukes.

Plus, if I went to the Dragon for help, I'd probably have to explain why I wanted to get into the Akasha. I was the worst liar ever, and he'd likely find out the entire Senior Council was MIA, and only a handful of scrappy apprentices were left.

Considering how many people seemed to have beef with the 'Council of the Seven Spheres', it didn't seem like a good idea to spill that particular tea.

Stefan flicked a doodled-on napkin at me. "Talk to the Fae. They owe you one, anyway."

"The Fae?" I frowned, smoothing the rescued napkin back out. "I don't think failing to find their murdered friend is something that deserves any kind of payback. Besides, why would the Faeries know about the Akasha?"

The Fae I met last month had been a lot of things. Charming, beautiful, clever, bordering on cunning, but they hadn't struck me as people who made deep studies about things. On the other hand, they knew enough about the Aether and how to manipulate it to their advantage to bankroll some key pop culture and change human perception. They went from being twee little beings with wings, to tall, pointy-eared runway models... so, what did I know?

Stefan squinted at me for long enough that it was uncomfortable, then shook his head. "Yeah, you didn't find him. He was probably dead before they ever even asked you for help. But you still *looked*. You gave a crap. Do you seriously not understand how rare that is?"

The urge to sink down into the couch cushions was almost overwhelming. I was tempted to tuck my head into my sweater like the awkward turtle I was, but managed to resist. "Anyone would have."

"No," he said, much too solemnly for my sketchy, annoying vampire roommate. "They wouldn't. Besides, the Fae live in the Akasha. Where did you think the Faerie Realms were?"

"Wait, what?" I shot upright so fast I almost fell off the couch. "What the hell? Why didn't you tell me that, like, a month ago?"

Stefan reared back like an offended cat. "I thought you knew. You got shitty training. How am I supposed to know what you do and don't have a handle on?"

Like most times when I spent more than fifteen minutes consecutively in Stefan's presence, a headache bloomed to life

27

behind my right eye. The worst part was, I couldn't even be mad. My training *had* been crappy. Cornelius had done his best, but after a couple of weeks of me sucking, he simply dumped a packet of his memories into my skull of the things he thought I might need.

It had worked for a while, even if not in the way he'd thought it would. But that too had faded a few weeks back, leaving me so far out at sea that I didn't even know enough to understand what I didn't know.

Now I felt stupid for not piecing it together myself. We'd literally travelled from Franklin Park at night to some crazy magic forest with enough crap floating in the air to look like an eighties fantasy movie and furniture that looked like it had been grown, not made.

Suddenly tired, I rubbed my eyes. "Yeah, okay. Could you see if they'd meet with me? I don't really know how to contact them."

Stefan shifted and chewed his bottom lip. A hint of fang peeked out before he gave a curt nod. "Yeah. Yeah, okay. I guess."

I knew it took a lot for him to agree, but I didn't want to thank him and make it weird. So, I nodded and turned back to my papers—as useless as they were—and sat quietly until the tension eased out of him.

He needed time. I knew that. Luckily, as a vampire, he had a lot to spare.

CHAPTER FOUR

*T*here was nothing like a pot roast on a cold November night. There was especially nothing like a pot roast I didn't have to make for myself.

It wasn't that I didn't know how to cook. My parents had done their best to send me out into the world with actual life skills. I just usually couldn't be bothered. Stefan didn't eat, and cooking for one was either tedious, or I ended up eating left-overs for a week straight.

And until extremely recently, I never had the time.

Why make a casserole when I could stand over the kitchen sink and inhale a can of tuna with a fork? Way faster and almost no dishes.

It was a win no matter how I looked at it.

But that didn't mean I would turn down a chance at something a bit more substantial. So, when Dad called me and 'oh so casually' dropped that he had a pot roast in the slow cooker, I was mentally rearranging my calendar to make it to my parents' place that night.

The smell alone was worth the trip to Cambridge as I let myself in the back kitchen door. Beef and red wine and herbs had saliva pooling in my mouth, and I had to swallow twice before I could speak.

"Hey, Dad." Habit born out of years had me stomping off my boots and hanging up my coat on the rack by the door. "Need a hand with anything?"

Dad straightened from sliding a tray of rolls into the oven and smiled at me. The skin around his eyes crinkled, and he ran a hand over his head, messing up his faded red hair. It was funny to me that he looked the most like a mad scientist in the kitchen, and not in his lectures or laboratory. The flour smeared on his cheek didn't help.

He hummed. "That depends. Do you think you'll actually help, or will you hang around the counter sampling everything?"

"Quality control is a very important process," I protested, trying to look innocent. It hadn't worked since I was six years old, but I might get lucky. "Fair enough."

There was a second crock pot set up, and I drifted over to it to lift the lid and gave it a curious sniff. "What's this one?" A rich, earthy aroma wafted out. It wasn't as good as the pot roast simmering away, but it only lost by a hair.

Dad glanced up from where he was peering anxiously through the oven window at his rolls. "Portabello mushrooms. For Lindsey."

Yeah, that tracked. My sister had been a vegetarian for years, and while she let her son eat pretty much whatever he wanted—so long as it wasn't full of *chemicals*—her husband mostly went along with her.

Mom must have dropped a comment about how it would be 'nice for the family to get together' for my dad to go all out like that. Nothing would lure us all to one place like food.

It wasn't like we didn't get together regularly, but with grad school, and then all the Magi nonsense I'd been dealing with, and Lindsey being a mom and having hobbies and classes that kept her busier than most CEOs, it was hard to find the time.

None of us were above bribery.

Mom was the next to arrive, breezing through the doorway in her surprisingly feminine, rich plum suit. She dropped a welcome kiss on my temple before heading into the kitchen to do the same to my father. Lindsey arrived with Scott and Conner not long after that, and it became a joyful, if a little chaotic, jumble of trying to wrestle Conner out of his snowsuit while he tried to squirm free and say hi to everyone.

Scott and Lindsey ran an almost seamless tag team getting him unwrapped, and Conner threw himself forward to wrap his arms around my legs.

"Aunty Ash! Do you want to see my dinosaur?"

I had no idea what he was talking about since he didn't seem to be carrying one, but my answer would be the same either way. I mean, who said no to that kind of ask? I wasn't a monster. "Of course I do."

"Okay!" He abandoned me to sprint full tilt into the kitchen to hug mom and dad, no dinosaur anywhere to be seen. Kids were weird.

Lindsey straightened, smoothing her hair back from her face. "Conner, what have I told you about running in the kitchen?"

"Check for knives," was the faint squeal that drifted back to us.

She sighed, and Scott laughed as he hung up their coats on the rack in the hall.

Lindsey and I were pretty much visual copies of our parents, just the mix and match version. She had mom's sleek chestnut hair, but dad's blue eyes and height. Whereas, I got mom's far less impressive height, her curves, and dad's unruly mop of hair.

Genetics were wild.

When we all settled around the table, I couldn't help but be kind of smugly pleased when Conner insisted on climbing into the seat next to mine. Did it mean I had to help him cut up his meal? Sure. Was it also a bit sad I was that happy a five-year-old thought I was cool?

Also, yes.

Still, I'd take my wins where I could get them.

Conner's little brow wrinkled up as he looked between my plate and his, and Lindsey sighed and put a chunk of juicy roast on his plate before he opened his mouth. He settled down and ate happily once he and I were eating the same thing.

Lindsey rolled her eyes at me and popped a very prim bite of her braised mushrooms into her mouth, like she was proving a point. "How's work, Mom?"

Shop talk was banned at the dinner table, but technically that rule had only included Dad and me. Once we got going about some theory or another, it could consume the entire evening. Lindsey once complained that no one could under-stand what the hell we were talking about, but that wasn't fair—Mom understood.

She had simply heard it enough times to tune us out years ago.

Mom worked as a clinical psychiatrist down at the hospital and since the family understood brains better than harmonic resonance and particle acceleration, I didn't call party foul.

Mom chewed carefully and dabbed at her mouth with her napkin before she answered. "We had a man come in who needed to be admitted. He was convinced a monster was stalking him and was absolutely panicked. We had to sedate him. I was worried his heart was going to give out." She shook her head. "I'm just hoping we can find a treatment that will help make things easier for him."

Lindsey coughed, and I almost choked on a badly timed sip of water. There was a heartbeat of really awkward eye contact before I snapped my eyes back down to my plate.

Back at the beginning of the month, Lindsey accidentally found herself caught up with... I didn't want to say cult, but it was a cult. They'd been led by a crappy Magi who had hurt feelings because he wasn't strong enough to reach the Aether properly. He started hunting Aether-born to live out his little megalomaniac dreams and had recruited a bunch of mundane people and convinced them they were protecting the world from monsters. Manipulative as he was, he got them to help with the dirty work of killing things.

Lindsey had been a latecomer, thank hell, so she never actually hurt anyone. But she'd gotten sucked in pretty good, right until she realized the person the group was going to kill was my roommate.

Sure, Stefan was a vampire, but Lindsey didn't know that. And let's be real, a not too sharp piece of wood through the chest would kill a lot of things, vanilla human included. It had been a huge wake up call, and she was now convinced the entire thing was a hoax thought up by a sicko.

I hated gaslighting my sister, but I didn't know how to explain that—yeah, no, *the magic part is real, but don't go around killing people for being supernatural because a lot of them are just people.* Heck, I couldn't even convince the other Magi of that one.

Mom had half stood from her chair at the implosive coughing from us, her eyes wide. "Aisling? Lindsey? Are you all right?"

I cleared my throat. "Yeah, sorry, went down the wrong tube. That, uh, that sounds really hard, mom. Do you think he'll be okay?"

She still looked suspicious, especially with how Lindsey was staring at the tablecloth like the mysteries of the universe were written on it. But she eased back into her chair. "I think so. He came looking for help, and that's the hardest step sometimes."

Scott murmured something to Lindsey while rubbing her

back, and she gave a fake sounding little laugh. No one in the entire family could lie worth a spit, I swear.

It only got better when Dad looked up from chasing a bit of carrot around his plate to ask innocently, "How's your ceramics class been going, Lindsey?"

I choked again.

Lindsey glared, which I wasn't sure I deserved.

Okay, coming up with a late-night ceramics class as a cover for where Lindsey had been disappearing to was, in retrospect, not the best decision, but what other option did I have?

Not roast my sister? Please.

"It wasn't for me," she said tightly, way too many teeth exposed by her smile as she glared. "I took up hot yoga instead."

"Hot yoga?" I frowned at her, my fork paused halfway between my plate and my mouth. "Isn't all yoga hot? And I thought you already did yoga."

She rolled her eyes at me. "I do Vinyasa yoga. This is totally different."

"I like the one with goats," Conner chimed in, his little face smeared with gravy.

I was pretty sure he wasn't kidding. I didn't know enough about kids to say for sure, but I didn't think they were capable of a deadpan delivery when they were screwing with someone.

"Goat yoga?" There had to be a punchline, right?

Lindsey reached for her water. "I haven't been able to find a place that offers goat yoga locally. We'd have to leave the city for it."

I was officially sorry I asked. Lucky for me, I was an old hand at drowning out my sister's rambling by shovelling food into my face. Buttery soft potatoes made everything better—even goat yoga.

"How's your roommate doing, Aisling?" Mom reached for her water glass, careful to keep her sleeve away from her plate. "Is he feeling any better?"

Lindsey choked on a bit of mushroom, and it almost dribbled back out of her mouth. I needed to change the subject before someone ended up asphyxiating. Who knew awkwardness could be so dangerous?

"He's fine, Mom. He's not sick, he's just become a shut in." I grabbed my glass and chugged, scanning for someone safe to talk to. Scott was checking on Lindsey. Dad was mopping at a drop of gravy on his sweater. And mom glanced between us, her eyes narrowing like they did when she was sure Lindsey and I were up to something.

To be fair, we usually were.

With no better options, I turned to Conner, who was eating bits of pot roast with adorable determination. "So, where's this dinosaur you wanted to show me?"

Conner didn't even look up, his head tilted to one side as he kicked his feet. "He's not here. He's at home."

"And what kind of dinosaur is he?"

"I dunno." Conner shrugged. "He's not in any of my books. But he's as big as me and covered in long feathers. He lives in my closet."

"So, he just chills in your closet all the time?"

"Yup." Conner frowned in concentration, carefully spearing a bit of mushroom on his fork. "He comes out at night sometimes, and he eats bad dreams. And socks."

Lindsey beamed, a soft look in her eyes as she watched Conner. "Isn't he creative? I hear him all the time, talking with his dinosaur friend."

"Yeah," I said, trying not to sound as suspicious as I was.

Imaginary friends were a lot cuter before my whole 'magic is real and there's another layer of reality' nervous breakdown back in September. Not to mention that when my crow buddy, Percy, crashed a family night, Conner understood what she was saying, which was worrying.

He was only five, and that was way too young to get mixed up in the nonsense the Aether could spit out.

Percy said some kids were just like that, which made sense. Everything must seem possible when a person is brand new. Talking animals and magic spells are at least as plausible as gravity and saying please and thank you. Maybe we were all born with the wonder the Aether brings, and the world just stamped it out of us.

But I was still super suspicious. There had better not be some critter hanging around my nephew's bedroom, or I would commit arson.

I was mopping up the last of my gravy when my phone rang.

Normally, I'd have ignored it. It wasn't some holdover 'no phones at the dinner table' rule or anything. I just hated talking on the phone and used any excuse to not do it. This call was different for a couple of reasons.

The first was that I turned my phone off earlier to save battery life. The fact that it still rang was worrying. The second was that the number on the display was 911. The back of my neck prickled, the hair standing on end. Whatever it was, it wasn't good news.

"Ash?" Dad put his fork down. "Is everything okay?"

"Yeah, I just need to take this," I said absently, pushing away from the table.

I ducked into the kitchen and accepted the call. "Hello?"

A burst of static had me yanking the phone away from my ear, but I could still hear the panicked, tinny voice coming over the line. "Aisling? Are you there?"

Young and female, but not Tessa. I didn't really chat with any other female Magi, and Tessa was just as likely to call me through a mirror shard as she was to use my cell. I didn't know who else could force a call through like that, though.

"I'm here. Who is this?"

"It's Caitriona. I need help."

36

As little as four weeks ago, I probably would have hung up as soon as she said her name. Caitriona was part of the group of apprentices who followed Cornelius's other apprentice, Mason. They'd been way more interested in forming the 'New Council' and giving each other ego massages than trying to find our missing mentors or, you know, saving the world.

Caitriona and I had never been friends. Our personalities just didn't mesh.

We were like oil and bitchiness.

But when I had to face the assembly of scary Magi, she showed up at my door and helped me get ready. She'd said it was to ensure I didn't embarrass the Council, but even so, I appreciated it. Just because I was clueless about haute couture and knowing what products kept my hair in pretty waves and curls instead of a frizzy helium cloud, didn't mean I didn't see the value in it.

She'd dressed me to impress, so I wouldn't look out of place among the scary, powerful people, and whatever her motivations were, she'd done me a solid. The little sob that she tried to stifle at the end of her sentence was also convincing.

I clutched the phone hard enough that the casing creaked. "Where are you? What's wrong?"

I could almost hear her trying to regulate her breathing, to force the words out as calmly as she could. "I'm at Mason's. Something's wrong with him."

Again, a month ago, I would have snorted and said something like, "*Obviously*," but I didn't. That was called personal growth.

"What's wrong with him? What's going on?"

Her shaky breath ghosted over the line. "I don't know. He hasn't answered my calls in days, and I can't get in the house, but it feels... shit. Please, please help. I don't know who else to call."

I held the phone away from my face and stared at it in shock.

I didn't know what was more disturbing, Caitriona asking me for help, or that she dropped a cuss word for the first time. It was impressive, considering she once turned up at my place with Mason to try to murder me, or maybe just beat the hell out of me, and got their butts handed to them by Stefan.

The whole situation was so uncomfortable, and there was a very good chance I was about to walk into a trap. But there was no way I could listen to her trying not to panic cry, begging for help, and just say, *sucks to be you*, and hang up. Not happening.

If I got murdered, Stefan would laugh at me so hard.

"Give me the address. I'm on my way."

Dammit.

CHAPTER FIVE

*A*pparently, Mason had a place in Beacon Hill because *of course* he did. It wasn't that the area wasn't beautiful, with its narrow, tree-lined streets and brick sidewalks. The gas lamps gave it a kind of old-world charm alongside the wrought-iron balconies on the row houses that ran the length of Chestnut Street.

Mason *'of the boater's tan and Rolex collection'* Stanford would never slum in any place that wasn't the most affluent neighborhood in Boston.

Of course, some of my attitude might have stemmed from the street parking only situation. The road, never spacious, was narrowed to a single lane, and I had to legitimately use magic to parallel park there with any urgency.

My fifteen-year-old Jetta didn't look out of place at all. No, sir.

Caitriona waited for me on the front step wearing a long, white wool coat that was so high-quality it almost glowed in the dark. She had her arms wrapped around herself, clutching like that was the only thing keeping her from breaking into pieces.

Relief flashed over her face when she saw me hurrying up

the walk, and that made me feel extremely weird. Then, the full whammy of the wrongness emanating from Mason's place slapped me in the face, and awkward social encounters plummeted down my priorities list.

I gagged. It was like getting a bucket of sewage tossed in my face. "What the *hell?*"

Caitriona bit her lip. "I don't know. I can't get inside, and he's not answering my calls. I don't know what to do."

She looked rough. Her skin was yanked too tight over the fine bones of her face, and the best make-up that money could buy was the only thing keeping her from being a blotchy mess. Either the effect was cumulative, or whatever was going wrong there was hitting her a lot harder than me.

Tess had said something once—that Caitriona's magic took a subtler direction. She was more attuned to the world around her, felt things stronger than others. Maybe that was why she had such a diamond-hard wall up all the time.

No wonder she was struggling so much.

I glanced at the building stretching up four stories into the evening sky. There were a lot of windows, but none of them had any light coming from them. The house was totally dark. If it wasn't for the rank vibes coming from it, I would've thought it was deserted.

As deserted as a piece of real estate in one of the most sought-after neighborhoods in the city could be, I mean.

"You haven't gone in? Are there wards up?" Just reaching for the door made my lips peel back off my teeth. It felt like when I had a dissection lab in first year, and I had to reach inside the chilled fetal pig's body.

The slimy wrongness of it had my stomach roiling.

Caitriona looked like she might be sick just thinking about it. She swallowed hard. "It's taking everything I've got to stand here. Going inside... no. I just... I can't. I'm sorry."

"It's fine." Beating herself up over it wouldn't do any good. I

ARCANE FELONIES

was about as sensitive as a lump of cheese, and *I* didn't want to go in there, so I got it.

Whatever the hell was up, it clearly wasn't going to sort itself out. I had to go into a cursed house to save a guy who tried to kill me at least once, possibly twice. Sure, he had his reasons, but I was still damn salty about it.

I really did not want to go into that house, and certainly not for Mason fricking Stanford.

But one look at Caitriona trying so hard not to cry, and I knew I would.

And if I took a kind of perverse enjoyment of winding back and lashing out with a burst of kinetic force that blew his pretty mahogany door right off the hinges, well... no one had to know but me.

The door crashed to the marble floor of the foyer and slid ten feet. Caitriona must have been more worried than I thought because she didn't say one thing. She clutched at her throat and paled as the dark miasma coating the house rolled out the open door like an oil slick.

I tugged the sleeves of my coat down over my hands, wanting as little skin exposed as possible. "Make sure no one calls the cops, please."

She nodded and took a step back. "Yes. I will."

There was nothing else for it. I steeled myself and stepped through the door.

My boot came down on a pile of mail that someone must have been pushing through the ornate slot in the door, and I slid a couple of feet before catching myself. It looked like Caitriona wasn't the only one Mason was ignoring.

That didn't fill me with good feelings.

The foyer looked like something out of *House Beautiful*, with its ornate staircase and veined marble floors. There was a wooden table, and a bench opposite it where someone could sit to take their shoes off. There was also a large mirror in a metal

41

frame—the kind that people got because it looked impressive, not because they liked it.

It really looked like the setting of a photoshoot. There wasn't a sign of personality or homeyness in the whole thing. Even the little pewter dish on the table for someone to put their keys in looked staged. The gross, clinging energy that brushed over my skin like rot and cobwebs didn't help the feeling.

My hands itched to scrub my face, but I knew there wasn't anything there to wipe away. That didn't stop the oppressive feeling from crawling down my throat, coating the inside of my mouth with a sour, metallic taste. The air felt thick, like I was swimming instead of walking.

No point in going upstairs before I checked the main floor. If Mason was just passed out in a Franzia haze or something, I would turn him into a salamander. I didn't care if I had to take an intensive zoology course to do it—being there was ten kinds of disturbing.

Something flickered in the corner of my eye, and I whipped around so fast my hair lashed at my cheeks. My heart was thick in my throat, the pulse heavy. The mirror. Something had moved in the mirror, but it hadn't been me.

Every part of me wanted to dust my hands off and power walk right back out the door. This spooky shit was not my scene. I didn't even like haunted house rides, and that was *before* I found out ghosts were real.

They weren't actually dead people. They were the Aether capturing a dearly missed, legendary, or dreaded memory and making it visible—energy projected into the light spectrum. Still, I carefully averted my gaze anytime I went past a grave-yard or a really old building. I didn't want to know what I might have caught sight of these days.

That the shadows were even darker in the silver reflection of the mirror was not a great sign.

"I hate this, I hate this, I hate this," I muttered to myself as I inched through the doorway into the next room. I fumbled along the wall for the light switch but flicking it back and forth a couple of times proved that—yep, all the lights were out. Of course.

"Yer a Magi, ye daft girl," my mean little inner voice chimed in. *"Make yer own light."*

The dry tone made me almost not want to, but since I was literally just spiting myself, that seemed a bit much. I had no idea why the voice in my head always sounded like my gran, Dad's mom. It could've been worse. It could've sounded like grannie, Mom's mom.

She smelled like mothballs and pinched me once.

Light was dead simple to make. The easiest way for energy loss to express itself was through light or heat. That was why I spent my first few weeks as a Magi trying not to commit felony arson every time I turned around. The tricky part was keeping it to a reasonable degree.

Searing my retinas would be both painful and unhelpful.

I barely had to think about it to have a little orb of copper-colored light bobbing around over my shoulder, casting stark shadows into angular lines on the floor. If I thought Mason's living room might look more like someone actually lived there, and less like someone told an expensive interior designer their favorite color was taupe, I was doomed to disappointment.

Everything was so bland. It was like a hotel room more than a house.

Cornelius' house in Marblehead was even fancier, but at least it had style. His style was 'I keep buying things that catch my eye over the centuries and jam it all into one room like the Victorian's did', but it was still a style. Mason's spindle-legged couch didn't even look comfortable, like padding was for poor people or something.

The house was silent. Not a creak, not a drip. Nothing.

It felt tense, like the building was holding its breath.

Well, if I was going to do it, I figured I may as well live out the haunted house stereotype. "Mason? You good?"

I pitched my voice to carry, but the house swallowed the sound and sent it back as barely more than a murmur.

"Holy shit, I hate this." I sent my little light bobbing ahead of me, lighting up the corners to make sure nothing was lurking there. The memories of pyrotechnics were still very fresh in my mind, so I was careful to keep it away from the walls and the ninety-inch television that hung across from the couch.

Dang. I whistled. That and the stereo system were the only signs that I wasn't walking through a movie set. I guess Mason liked his media.

There was gray dust on the wooden coffee table, and more drifting over the television screen, like neither had been used recently. Every step forward felt *wrong*, like I shouldn't be there. My skin was jumping in the still air, feeling too big and hyper-sensitive. Gooseflesh ran down my arms under the sleeves of my sweater and coat. The air was colder in the house than it had been outside on the porch.

I didn't have any better ideas—other than to run screaming out of the place, and maybe have it condemned—so I kept going into the next room.

I found a kitchen with an honest-to-goodness breakfast nook. And when I sent my light bobbing ahead, I saw through a darkened doorway across from me that there was a dining room. Few houses had a dedicated dining room these days, but it was actually set with linen and place settings—all of them covered in that layer of pale dust.

Whoever Mason paid to clean up hadn't been by in a while.

The kitchen was gorgeous. My dad would have been filled with joy at the huge island and the butcher's block over in the corner. There were gleaming copper pans hanging from a rack on the ceiling, and glass-fronted cabinets showed off every kind of dish or plate that I could imagine, and a few I couldn't even name.

Nothing looked touched.

My dad was a stickler for kitchen cleanliness, but it still showed signs that he worked and prepared things in there.

I couldn't tell if Mason's kitchen was like that because he was super strict about tidying, or because no one had ever actually used anything in the room. I was leaning toward the latter.

It was possible Mason was secretly a hobby baker, but I doubted it.

The shadows in the room clung harder, sullenly peeling away from the walls when my light came close. The sour, metallic taste was back, sliding down my throat and into my stomach. It made me want to spit.

"Mason?" It came out as less than a whisper. My ears rang with the silence. It pressed down in a smothering wave, like someone was holding a pillow over my face.

Jerk or not… if Mason was actually in there, I needed to get him out, and fast. I was crawling out of my skin, and I'd been in there less than five minutes. The idea of *living* in it had my stomach doing a somersault.

There was another doorway off the kitchen, other than the one to the dining room. I didn't really want to go into the little closed off room with the table set for guests that weren't there. It reminded me of those fake houses they used for bomb testing sites.

Instead, I sent the light in and checked from a distance that Mason wasn't sitting in there, alone in the dark. When I confirmed that, I turned toward the last door.

The shadows didn't want to let me through.

The logical part of my brain knew that was stupid. Shadows weren't anything… they were simply an absence of light without mass or weight or intentions.

Walking through them would be nothing.

But that didn't seem to matter. I pushed forward, straining against the thick, membranous feeling of the dark, and felt it pushing back. My light couldn't get through, either. The dark swallowed it up.

There was a faint, hissing whisper… just a breath of sound. I couldn't make out the words, but I could hear enough to know that there *were* words. I froze, my skin running cold, my breath catching in my throat.

The whisper came again, and then another, layering on top of each other in waves. I didn't want to hear them. They hurt my ears, dripping inside my mind like poison, so cold they burned. I didn't want to know what they were saying. If I kept pushing, I'd have to listen. If I forced my way through, I'd hear them.

I couldn't sense anything in there when I dared to take a magical peek.

It was an empty void beyond the doorway.

No, that wasn't right. I felt the Void. I carried a piece inside me, and it was nothing like that. The Void was absence. It was nothingness. But it didn't *hunger*. The darkness I felt on the other side of the doorway had a *want* to it. The only word I could think of was greed.

Okay. There was a very good chance that Mason was on the other side of that door, which meant, unfortunately, that I had to get in there. Not for him, and not for Caitriona, but because if I turned and ran, I didn't think I'd ever be able to look at myself in the mirror again. And that was already hard enough to deal with because of my hair.

"No way out but through."

"Yeah, thanks," I muttered, and cracked my neck.

So, if shadows were an absence of light, it was time to see how they held up to illumination.

It wasn't anything I'd tried before, but human bodies put off energy all the time—heat, general bio energy. We put out quite a lot into the world. Any large, complicated system would. It just took a little mental twist to change from heat to light.

My skin glowed faintly, and then stronger and stronger. I had to squint against my glare, and the warm pressure all over my body told me maybe it wouldn't be smart to keep it up for long. But I needed to get into that room, and I needed in *now*.

I took a couple of steps back, ducked my head, and charged.

The shadows held me back for maybe a second before they shredded.

I staggered forward and almost went sprawling, the light pouring into the room with me. It didn't banish the darkness, but it forced it to retreat to the corners, where it writhed and twisted like some deep-sea creature.

The den seemed to be the only place in the house so far that had comfortable, usable furniture, a couch, and an easy chair in dark leather. Mason was sprawled on the couch in jeans and a button-down shirt that looked like it had been worn for a few days. Blond stubble dusted his jaw, and his skin was horribly sallow, with dark bruises under his eyes. The empty bottles stacked on the coffee table and floor might have had something to do with why he looked like a microwaved corpse.

But it was the amorphous mass of shadows wrapping long, choking tentacles around him that had my bet.

Harrower.

Out of all the horrible things that I'd seen the Aether puke up, of all the monsters and madness, the Harrowing was hands down the worst.

They were the living manifestations of humanity's fears. If there was something in the world that had terrified a person, made them curl up with despair, made their heart pound like a trapped thing—then somewhere, a Harrower that represented that fear existed. If given the opportunity, they fed on people, their fears, and their deaths.

But their favorite prey were Magi.

Not only did we have more energy than the average person, but when Magi lost control, lashed out in a panic, or straight up died, we tended to do it in an explosive way.

Literally. Not figuratively.

And that kind of collateral damage was too much for the monsters to resist.

One had been sent after me the first night I awoke to magic. If Cornelius hadn't saved me, I would never have survived that night. I lost a friend to another. It had crawled into her home, taken advantage of her weak spots, isolated her, and eventually killed her. I made it pay, but that didn't bring Jamie back.

The madman who used the Harrowing to hunt our fellow Magi was gone, blown up by his own frigging hubris. Good riddance.

But there was still one of the bastards right there, curled around Mason like a lover while he stared blankly at the wall like he was already dead.

It was hideous, even for a Harrower. It looked like a blob of crude oil more than anything else. Foul, dripping tendrils wrapped around Mason's limbs, his neck, and oozed across his chest. Dotted across its body were dozens of eyes, and hundreds of tiny mouths, all of them whispering. The words rushed over each other like the tide over the beach, a hissing current that filled the room.

You failed them.

You won't be able to hold them together.

They hate that they followed you.

They hate that they trusted you.

She can't stand the sight of you. None of them can.

Weak.

Useless.

They'd be better off without you.

I didn't like Mason and had never been subtle about it. We

had scrapped physically a couple of times, and that wasn't something I did without extreme measures. I might've hoped he'd stub his toe on a doorframe every day for the rest of his natural life... but seeing him there, with that *thing* dripping poison into his ears, feeding on him, sent a hot rush of fury roaring up my spine.

My hands curled into fists at my side. The Aether trembled at the edge of my awareness, churning with my anger, ready to be unleashed.

"*Hey, asshole.*"

Both Mason and the Harrower snapped around in surprise.

"Oh, you both looked. Wow." I took another step, and the shadows flinched back from the light pouring off my skin. "Get your gross-ass tentacles off of him."

Of course it didn't. If anything, it tightened its hold. But it trembled, shying away from me. The fear monster was afraid of me.

I should have probably been worried about how satisfying that felt.

There was no way for me to be normal about Harrowers. They attacked me twice when I was alone and vulnerable. They killed my friend. They helped a madman murder many new Magi. They crept in and fed on us... disgusting parasites, glorying in misery.

I knew the fear coiled so damn intimately around Mason. The fear of rejection. The fear of not being enough. I hadn't thought anyone who danced so close to the edge of narcissism would worry about that kind of thing, but seeing him there, a shell of the man I knew, gave me an uncomfortable perspective that I would've been happier without.

I didn't like the guy, but I wasn't about to let his fears consume him. The thing about fears was they couldn't stand being dragged into the light and confronted.

The smile that curled my lips wasn't friendly. The Harrower

was as tightly coiled as ever, probably banking on the idea that I couldn't attack it without risking Mason.

My hand rose, fingers sketching quickly in the air. Planck's equation for photon intensity blazed to life in the shadow-drenched room.

I pointed my finger and a beam of searing light streaked across the room, and the hole it burned through the Harrower was smaller than a dime. I spent years working with lasers, light concentrated to a searing pitch. And hey, there I was, months after getting kicked out of my PhD program, finally putting my thesis into practical use.

The Harrower *shrieked*, all its venomous little mouths howling in different voices. It tried to squirm down behind Mason, who'd curled up, his palms clamped over his ears. I readjusted my aim and blew a tentacle off it next.

That was the beauty of working with something with pinpoint focus and accuracy—there was no way for the monster to get away from me.

Three more shots, and it finally realized that maybe the guy I barely tolerated wasn't a good meat shield after all. It lurched behind the couch, trying to dive for the darkest corner of the room.

That was a mistake.

It wasn't a spell, or a formula, or even an equation. I just took all my fury, all my fear, all my disgust, and I let it erupt out of me in a burning wash of light. Mason had already crumpled to the ground, so the only possible casualty was the couch, and he could bill me for it.

Everything went white. Even the shadows burned. I closed my eyes a fraction too late to totally save my vision, but I didn't need to see clearly. I knew I hit it because the Harrower screamed in its many layered voice.

Until it didn't.

For a few seconds after it stopped, I stood there with my

watering eyes closed. The house felt different around me, even without looking. The toxic, haunted atmosphere was gone, like a bubble had popped and all the creepy wrongness had gone with it.

I heard the traffic on the street again, and Mason's shaky breathing.

I felt scraped out and hollow inside. Like after a wound is lanced and all the poison has been leached to let things finally heal. It didn't feel bad, just odd. It was kind of nice not to be anxious about something, for a few minutes anyway. I didn't have a lot of hope of it staying that way for long.

When I finally blinked my eyes open, shadowy afterimages swam across my vision, and I wiped the tears off my cheeks. Mason was lying on the floor in the narrow strip of space between what was left of the couch and the coffee table. He was blinking, looking around like a man who just woke up from a nightmare.

And, oops... I kind of destroyed the one wall.

Paint chips and blackened drywall dust drifted through the air. Parts of the wall had bubbled, damaged within an impressive scorch radius. It also had streaking tentacle shadows stretching off it. The Harrower may have tried to make a run for it and hadn't gotten far.

Luckily for Mason, he was a Magi. He probably wouldn't even need to hire a general contractor. Too bad about the couch, though. It had looked comfy.

"Aisling?" Mason's voice sounded terrible, like he'd been gargling rocks and broken glass. "What are you doing here?"

"Your... BFF called me in. I don't really know what your relationship is, but Caitriona needed help. And on that note..."

I pulled out my phone and—lucky me—it hadn't fried. Caitriona picked up before the first ring was through, her breathy, "Yes?" tight with fear.

"He's alive. It's safe, I think. You can come in. We're in the den."

I would sweep the rest of the house but didn't think there were any more. Harrowers seemed to be territorial about their meal. I'd rarely seen them pack up. Other than the cloud of them that crowded into the crappy new age shop the cult set up.

I guess there'd been enough fear of death to go around.

Ugh.

The lights flickered back on in the house and I winced, letting the glow on my skin slip away. The rapid tapping of heels on expensive hardwood echoed as Caitriona hurried into the room and dropped to her knees beside Mason.

"Are you okay? What happened?" Her hands hovered over him, like she was afraid to touch him. And maybe she was.

"It was a Harrower." My voice came out more clipped than I meant it to.

With the way the house had relaxed, the bad horror movie feeling drained away. I was confident there weren't any other evil little surprises waiting. I would do a quick search before I headed out, just in case.

Caitriona's nails dug into Mason's arm. He flinched, and she jerked back, finally just gripping the sleeve of his shirt.

I turned to Mason, who seemed to be slowly piecing his wits back together. It was like watching someone come awake from a deep, deep sleep. "Do you know how long it's been here? It had its hooks in pretty deep."

"No." He squinted up at me like he was having trouble seeing.

"What was the last thing you remember?"

He sighed. "I just talked to Cait…"

"Mason," she said gently. "We talked almost a week ago."

Mason stared at her before a shudder worked its way up his spine, his back convulsing. "It… it wanted me to…" He swallowed hard, his throat bobbing. I could see the tendons in his jaw straining as he clenched his teeth.

I felt like a voyeur. Mason and I didn't like each other, and we sure as hell didn't trust each other. But seeing him like that felt unfair, like I was prying open his ribcage to take a peek. So, I turned my back to give them at least the illusion of privacy.

"I'll check the rest of the house and ensure there isn't anything else hiding." My voice was way too loud in the room, and I winced at the sound of it.

No one answered me either way, so I power walked away from the awkward situation to the best of my ability, heading back to the stairs that would take me to the second floor. I could hear Caitriona murmuring something in the den, but I couldn't make out the words, and that was probably best for everyone involved.

CHAPTER SIX

I dragged myself up the stairs, fumbled my keys out of my pocket, and opened the apartment door on a home front massacre.

Chunks of cardboard, waxed packaging and dry cereal were flung everywhere. The victim—a family-sized portion of off-brand sugar flakes—lay on its side on the counter, a hole torn right through the box as a large black crow hunched over it like a vulture over a carcass.

The crow turned her head, looking up at me with one beady black eye. "You're out of the fruit ring kind."

I pinched the bridge of my nose, forcing back the headache growing there. "Noted."

Satisfied, Percy shifted awkwardly on her club foot and used the claws of the other to rip the hole larger. More garbage and spilled cereal drifted to the floor as she rooted with her beak. At least she hadn't gotten into the rice again.

There wasn't any point in getting mad at Percy.

She helped me save the world and keep track of the entire city, so it seemed petty to begrudge her a few dry goods. And at least she'd stopped storing things she thought were neat in my pillowcase. I still didn't know who'd been more alarmed that morning, me or the snail I found in my hair.

Honestly, I worried about Percy. The logical part of my brain pointed out that she had survived just fine, long before she met me, but her clubbed foot made things more difficult. Even just perching properly was a chore… and it was getting colder, especially at night.

That was what drove me to rig up my bedroom window like a magical cat door. The little red bead on a string that Percy wore around her good foot meant that she could get into the apartment anytime she wanted. Also, apparently the other crows were jealous of her stylish accessory.

I grabbed a broom and started cleaning the area of destruction around the counter while Percy happily crunched away. "Are you here for anything, or just stopping in for a snack?"

"Snack," she said, her head still in the box of cereal.

Well, at least there wasn't a hole in reality in the middle of Roxbury.

That was something.

I grabbed the dustpan, and something in my gut twisted.

It didn't hurt, exactly. Almost the opposite. A gentle numbness pulsed in the middle of my body, slowly spreading. I fumbled the dustpan, and it clattered to the floor as I pressed a hand to my tummy. "That was… weird."

"Wow, ye really inherited yer father's brains, didn't ye?"

I ignored my inner thoughts and listened to my body instead. The numbness wasn't spreading any further, but I didn't like that I'd felt it at all. People drowned out most of the things their bodies told them, because otherwise we'd be constantly deafened by a lot of complex systems working as one.

But normally, the human equivalent to white noise was not a great thing.

Percy twisted her head nearly upside down, sugar dust coating her beak. "You okay?"

"I think so." It was probably a coincidence that the weird feeling was spreading from the same place where the Void seed sat. Nothing to worry about. Nope. Not at all.

Well, I'd known even as I did it that there would be consequences for sharing that little brush of Aether with Bastian. I'd just have to make sure those consequences didn't involve me turning into a big pile of black ash.

I waved a hand Percy's way. "I'm fine. I've got to make a call."

If there was one thing I learned since all this crap started, it was that no matter how many crises you strung together, life kept happening. Usually all at once.

I knelt beside my bed and eased the carefully wrapped shard of glass out from between the mattress and the box spring. Once, it had been part of a fancy-ass mirror in Cornelius' house. The other apprentices and I—the ones who gave a crap about tracking our mentors—took the shards to build a beacon for them to navigate their way home, like a lighthouse.

It hadn't worked.

Or they hadn't been able to follow it.

Or, it had been sabotaged from the beginning, since Oliver—who we'd thought was on our side—ended up being a hubris-riddled jerkwad willing to destroy the world and kill everyone if it meant he could have the Aether all to himself.

Who even knew what happened to his piece?

The shards also doubled as a way for us all to communicate without needing phones or incurring roaming charges. With my pillow cushioning my back against the wall, I sent a brief pulse of energy through the glass and waited for the words weirdest video call.

It took less time than I thought it would for the gang to assemble. I was half dozing, my head tipped back against the wall, when the others started popping into their mirrors. Either because it was broken, or because I really hadn't known what I was doing... everything showed up blurry in my shard—like there was a layer of grease on the inside of the glass.

Sean was first in, as usual, even though he was all the way over in Ireland. I had no idea what time it was there, but he looked as awake as he ever did. His dark hair was pushed back from his face, as he obnoxiously chewed on something. "Aisling, what's the craic this fine day?"

Will was next, flashing across the shard in a fuzzy blue flannel. "Is everything okay?"

As one of the more mobile members of the group, Will played our knight errant more often than I was strictly comfortable with. He could move through a door and step out somewhere miles and miles away. And if I had a nickel for every time he saved my life, I'd have two nickels.

Technically, not that much, but still twice more than I liked.

"What kind of greeting is that?" Sean flicked the surface of the glass. "Maybe Aisling just missed our delightful company."

Will peered into the mirror, a worried wrinkle creasing his forehead. "That would be fine, but *are* you okay?"

"Yes?" It didn't even sound convincing to me, so I tried again. "I think so. We had a situation, but it's handled. I just wanted to pass the word."

Our last two members popped up, one after the other, before I could explain anything. Tessa, who was a surgical resident up in Vancouver, and Koji, who was a homicide detective in Tokyo.

Tessa looked tired enough that I could see it even through the horrible bacon grease filter on my mirror piece. Her warm brown skin had an almost grayish hue, and her ringlets—way nicer curls than mine—were flat. Like all the bounce had drained out of them.

I winced. "Long shift?"

She sighed, a long, gusting sound.

Then Koji popped into view, the left side of his face a mass of purpling bruises, and I sucked in a sharp breath.

"Holy crap, dude!"

Sean whistled. "Hope the other guy looks worse."

Tessa immediately snapped into professional mode. "Do you need help? Have you been checked out? There's a chance of an orbital fracture in the–"

"I can get us there in five minutes, Koji," Will cut in. He grabbed the leather sheath of his honest-to-goodness *sword*, getting ready to strap it to his back.

Koji waved them off, looking flustered. He raked a hand back through his hair. "It's fine. There was an... incident, but it's been handled."

"An incident that's been handled? Care to share with the group?" I ask, in the most upbeat, pleasant tone I could manage.

Hey, why should I be the one always on the hot seat?

I probably deserved the look Koji gave me, diluted as it was by thousands of miles and wonky magic glass, but he sighed and grudgingly explained. "There was another magical girl awakening."

Sean hooted. "An anime trope kicked you in the face?"

"Wait, wait." I tried to remember what he'd said about the whole situation when the cleanup after the Aether Storm was in full swing. "You said teenage girls with superpowers? Why were you fighting a teenager?"

"I wasn't," he said, every word dripping with bruised dignity. "I was trying to keep a teenage girl from being eaten by a soul gaki."

Sean fumbled with something off the screen. "Hang on, let me Google that really quick. Oh, yikes. Yeah, that's bad."

I wasn't even sure I wanted to know. "So, the... what did you call it? Gaki? Hit you?"

Koji tossed back a drink, and I could just make out the bob

of his throat over the mirror. "Have you ever seen a magical girl transformation sequence?"

"N–" I didn't even finish the word before Sean texted me a video, and everyone waited while I watched a minute and a half of spinning, glowing costume change. "Oh, wow."

"They're going to get *killed*." Koji gripped the sides of the mirror like he wanted to shake it. "You can't take three minutes out of a fight to just spin around in the air! She was two seconds from getting gutted by a monster that eats *souls*."

I did a quick calculation in my head and waggled my hand back and forth. "I mean, probably not. If what I'm looking at is the usual, she'd probably be untouchable while spinning around like that."

Koji squinted at me like he was waiting for, and dreading a punchline. "What?"

"Well, look." I shifted, curling my knee under myself on the bed. "She's being lifted into the air by *light*. For the photon intensity to be strong enough to lift a full-sized teenager into the air like that, it would probably vaporize anything trying to reach her. She'd be impervious to outside interference."

Koji stared for a few awkward seconds. "The initial blast *did* knock both of us flying."

"It's not that I'm not interested," Tessa broke in, "but I just finished a sixteen-hour shift. Ash, did you need us?"

With any luck, the weird film on my mirror shard kept all of them from seeing the flush crawling over my face. "Right, sorry. Well, first off, no one died."

"Oh, it's one of those meetings," Sean muttered.

"Someone could have died?" Will held the mirror up closer to his face, like that would get him answers faster.

"But they didn't," I stressed. It was better to get that clear right off the bat. "Mason got attacked by a Harrower. It was bad, and I wanted to give you all a heads up to be extra sharp on the lookout. Check all closets and under all beds."

My joke landed like a dying fish doing an awkward flop.

"What happened?" Koji fell into what I thought of as 'detective mode', which he probably wouldn't appreciate if he knew I called it that. There was a sharpness to him, the skin of his face pulling a little tighter over the bone.

It made the bruise on his face look even more lurid.

I gave them the Coles Notes version of what I walked in on after Caitriona called me, skimming some of what I felt were more personal details. No one needed to know what kind of Harrower weaseled under Mason's armor of self-interest. I wrapped up with what little of the aftermath I saw before I awkwardly slunk out the door.

There was quiet over the line for long enough that I worried I dropped the call.

Sean was fiddling with something I couldn't see clearly, but experience told me it was probably an unlit cigarette. "Well, shit."

"You said it." Will's drawl was more pronounced than usual, which was a good sign that he was upset. "All right, everyone. At the first sign of something not right, call me and I'll be there in two shakes."

"I don't like it." Tessa tugged on her hair, pulling the curl almost straight. "The Harrowing have almost never dared to attack a Magi like that. Not an experienced one like Mason. How did he not sense its presence? I know Jamie–"

Her voice cracked on the name, and she stopped to collect herself before continuing. "Jamie was compromised, and Oliver was helping to hide them, but he's gone now. Why would they take the risk?"

The pieces turned together in my head, clicking into place. "There have been a lot of team ups between Magi and Harrowers the last few months, haven't there?"

Oliver, then the idiot would-be cultist, Gregory. What were

the odds of it happening a third time? Pretty good from where I was sitting.

"You think someone sent them to target Mason deliberately?" Koji stifled a wince at the words. The bruise must have pulled at his jaw.

Was that what I thought? It was plausible. I started carefully, thinking as I went. "I think the Harrowing knows the Senior Council is gone and they're circling the rest of us like hyenas, waiting to pick us off."

Sean cursed. "Well, that's fuckin' grim. What the bloody hell are we supposed to do?"

I took a deep breath, ready to set foot on well-trodden, if extremely awkward ground. "We need the Senior Council back. There is a big power vacuum in the world, and I am pretty sure I didn't fool anyone at that weird Dragon summit. The other Magi know something is up, especially Baba Yaga and Ceridwyn. They seem to have some serious grudges going on."

"You could say that," Koji muttered.

Tessa shifted, her voice as brittle as the mirror glass when she spoke. "And what are we supposed to do about it? You're not the only one who wants them back. You knew Cornelius for what, a few weeks before he vanished? Imani trained me for *years* before she admitted me to the Second Circle. She wasn't just my mentor—she was my *friend.*"

I winced. There was a reason I preferred to be in a lab. Most of my communication was done through reports or emails, where I could write things down and go back over it again and again until it was right.

"That isn't what I meant." I knew Tessa and the others spent years with their mentors. And I certainly never meant to imply they didn't care as much as I did. But they all seemed to have a growing certainty that everyone was dead, and I just... wouldn't accept that.

I refused.

"I *know* you all want them back. But either they can't get back on their own, or something is stopping them. Maybe some*one*."

I rubbed my tired eyes. The night was catching up with me, *hard*. I really wanted to slide those few extra inches down and take a nap. I couldn't solve an equation where half of the numbers were missing. There were too many unknown variables.

I let out a long breath and hoped it didn't sound as petulant as I felt. "Look, I get it makes you all uncomfortable, but I need you to talk to me about the Akasha. I think the Senior Council is trapped between worlds."

Normally, I needed some serious empirical evidence before I came to a conclusion. I didn't have any facts. All I had was a gut feeling. Something told me that if the Senior Council was still alive—and they had to be—then they were in the Akasha.

But I couldn't frigging do anything about it if no one would *tell me* about it.

Will scrubbed his face. "Ash, we're not being weird about it to be difficult. There's a lot about the Akasha we don't know. The Council of the Seven Spheres has decreed that passing into it is forbidden. We're supposed to minimize any damage to it at all."

I fought the urge to look at the knife Bastian gave me. The blade looked like it was carved out of volcanic rock, and it could cut through anything. I had to be careful how I put it down. I already lost a full corner of my nightstand to it.

Sean's image bobbed. He must have been jangling his leg up and down, jostling his shard. "Cornelius was considered a bit of a bleeding heart. He tried to push Aether-born back through before sealing the rifts. Most Magi on the Council just killed them and did their best to patch the holes."

"From what I understand, there was some fear that the more

things rattling around in the Akasha, the more unstable it would become," Tessa said, sounding tired.

I ran my hand through my hair, barely resisting the urge to yank. "The Dragon has a frigging summer house in the Akasha."

"And there's a reason he and the Council have never gotten along," Tessa pointed out.

"Is there an example, or proof, or a written account on why they think this is the case?"

It got quiet, other than some shifting around.

"No," Will admitted. "Not that I've ever heard. But that's what the Council has taught, for more years than any of us have been alive. Heck, maybe more than all of us combined."

Great.

I wanted to dismiss it as an old wives' tales. Problem was, sometimes those old wives knew what they were talking about. I hated not having all the facts, but with the other apprentices not having any answers, and the fact that I would rather eat glass than asked Mason for help, it looked like reaching out to Stefan's friends might be my best bet.

The Dragon was also a possibility, but I would reserve him as a very, very scary Plan B.

The conversation died while I chewed my lip, thinking, so after a few warnings to watch their backs, we said our good-nights and I put the shard back into its hiding place.

"What the fuck?"

I poked my head out of my bedroom door to find Stefan and Percy having a stare down over the ravaged carcass of a cereal box.

Stefan shook his head. "Live with a Magi, I thought. It's good protection, I thought. Should have thought about the chaos."

"So, you don't want some?" Percy asked, spraying crumbs from her beak.

Stefan made the face people usually reserved for cat vomit. "That's a hard no from me. As much as I love the idea of barfing up hunks of sugar and breakfast particle board, I'd hate to deprive you of your lawful kill."

I came further into the room, looking Stefan over as he shrugged out of his gray wool coat. There was an ivy leaf, bright green and almost waxy, tucked behind his ear, and the circles beneath his eyes looked like thumbprint bruises.

"You good?"

"Peachy," he groused, checking the three locks on the door. Shimmering bronze equations flared along the doorjamb warding our apartment to keep out trouble. "You have a meeting for tomorrow."

I blinked. I'd figured it would take some cajoling on Stefan's part. "That was fast."

"For a Magi, you really don't know much about myths." Stefan rolled his eyes at me as he took an exaggerated step over the cereal massacre. "Fae don't like debts. It nags at them. They're very much into not owing or being owed, and this is the only thing you've asked from them since you helped them."

"I didn't do anything," I reminded him, frustrated. Stumbling around SoWa and failing to find their friend didn't seem like the kind of thing that needed to be paid back.

He shrugged, a lazy roll of his shoulder. "Doesn't absolve them one bit in their minds. Deal with it. And trust me, this is way better than them trying to guess what you want as repayment." Stefan shuddered. "There lies the way of walking sticks that make every sheep in the field have twins, or a baby that never grows up."

That was horrifying. And weirdly specific.

"Whatever. I'm too tired to deal with this. Thank you. Goodnight." I waved over my shoulder as I dipped back into my room. "Percy, there's another box of fruit rings in the cupboard by the fridge."

My door closed on her pleased little caw.

I couldn't help but hope to see Cornelius waiting for me

when I closed my eyes, even though it had been weeks since I'd been able to see the rose garden in my dreams. I needed his advice, and as much as it annoyed me to admit it, his wisdom. I didn't know what to do.

But I didn't find anything except darkness behind my eyelids that night.

CHAPTER SEVEN

*F*ranklin Park looked like something out of a fairy tale under its veil of moonlit snow. The bare branches of the trees were gilded silver, and the drifts of snow, churned by hundreds of feet over the course of the day, looked like piles of diamond dust.

I would have been able to appreciate it better if the frigid air wasn't creeping down the back of my jacket every chance it got, and my nose hadn't started to drip ten feet from the parking lot.

By the time we reached the arbor near the castle, my toes were all little numb blocks of ice, even with the two pairs of socks I was wearing. All I wanted was to go home, curl up under seven blankets, and have something hot to drink.

But I really, really needed to understand what was up with the Akasha, and the fearmongering, 'things man was not meant to know' take that the Magi Council had apparently handed down to everyone, was about as helpful as a screen door on a submarine.

So, I didn't complain too much as I followed Stefan to the nearly bare arbor stretched over the path, only a few sad, brown vines clinging to the wood. I waited with as much grace as I could, trying not to bite my tongue while my teeth chattered. Stefan rooted in his pockets before pulling out a softly glowing leaf key that looked like it was made from hammered gold.

Stefan held out his hand, and I gave him an unimpressed look.

His eyebrow climbed higher and higher, and he waggled his hand at me impatiently.

My hands stayed firmly lodged in the pockets of my blue puffy coat.

"I don't have vampire cooties," he snapped. "Why are you being so weird about this?"

"Some of us still have core body temperatures to preserve," I ground out, my jaw aching with the effort to keep my teeth from clacking together. I left the *idiot* as subtext, but from the way Stefan glared at me, it came through loud and clear.

"Oh, for fuck's sake," he muttered, grabbing my elbow to yank me forward.

I slid in the snow and let out an embarrassing little yip before the space beneath the arbor flared with golden light, and then we were swallowed into the gentle tinkle of wind chimes.

There was a moment of disorientation, like when an elevator drops a few feet unexpectedly and sends my stomach shooting up into my throat. It didn't last long. Soon after, warm summer sunlight poured over my skin, seeking the chill that late November in Boston had sunk into my bones.

It wasn't any less jarring than the first time I passed through the gate, but at least with some experience, I knew better than to panic about my vampire roommate suddenly standing in full sunlight.

It wasn't really sunlight—just magic imitating it—but apparently the distinction was enough to keep Stefan from turning into a charcoal briquette.

I wouldn't pretend to understand how it all worked.

The glade where we stood was so perfect it looked fake,

which was my entire experience of dealing with members of the Fae. I'd never met anyone—not even other Aether-born—who looked more like they were under a social media filter in real life.

The grass was a little too green, like someone had hyper-saturated a picture. The sky above was a perfect robin's egg blue with fluffy clouds that would have been depicted drifting across a chapel ceiling.

It was all so very perfect it was irritating.

There were bits of furniture scattered around the glade, all of it made from wood or moss so soft and plush-looking it could have been emerald velvet. Little white flowers dotted the ground, filling the air with a faint sweetness.

The only chair looked like it had grown there deliberately instead of being made, and was currently occupied. A long and lean man—utterly gorgeous—was doing whatever the classy version of sprawling was, one leg thrown over the woven root arm of his throne. His hair was shimmering golden silk swept back over one broad shoulder, with just a hint of one pointed ear peeking through. His clothing included a lot of billowing cloth and tightly belted leather, landing somewhere between pirate and punk, except for the half circlet of golden icy leaves that curled around his head.

Thalian, the King of the Fae, or as close as I would get in Boston, smiled as Stefan and I stumbled through the gate. "Be welcome," he said, in a rich, low voice, still lounging in his seat like a non-Euclidian fluid.

Seriously, how could any being that possessed bones just... drape like that?

Like any time I was confronted with ridiculously pretty people, my awkward meter shot into the red zone. "Um, I really appreciate you agreeing to speak with me. So... thanks."

Stefan gave me a withering look that I deserved but ignored, anyway.

Thalian smiled, his full lips curling up. "The honor is mine."

That was when I had the unwelcome realization that he was hot. I'd known it objectively since I clapped eyes on him the first time—I wasn't that oblivious—but it had simply been information to be filed away. The sky was blue. The snow was cold. And Fae kings were stunningly beautiful. It wasn't anything I had to do something about.

Stefan was equally attractive, in a swooning heartthrob kind of way, but he'd been firmly slotted into the 'no thanks' category of my brain. Him looking like he'd been chiseled out of marble by the hands of a master sculptor didn't change the fact that he was my roommate or make him one ounce less annoying.

The last time I was there, the sense of *presence* Thalian and his troop possessed had affected me to a degree. His attention had a weight to it. When he looked at me, I felt it like summer sunlight against my skin, a warmth that spread over my body.

Stefan called it a *glamor*.

It had been distracting the last time I was there, making everything about the Fae sharp and present and impossible to ignore. But it was worse with just Thalian there, with his attention solely on me. I felt his gaze like a touch.

Awkward.

At least Stefan was still with me.

Which was, of course, when he said, "Okay, you two talk magic crap. I'll go see what everyone else is up to."

And then he stalked away toward the trees at the edge of the glade.

I could've strangled him.

Thalian rose to his feet, over six feet of leanly-muscled grace, and stepped toward me, still smiling. "Stefan said you had questions."

Right. Yes. I was there for a reason. One that didn't involve staring for socially inappropriate lengths of time at pretty people.

"Yes. Yeah, I do."

Deep-seated curiosity helped me finally turn away from his face, scanning the glade for the first time. It felt so *real*: the grass whispered against my jeans with every step I took. The ground held firm beneath my boots, the breeze was warm and sweet enough that I had to undo my coat or risk roasting to death.

The first time I was there, I hadn't thought about where we were. Cornelius set up a Way for me when we first met, and I could step from the Cambridge public library, right into his backyard rose garden in Marblehead. So, when Stefan brought me here, the idea that we zapped somewhere far away hadn't really thrown me.

Now, knowing that we were standing inside the Akasha, it changed everything.

The whole place, the matter, the system of it, had been carved out of nothing but magic and willpower. No wonder I felt like I was breathing pure oxygen just standing there. It felt exhilarating, like I could run for miles, or jump over a mountain, but it was just as likely to burn me out and turn me to cinders.

I waved my arms in the air, trying to take in everything with the gesture. "How did you do all this? How is it even possible?"

He shrugged, a languid, fluid gesture. "The Akasha is the barrier between worlds. There's far more of the Aether here than there is in the mortal world. With will and a vision, it's possible to carve reality out of raw creation." Thalian smiled, his lips a little too tight. "What is far more difficult is holding it."

I nodded slowly. "Yeah, no. You're going to need to back that one up for me."

His laughter was like music, and it sent a shiver down my spine. I hunkered my head down into the collar of my coat, like a turtle yanking itself back into its shell. It was weirding me out how much he was affecting me.

"The Akasha is not reality," he said, somehow managing to

not sound patronizing, which was a bigger act of magic than pretty much anything I'd seen. "When the Aether touches the world, what it creates lingers until it is altered. It becomes real. The Akasha is far more fluid, raw creation rolling between worlds like a thunderstorm. It takes only the smallest effort to shape it. But to force it still? To command it to be static? That is the challenge."

My hands ached for my notebook. What had I been thinking, coming without it? "So, the Akasha wants to be in a state of flux?"

Thalian hummed. "Want is a strong word. It simply is."

He was doing me a favor, so I didn't roll my eyes. Plus, I remembered the last time we met, he mentioned giving people donkey heads, and that wasn't something I wanted to risk, even if he had been joking.

He made a grand gesture toward the glade and the woods, and the arbor Stefan and I passed under to get there. "I created this, a place for my people to be safe when the world changed around us." For a second, that perfect, immortal face twisted with grief, and I knew he was remembering the one they lost. It was gone so quickly that part of me wondered if I'd really seen it, hidden again behind a serene mask.

"We made this place, built the gate together, all. But it is *my* will that holds it."

There was a lot to unpack there, and since I didn't know how long he would humor my little Q and A session, I let it go, no matter how much it grated. I turned toward the arbor instead. In Franklin Park, it had been almost bare. Just some frost and a few dry brown leaves stubbornly clinging to the wood. But there, in Faerie, it was covered in lush greenery, with huge pink and white blossoms dotting it, like something out of a painting.

"Can we talk about the gate? All the times I've seen tears in the Akasha, they weren't anywhere close to stable. They kept threatening to rip further." The cuts I put in it with the knife Bastian gave me did the same—like once there was a tiny hole, the entire weight of the Aether bore down on that point until the Akasha buckled under the strain.

I wanted to rescue Cornelius and the others—I wasn't sure I'd ever rest if I didn't—but I could never live with myself if I ripped a hole in the Akasha and finished what the Aether Storm started... incinerating the planet.

Cornelius wouldn't thank me for it, either.

But the Gate was stable. It even had a key, so every rando walking through the park didn't stumble into Faerie. There had to be a trick to it, or at least something I wasn't getting.

Thalian's smile edged toward more of a smirk. "Think of it more like parting a gauzy set of curtains instead of kicking in a door. The Akasha isn't a solid thing, it's layers upon layers. The trick is to sift through them... just enough. But trust a Magi to think they have to bull their way through."

Well, that was rude. Not entirely unfair, but rude.

Still, it reminded me of when the whole mess first started, when I demanded Cornelius tell me how in the world he sent me almost twenty miles in a single step. He had looked at me over the rim of his silver spectacles, far too pleased with himself, and said to think of it like running between the raindrops.

It infuriated me at the time. I wasn't exactly thrilled about it now, either. I liked things to be logical and repeatable. Magic made the scientific theory sit in the corner and have a panic attack.

Still, I understood the idea of sifting through existence, letting the space between molecules drift past while not quite occupying the same space, even if it gave me the shivers. It was something I could practice and work toward.

Of course, getting through was only the first part of the problem.

I barely resisted the urge to chew at the edges of my thumb nail. I refused to gnaw on myself while standing beside a literal Fae king. There was only so much my dignity could take, and that was one step too far. But I itched to have something in my hands, something to do.

"All right. And how do beings go about navigating the Akasha?"

Thalian turned, his brows pushed together over the bridge of his perfect nose. He looked at me, somewhere between confused and alarmed, and I wish I wasn't so familiar with that expression. It made me feel like I said something wrong. "What do you mean?"

"You know." I flailed my hands, gesturing to the trees. "If I came through the Akasha here, and then wanted to go somewhere else, how would I do that? If I were say... looking for someone who was also in the Akasha."

He didn't say anything for a long moment, staring off into the middle distance. It reminded me of talking to fellow grad students who didn't speak English as their first language. Sometimes they needed an extra second to run the translation through their heads, to make sure they got it right.

"The Akasha is not a static place," Thalian said slowly, like he was picking his way across uneven ground. "Pushing between claimed demesnes would be much the same as entering in the first place, assuming there are no protections in place. But there are no maps or stars to guide travellers. What you are suggesting is not something that has been done, to my knowledge."

Well, if there was ever a way to get me to charge full speed ahead, it was to tell me something couldn't be done. "But it's not impossible. How could it be?"

With the Aether, belief and will could shape reality, bend it into new shapes. And I *was* going to find Cornelius and bring him home. I felt it in my bones. I owed the old man that much.

Thalian tipped his head to the side, the golden silk of his hair sliding over his shoulder. He gestured for me to walk with him, and I had to take two steps for each one of his to keep pace. We walked through a small forest that was so perfect it looked more like a movie set than anything nature spit out.

"I would say very few things are impossible," he said, gently chiding. "But difficult, certainly... and dangerous."

I did my best not to get offended by the tone. It was probably hard not to talk to people like they were little kids when you'd been alive for centuries. I mean, Bastian never did. Neither did Stefan. Okay, so maybe I was a little offended.

I kept a stranglehold on the fact that he was technically doing me a favor and took a breath before I spoke again. "Dangerous how?"

Thalian gestured toward one of the trees as we passed it, and golden light flared up through the cracks of the bark before forming some kind of sigil that wasn't any language that I'd ever seen before. The symbol was fluid, looping back on itself, and had something that almost looked like a sideways umlaut. Before I got a good look at it, I had to turn away, blinking to clear the dark spots.

It was a bit too bright to look directly at.

"The Akasha is much closer to the Aether than the material world—it'itss power rests more heavily here. Domains don't just hold space, they shield those within from the might of creation. Travelling between them would involve leaving that safety, like stumbling into the desert and never knowing how far it is to the next oasis."

As we walked, I studied the trees. They were all marked with glyphs to help hold the little pocket world in place, and to have the Aether flow around it rather than through it. I understood their purpose, even if I couldn't read them.

It almost reminded me of a faraday cage being used to ground out electricity.

Unfortunately, he raised a good point—one I hadn't considered. I'd seen what happened to Magi who lost control, when the Aether ate them from the inside out, incinerating their bodies. I had zero desire to set off on a rescue mission, only to immolate myself right out of the gate. There had to be a solution.

"And then, of course, there is the Akasha itself."

I jerked myself free of my thoughts when he spoke again, just in time to realize he had stopped walking. I almost crashed into his back. Clearing my throat, I tried to will the embarrassed flush off my face, and turned my attention to the weird tree we stopped in front of. Ha. As if that would keep the King of the Faerie from noticing I'd turned scarlet to my hairline.

The tree was actually *two* trees, their trunks gracefully arching until their branches wove together into a near perfect circle. Golden fireflies, or something close to that, hovered around the tree gate, lighting the space beneath the canopy.

Thalian stepped up close to the gate and laid his hand on the curved trunk. The space between the trees shimmered and changed, and suddenly, instead of looking out into the sun-dappled depths of a forest straight out of a Disney movie, I was looking out into...

Well...

There were no words. Shifting light and patterns made my eyes ache. Floating fractals of reality were little windows into strange worlds dancing on cosmic wind.

Everything pulled slightly to the left, and I staggered off balance.

It reminded me a little of Bastian when he was in his most cryptid state. The world felt like it had a dozen more dimensions to it, and everything was weirdly flattened around him.

There was a sound that was also silence, an orchestra building to an imploded crescendo, and I had to tear my eyes away before I did something humiliating like giggle or burst into tears.

It wasn't upsetting. It was strange, sure. But it felt like it was too much stimulation for my brain, and if I didn't vent some chemicals in a hurry, I might pop a gasket.

The gate went dark, then filled with gentle sunlight and the green shadows of an old-growth forest once again.

I was shaking. My eyes stung, tears pooling on my lashes as my entire body sent out contradictory alarms, trying to figure out what the hell had my lungs feeling like rocks in my chest, and my pulse hammering hard enough that it felt like my ribs were bruised.

I stared at the Faerie king, and he watched me with something that was uncomfortably close to pity. "The Akasha is a twisting labyrinth of all that is, or was, or ever could be under creation. It's not a path that can be mapped and strolled down."

Thalian sighed, and the breeze sighed with him, tugging at my hair and the end of my scarf. "Whatever it is you are searching for, Magi, if it is within the Akasha, then it is well and truly lost to you."

CHAPTER EIGHT

I spent a lot of time in my head. When trying to work through a particular problem, I could easily spend hours staring at the walls, jotting down the occasional note. It was like teasing apart a knot, taking the end of a string and unwinding it until I got to the heart of the matter.

I liked to do it at my own pace, with no one around to bother me or demand my attention. When I didn't have some sort of magical disaster breathing down my neck, or people's lives on the line, of course.

Being told that navigating the Akasha was impossible was a letdown, but it wouldn't stop me from trying. One thing I had noticed since becoming a Magi is that people accepted things they were told and embrace them as an absolute. No one thought to push or test things for themselves, and that drove me absolutely fricking bonkers.

No one had done it before. Okay, so there was always a first. If no one tried anything because they thought it couldn't be done, we'd still be sitting around in mud huts with no electricity, hoping we didn't get eaten by a bear.

It's not like I wanted to be reckless, or do something that

might evaporate the whole planet—cough Oliver, cough—but did Thalian really expect me to meekly nod and go home to mourn my lost mentor because he didn't think something was possible?

Come to think of it, that probably *was* what he thought.

I was sure he thought he was helping me… in his way. He probably didn't want to see me chewed up and spat out again by the cosmic tumble cycle of the Akasha. But if I was the kind of person to accept things and stay home, I would've been eaten by a giant steel praying mantis a long time ago.

I hated that the mantis was a thing to be referenced at all.

What happened to my life?

The point was, after Stefan and I headed back to the apartment, I shut myself in my room, dug out my notebook, and got to work.

Time passed, and I couldn't have said how much even if someone had me at gunpoint. I took breaks to use the bathroom and to shovel dry cereal into my face like a robot before diving back into it. I had some flickers of memory of Stefan watching me warily, like I was some strange predator he was worried might snap at any moment.

That was so damn ironic I would've laughed if I had the attention to devote to it.

I took a longer break when Percy scared the shit out of me by trying to stuff part of a pop tart into my mouth with her beak when I hadn't even realized she was in the room.

I sucked in a breath, and pastry with strawberry frosting shot down my throat. She flapped around the room cawing while I wheezed and did my best to get oxygen past the breakfast dessert and into my lungs.

I didn't know if it was the choking or the crow flipping out, but Stefan ended up bursting through the door to take in the fluttering papers, feathers, and wheezing Magi on the floor with a look I could only describe as resigned panic.

"Move in with a Magi, I said," he muttered as he hauled me up off the floor. "It'll be safer, I said. What the fuck was I thinking?"

Two solid smacks on my back had me spitting out a saliva-covered lump onto the carpet, and I sucked in a greedy lungful of sweet lady oxygen. I could have done without the snotty commentary, but I was glad he hadn't tried the Heimlich maneuver. I'd seen Stefan bend metal with his hands. If he heaved on my ribs, I might've puked up my entire digestive system like a toothpaste tube squeezed too hard.

As it was, my back throbbed with a tight, stinging pain.

Still not quite able to talk, I gave him a thumbs up, and he dropped me onto my bed with a put-upon sigh. "I don't even want to know what the hell is going on in here."

"Percy tried to kill me." My voice came out in a low rasp, my throat still thick.

She ruffled up her feathers and gave me an indignant look down her beak. "I did not! You hadn't moved in a while. A long while. I thought you forgot to eat." She cawed and flipped her wings to settle them. "See if I ever share again."

Honestly, if sharing meant having her carrion-picking beak in my mouth, I was fine with being cut off.

"I said I *didn't* want to know." Stefan tossed my phone onto my comforter next to me where it bounced once. "Also, answer your damn phone. The stupid thing's been going off constantly, and I'm trying to watch T.V."

"Oh, sorry, did I interrupt you binging on gothic brides and castles?" I slid my thumb over the screen of my phone. Okay, there were actually a lot of missed texts and calls... and I only had about six percent battery left.

How long had I been in my room?

"Wait." My eyebrows pulled down with my scowl. "Why is there a twenty-four-minute conversation with my mother on here?"

AVA L BISHOP & AUBURN TEMPEST

Stefan glanced toward the floor and fidgeted. It reminded me of someone trying to hide a blush, which was ridiculous because he didn't have enough blood to waste on blushing, and he was a five-hundred-year-old vampire and not a teenager with a crush. "She'd been calling, and she was worried about you, so I told her you were fine, just hyper-fixating on something. And then she asked me about my day."

I jabbed a finger toward his face. "No. I mean it. No smiling. Do not hit on my mom. Bad vampire!"

The phone rang in my hand, and I almost dropped it before managing to answer. "Hello?"

"Hey."

That familiar low baritone rumbled across the line, sending a shiver down my spine like someone had traced it with a finger. I couldn't have stopped the smile that curled my lips if I'd tried. "Bastian, hey. What's up?"

It was still weird knowing he had a phone and knew how to use it. Which was ridiculous, since he'd been alive since before phones were invented. Why wouldn't he use one? And it sure beat the hell out of having to go out and cause some property damage to create a *nothing* and hope it drew his attention.

Stefan recoiled at the name, curling in on himself, and I rolled my eyes. Bastian helped me save Stefan's life, so I didn't understand why the vampire was so freaked out by him or why anyone was. The scariest thing I'd ever seen him do was fill in the New York Times crossword in pen with no mistakes.

Well… that and turning Harrowers into fine black sand with a look. But that saved my life, so who was I to kick up a fuss?

"Are you busy?"

I glanced around at the destruction that had been wrought by hurricane research and lied blithely through my teeth. "No. Is everything okay?"

There was a pause, and his voice was careful when it came across the line again. "Does it need to be not okay?"

80

"What?" I was puzzled for a second before I realized what he was actually asking. We'd never just called each other before. It was always some disaster, or some fight, a warning, or asking for backup. Never just to say hi. "No, no, I was…"

I sighed and pinched my nose, glaring at Stefan as he gave a high-pitched whistle and made a gesture like a plane crashing. I was not good with words, especially not on the spot. I needed to go over emails three times before I sent them, just to make sure I got the tone right.

But I really didn't want to screw anything up. I liked Bastian. I liked his company, and not just because when he showed up, the bad guys—and the good guys, actually—tended to wet themselves and run away.

"Sorry. These days, I assume something is on fire. What's up?"

The thread of warmth was back in his voice when he said, "I was wondering if you wanted to meet me somewhere." And it was only when something inside of me relaxed, that I realized it had been tense.

Stefan, with his stupid super hearing, scowled and slashed his arms through the air to form an X over his chest. "No," he mouthed repeatedly.

Like he got a vote in what I did.

I narrowed my eyes at him and thrust the phone toward him. He gave a little yip and bailed out of the room like I'd shoved a crucifix in his face, and I just barely smothered a snort before I answered. "That sounds great. Where and when?"

Bastian gave me a time and an address, and I was still smiling when I hung up.

Percy watched me from the bed, her head cocked to one side until it was almost upside down. The look in her beady black eyes made me self-conscious, and I fought the urge to squirm.

"What?"

She clicked her beak like she did when she was thinking

hard about something. "If you're going out, maybe brush your hair."

Alarmed, my hand shot up and met the Gordian knot of tangles that I'd worked my hair into, and I grimaced.

Percy laughed so hard she fell on the floor in a flurry of wingbeats.

~

About a century ago, the power station south of Washington Street was large enough to run the West End Street Railway. More recently, it was painstakingly restored to its 1890 glory, and was now mostly used to host events, weddings, and fundraisers. But every year, in late November and December, it was used to hold the Winter Festival.

I'd been a STEM girl all my life: catching tadpoles to observe their transformation into frogs, or creating chemical weapons by seeing what happened when I mixed cleaners together, or the time I dissected a Furby and only made it more horrifying.

It had only been half a joke when my parents dubbed me their very own little 'mad scientist'.

But the SoWa Winter Festival had been one thing that had me believing magic was real, years before it snuck up and bit me on the ass.

The entire building was lit up, and the crowd of people waiting to get inside stood laughing and bouncing to stave off the chill in the air. Long strings of Christmas lights hung draped down the corridors. Projectors cast rippling purple lights over the brickwork, glinting off the windows, making them almost look like they were underwater.

There was a low hum of cheerful voices all around that faded into a cheerful white noise. I did my best not to snuggle into Bastian's side. Partly because I wasn't sure we were there yet, and partly because he didn't seem to have all that much body heat to share.

I was huddled down into my dark wool coat—which I had broken out of the back of the closet to cosplay being a responsible adult—and pulled my sage green scarf to just under my nose.

Bastian didn't seem to feel the cold, which—rude. He'd worn a short black coat, likely only because people looked at you strangely when you wandered around in just a dress shirt with the sleeves rolled up during a Boston winter.

His camouflage had worked better than normal, though. I almost walked past him when I first got there. I was accustomed to the black hole sink of his presence but didn't feel his ringing stillness until I practically walked into him.

Bastian didn't look any different than he usually did—I wasn't sure he *could* look different—but there was a hint of rose on his cheeks that hadn't been there a few weeks ago. His hair was also a tiny bit longer than his chin.

It gave me a brief flutter of joy in my chest.

I shouldn't have passed him that seed of the Aether without asking. At that moment, it had felt like the most natural thing in the world, but consent mattered. It was hard to regret it, seeing him smiling and relaxed in a crowd in a way I'd never seen before.

And if the Void seed I'd taken in return gave an icy little shiver in my gut, that was something future me could deal with, because I had plans that night.

I was riding high on just being there and hanging out with no one trying to kill anyone and no buildings on fire. It was enough to keep me from chattering my teeth into splinters while we waited to get into the market.

Boy, was I missing my down-filled jacket. It was ugly, but it was *warm*.

Bastian frowned at my 'freezing my butt off' dance, his hand hovering over my back before gingerly rubbing my coat like he was trying to generate some heat. "Are you okay? Do you want my coat?"

Okay, that was super sweet. I smiled and almost bit my lip bloody when I opened my mouth to speak. "No thanks. We're almost inside."

He didn't look convinced.

"Really, it's okay. I was contemplating this idea to bump my internal body temperature a few degrees so I wouldn't feel the cold as much, but, well…" I shrugged, my hands still buried in the pockets of my coat. "The chance of spontaneous combustion would put a damper on the night."

That got a laugh out of him, and I stood there basking like I'd won something.

Oh boy, I was in trouble.

Bastian's hand slid around my shoulder, encouraging me to lean into him, and I did it gratefully. It wasn't much warmer, but it was *really* nice. It made the whole thing feel like a date, and I hadn't been on one of those since my undergrad years, which— yikes. Who knew it would take the world almost blowing up for me to find something close to a social life again?

We shuffled forward under the arch of lights, surrounded by the chatter of the crowd. The press of people made things warm enough that my teeth stopped chattering and some of the muscles I thought were permanently locked into place thawed out. I couldn't remember the last time I'd done something for fun. It was nice to feel like a person for once, and not like I had a never-ending checklist of crap to get done.

I did my best not to burrow into Bastian's side, but it was a struggle. The fact that I fit comfortably under his arm didn't help me at all. "Have you been here before?" I asked.

The corner of his lips curled up. "I come every year. I love the people and the energy. The lights, the smells, the music. I could never stay very long—not without the crowd getting uneasy—but still." His head tilted down toward me, his eyes so dark I couldn't tell where his pupils ended and his irises began. "You?"

It took me a moment to realize what he was asking me about. Wow, way to go, O'Reily. A guy smiles at you, and your brain leaks out your ears? In my defense, he was a ridiculously, supernaturally hot guy who'd saved my life and risked his own on my say so, but still. *Ugh.*

My inner voice gave a little scoff that sounded way too close to my gran's displeasure for me to want to hear it while I was on a date.

"My family and I used to come all the time, when Lindsey and I were little." I smiled at the memories, feeling like some of the twinkling lights had taken up residence inside my chest. "It was always a great time."

"Why did you stop coming?"

I shrugged. "You know. Life happens, and then it was hard to find the time for us all to get together."

We hadn't been in years. Did Lindsey and Scott bring Conner? He would love every bit of the festival. I made a mental note to ask her. Maybe I could take him if she was too busy. But Lindsey was never too busy for Conner, especially if there was something he wanted to do.

Or maybe I could bully the whole family into making a trip.

If we couldn't find time, we needed to *make* time.

The crowd shuffled forward, and then we were through the big glass double doors, fogged over with condensation. The golden warmth of the building folded around us, and I could finally loosen my scarf and undo a couple of buttons on my coat to let the heat slip inside.

Bastian didn't move his arm, and I didn't mention it.

The first steps inside were a dizzying rush of voices and music and bright lights, colors, and smells. It was almost overwhelming, but we adjusted quickly, the crowd thinning out around us.

And while people didn't veer around Bastion like he was radioactive anymore, it was nice that they still seemed unwilling to bump into him. It probably had something to do with the fact that he was over six feet tall and had the shoulders to back it up.

Even into our mid-teens, Lindsey and I had to throw ourselves into the fray like we were doing roller derby, slinging elbows around to earn a couple of inches of breathing room when the crowd was at its worst.

Not with Bastian around. A girl could get used to that kind of thing. A girl could also seethe a little about needing someone to part the crowd for her instead of doing it herself, but I wasn't about to let it spoil the evening.

The market showcased everything the local artisans offered. SoWa was known for ceramics, sculptors, painters, and just about any creative thing I could imagine. I'd seen a lot of the studios a few weeks ago when I was searching for the missing Aether-Born, but I pushed the thoughts of a would-be cult and dead dreams as far away as I could.

Why was it so hard to just be normal for a night?

Dozens of stalls were lined up for people to walk past, everything covered in tinsel and little white fairy lights. The air was filled with mouthwatering smells of pie spice and apples and chocolate from the food vendors.

It was the closest thing to heaven I'd experienced in a very long time.

Bastian and I wandered through the marketplace, checking out the stained glass and the paintings with electric lights. He seemed to enjoy the colored glass ornaments a lot, taking them in from every angle, and watching the spill of rainbows dance over the white cloth draping the booth.

He was the same man who once lifted me out of a giant aquarium with one hand, like I was no heavier than a set of keys. He'd plucked me out easily. Almost absently. But he held the ornaments so carefully, turning them around and around, and cupping his hands like he could hold the fractals of light they gave off, rubbing his fingers together.

There was a refreshments bar against the back wall of the event space, and I got myself a cup of cider, letting the sweetness and spice pool on my tongue. It melted the last bits of chill lingering in my chest, other than the persistent little sliver of ice that seemed to hum in Bastian's presence.

There was a staggering amount of food. Everything from gingerbread houses, to bowls of chowder, to donuts. Bastian bought himself a pretzel covered in some kind of dull orange sauce. Just the smell of it had my eyes watering and the inside of my nose tingling.

"What is that?"

He finished chewing and held it out like he was offering a bite. "Some kind of hot sauce. They said something about Carolina Reapers."

My hands shot up, warding off the demon pretzel. "Yeah, no thanks. I like my face un-melted. How are you eating that?"

He blinked, like he didn't quite understand the question. "The usual way?"

And then he took another bite, chewing placidly like it was plain bread instead of two million Scoville units.

I laughed, even as the skin around my eyes burned. Trust the guy with the eternal Void inside him to eat what was essentially mace without even blinking.

When he moved on to a sausage on a bun and dipped it in a jar of artisanal honey, I grimaced. "Why?"

He shrugged, unrepentant. "You should try it."

"Hard pass." But I couldn't stop the corners of my lips from curling up.

Bastian's culinary habits aside, it was so much fun to meander through the crowd, not having to think about missing mentors, or fragile barriers between realms, or the Aether spitting out every errant thought made manifest from peoples' IDs.

And it was *really* nice to spend time together where danger wasn't imminent.

"This is great," I said, meeting his gaze. "I really needed a break. Thank you for calling me."

Just being there, wandering around, thinking about something that wasn't Aetheric resonance and the calculations of the cosmos had the cobwebs filtering out of my brain.

Bastian smiled down at me, and my breath caught in my throat. He really was unfairly handsome. He reminded me a bit of a picture I saw online of a sculpture of Lucifer that looked less like a warning to medieval peasants and more like a thirst trap.

But Bastian wasn't a devil, no matter what everyone seemed to want me to believe. I was pro evidence, and from that moment when he absently saved my life on his way home from the grocery store, right up until two seconds ago when he offered me a bite of his gross honey-dipped spicy sausage, he proved himself to be a good guy who liked to help people.

Even when they were cruel to him.

Even when they were afraid of him.

"I'm glad you could make it. I know it's not as exciting as our last outing," he said, his voice teasing.

I groaned and bumped our shoulders together. "I'm good without seasickness and ocean monsters trying to eat our boat, thanks." My brain burped up the memories of puking my guts out over the side of the ship while Bastian tried to keep my hair out of the way.

His laugh had my mouth going dry. I'd never seen him so relaxed, head back, leaving the strong column of his throat bare. Warmth that had nothing to do with the crowd kindled low in my belly, and I took a hasty gulp of my drink.

Yes, he invited me out, but that didn't mean anything. And

yes, okay, we'd shared one unbelievable kiss, but that was to literally save the world, and he hadn't made a move since. He probably just asked me because I was one of the few people in the city who would've said yes.

Bastian was lonely. He didn't exactly hide it. He'd been mostly alone from the moment he'd been created by a bunch of old shit-weasels who tried to make a perfect weapon to control. It had blown up spectacularly in their faces, but Bastian was still *other*, and people knew it, even if they didn't know they knew it.

People drifted away from him in public without even a glance. Magi and Aether-born could be outright hostile. Percy liked him, but she also liked me, so her judgment was suspect at best.

I wouldn't make it weird. If he wanted a friend, then that was what I'd be. Even if it took an act of will stronger than any magic I had ever cast to keep from staring at him like a creeper.

I cleared my throat. "But seriously, thank you. I've been shut up in my room trying to figure out how the hell I could track someone across a shifty plane of pseudo-reality that doesn't hold still. Given another fifteen minutes, I might've started barking at the ceiling."

He laughed again, but it was more of a surprised huff than anything else. "I've been alive a long time, Red, and I still can't predict what will come out of your mouth next."

"Sorry. That's the hazard of hanging out with me."

He tipped his head toward me, silky strands of ink-black hair sliding over the side of his face. "I didn't say I didn't like it."

And there came the blush. I took another drink of my cider, suddenly wishing it was a lot stronger. Then I unwished it in case the Aether was listening. I could fully make an ass out of myself dead sober. I didn't need any help.

"So, you're trying to track something through the Akasha?" Bastian slid his hands into the pockets of his jeans, a little wrinkle between his eyebrows.

I was always surprised by what he knew about the Akasha. Then again, the guy was a millennium old... possibly... he wasn't too sure. But it was unreasonable to think he'd never picked up anything to do with magic or the world in that time.

"I am."

We passed a table covered in cookies, cakes, and other nutritionally bankrupt delights, and I had to stop myself from drifting over. They weren't my favorite sticky buns, but they looked and smelled amazing, and there was a certain appeal to drowning my frustrations in carbs.

Mustering up the tattered remains of my self control, I turned back to its other biggest strain. "I have no idea how to go about it. Even if I get into the Akasha without ripping apart reality, which is a dangerous and real possibility, I still have no idea how the hell to find a man in a place I'm starting to believe is infinite. I can't exactly stand on a street corner and whistle."

Bastian smiled at my snark, but his face fell back into serious lines quickly. "What about the spell you used to find your vampire friend?"

"I thought about that." It had been a bit of a Hail Mary, using Stefan's energy to track him down when he was kidnapped by the cult. "I had Stefan's hair, a tie to his actual physical form, and was tracking him here. I don't have anything like that for Cornelius. I guess I could ransack his house, but I doubt his favorite armchair would let me follow him through magic's version of an event horizon."

He was quiet for a second, and I mentally kicked myself in the butt. Look at that, watch Ash bring down the entire mood, no magic spells required.

"Maybe ye should stick to askin' him how his day was."

I shook my head, trying to banish the judgmental little voice.

"If anyone can figure it out, it's you."

I almost tripped. That hadn't been what I was expecting at all. There was something in Bastian's voice—like he was stating a fact, not like he was trying to dismiss my problem. He really thought that I'd be able to solve it, even though, as far as I could tell, no Magi had ever even attempted it before. Something very much like hope fluttered to life in my chest like moth wings.

"Yeah? You think so?"

"Of course," he said simply. "You figured out how to stop the Aether Storm from ripping across the world. I mean, it was crazy and could have killed us both. But it worked."

"I would like to skip the almost dying part this time," I admitted. "And it wasn't crazy. It was genius. You can tell because it worked."

Bastian smirked down at me, leaning closer so he could lower his voice. "Oh, it was crazy. But that's okay. It's part of your charm. You're never boring."

There were a lot of ways that I could have taken that. Unfortunately, all of them had blood rushing into my face, and that had Bastian tilting his head to the side in a gesture that reminded me too much of Percy. He watched the creep of my blush like it was fascinating, and that had me remembering the stupid kiss again and how his hands had clutched at me like he'd been worried something would tear me away from him, and if I didn't rip my head out of the gutter I was going to spontaneously combust with no help from the Aether.

My drink was empty, and I didn't even remember finishing it. At least throwing the cup away gave me a minute of breathing room to keep me from making a giant social embarrassment of myself. I thought I heard Bastian chuckle, but it was probably my imagination.

A table caught my eye, and I drifted over to look. Dozens of candles in pretty glass jars had been arranged in tiers, listing all the scent variations available. One reminded me of pine trees; the bright, almost citrusy scent that cut through the sugar and spice of a nearby gingerbread stall.

A candle would be a nice present for Lindsey for Christmas,

actually. She had a million of them, but she burned them all the time for meditation or yoga practice, so she did go through them. Sometimes just being in her house gave me a headache, depending on the scent combination. It was a good thing Scott and Conner didn't have asthma. That's all I was saying.

Of course, picking the right candle would take some research. Nothing too sharp or cloying. Something mellow, good for relaxation, and nothing that would make me want to puke if I ended up being around when she burned it.

There were a few that were nice, but others made my nose wrinkle. One was labeled 'Ocean Breeze', but it reminded me of salt. It was probably for the best, really. I remembered exactly what the ocean breeze smelled like out in the harbor, and it had mostly been fish and seaweed. I put it down, disappointed, and picked up 'Sugar Cookie' instead.

Sweet. Inoffensive. But not quite right.

I turned to Bastian and held out the jar. "What do you think?"

He glanced down, one brow ticking up. "About candles? In general?"

I ugly-snorted a laugh, and if I'd had a hand free, I would have slapped it over my mouth at the horrible sound. "No, of this scent in particular."

He leaned forward, really taking his time, looking like a sommelier judging a vintage instead of a man smelling a Christmas candle. "It's okay. It just smells sweet, not like actual cookies."

"You're not wrong."

The next candle I grabbed was a light biscuit color and was labeled 'Butter Toffee'. I held it up to my nose and breathed deeply. The rich smell of caramel and sugar filled my head, and I exhaled a punched-out little gasp. It was delicious, perfect. Part of me wanted to take a bite, even though I knew darn well it was made of wax.

The memory hit me like a sledgehammer... Lindsey and me in the kitchen with my gran. I had only been about eight, but she'd been teaching us to bake toffee cookies, and we'd turned it into a game of taking turns distracting her so the other could steal a bit of the dough. Gran had played along, exclaiming about the Faeries stealing the batter. She'd shaken her rolling pin in the air to 'scare them off' while Lindsey and I had giggled behind our hands.

If she was alive and found out I spent an afternoon in 'Faerie', with their king no less, Gran would've made me wear my clothes inside out for a month. She maybe hadn't believed all the old tales she brought with her when she moved to America, but she had always been pragmatic about it not being worth the risk of ignoring them.

It was funny how smells could trigger memories like that.

I jerked like I'd been electrocuted and only just remembered to put the candle back down before spinning around to face Bastian. "That's it! That's how I can do it!"

Bastian nodded sagely, still holding my elbows that he caught when I turned fast enough to stagger. "I'll need a little more context than that, Red."

I grabbed the front of his jacket without really meaning to, ready to burst at the idea lighting up my frontal cortex. I needed my notebook. I needed a pen. I needed to get the thought out before it wisped away like fog burning up in the sun.

"The memories! The ones that Cornelius gave me when he was trying to train me. They've faded, but they're still in there somewhere. If I can configure them again, isolate them maybe, then I can use them to find him. What the hell could be better than a piece of him?"

I was dimly aware of Bastian using my grip on him to shuffle us out of the way of the crowd and into a little alcove between a handmade card stall and a truffle display. I didn't care. I was ready to squirt out of my skin with excitement.

Bastian blinked down at me. "Cornelius gave you his memories?"

Oh, right. I hadn't told anyone that part.

I had a good reason in the beginning, but then I forgot people didn't know. I tugged on the front of his jacket impatiently. "Yes, to try to teach me how to work with the Aether in case something happened to him. He downloaded all his memories about magic into my head, and they kind of made a subconscious copy of him in my brain. It faded or absorbed or something, but if I can use them, then what would be better than using a literal part of him to track him?"

It was so much better than a strand of his hair or his favorite teacup. I was bouncing on my toes in excitement, and I couldn't wait to see if I could make it work.

Bastian's grin crept across his face like molasses, and he gave my elbows a little squeeze. "I knew you could figure it out. It's off the wall, unique, and so bizarre no one else would ever think about it. It's absolutely you, Red."

And only in my messed up, over-crowded brain could that string of words land like a compliment. But I knew that was how he meant them. There was admiration in that night-dark gaze, and something warmer. Something more than an interest in something new and strange. Something that had my laughter drying up and my pulse picking up speed.

Bastian let go of one of my arms and brought his hand up to the side of my face to smooth a strand of my hair back behind one ear. Even though his fingers were cooler than the average person, the touch left trails of fire on my skin.

I swayed forward, brushing against him, and the hand slid back into my hair to cradle my skull, his thumb sweeping over my cheek. A shiver worked its way down my spine, my pulse loud in my ears as that dark head bent toward me.

The blare of my phone ringing scared me so badly that I

jumped, and only missed head-butting Bastian because his reflexes were a lot better than mine.

The noise of the surrounding crowd rushed back in like the tide, and whatever moment there had been between us was absolutely destroyed.

"I can't catch a break," I grumbled as I yanked my phone out of my pocket.

Seeing my sister's name blinking up at me didn't improve my mood. How did she know? Trust an older sister to be punking me subconsciously. A vindictive little part of me wanted to send a burst of sound like an air horn across the line, but I stomped it down and angrily jabbed the button that accepted the call.

Still, my voice was just a few shades shy of homicidal when I spoke into the phone. "What?"

There was a moment of silence, and then a sniffle. "Aunt Ash?"

Something colder than the winter wind outside tore through me, and I clutched the phone to my face, jamming a finger in the opposite ear so I could hear better. "Conner? Sweetie, what's wrong? Where's your mom?"

He was crying in earnest then, wracking sobs that shredded my heart. "They don't believe me. I'm not lying, I'm not."

It was a struggle to just stand there, listening to him cry. My hands were shaking hard enough that I was terrified I might drop the phone. "You told mommy and daddy something and they didn't believe you? Is that it?"

He cried harder, but I made out something that at least sort of sounded like an "Uh-huh."

Somehow, my voice came out with a steadiness I did not feel. "Okay. I believe you, Conner. Tell me what's going on."

"Aunt Ash," he choked out, his voice filled with tears. "There's something under my bed."

CHAPTER NINE

I broke several traffic laws, and possibly the sound barrier, hauling ass out to Brighton. My fifteen-year-old car made some grinding noises that, under other circumstances, would've been concerning, but with my nephew's terrified whisper still ringing in my ears, I forced the pedal to the floor and dared anyone to get in my way.

If I thought I could concentrate hard enough, I might've risked creating an Einstein-Rossen bridge, or wormhole. Magi called it a Gate or a Portal or a Way, but it was the same idea.

I saw someone messily bisected by one, and I wouldn't be any damn help to anyone if I screwed it up, so driving it was.

I hadn't even hung up the phone once I started driving. Bastian gently uncurled my clawed fingers and took it from me as he folded himself down into my passenger seat. The low thrum of his deep voice as he spoke quietly to Conner was soothing, even if I couldn't make out the words over the panicked air-raid siren going off inside my head.

My sister lived on a quiet, narrow, tree-shaded street that I swerved onto on two wheels, fiercely glad it was late enough that I didn't have to worry about kids or dog walkers being out and about. My front wheels went up on the curb as I more or less parked beside a telephone pole, and I was out and running before the door finished closing.

I didn't bother with the pretty fieldstone steps that led to the cheerful yellow front door. I just ran up the slight hill to duck around toward the back of the house. I was about two seconds away from flattening the back fence when Bastian caught up with me and boosted me over the top of it.

Because of the way the house was built on an incline, Conner's bedroom was closer to half a story off the ground than a full one, but being less than average height and allergic to any form of cardio or strength training, it might as well have been on the moon for all the chances I had of climbing up there under my own power.

It took more effort than was pretty to beat back the panic and really think.

It was late, but not so late that Lindsey and Scott would be asleep. The smart thing to do would be to knock and tell them Conner called me and asked for my help.

But that would involve an explanation—assuming they humored me enough to let me in—and was just more time when Conner was alone with something that wanted to hurt him.

Fuck that.

Luckily, Bastian was right behind me. He saw where I was looking, and without asking questions, put his hands around my waist and lifted me up off the ground. It was good I had other things on my mind, or I might have really embarrassed myself.

A quick conversion of mass, and Conner's window crumbled back into sand. I scrambled over the sill, kicking grit out of my way as I stood, and took in the room.

It looked the same as the last time I'd been there—the same dinosaur wallpaper with the stacks of primary-colored milk crates Lindsey turned into a storage shelf filled with stuffies and building blocks, and what looked like a robot gorilla.

The headboard of Conner's bed was flush against the wall in the middle of the room to make space for a nightstand, and he had pulled the covers over himself to make a cave to hide in. The comforter was shaking slightly, and I could see the shine of a phone or a flashlight inside.

"Conner," I whispered, taking a step toward the bed. The wind whipped the curtains into the room, blowing sand across the carpet. "Sweetie, I'm here."

A lot of things happened really quickly.

Conner's head popped up out from under his blanket, his face tear-streaked, his hair a mess. He sniffled. "Aunt Ash?"

A long, spindly arm that looked like it had way too many joints in it snaked out from under the bed. Wormy fingers grabbed a fist full of comforter and tugged, like it could drag everything to the floor.

Conner made a high-pitched little cry and kicked out when he saw it.

The sickening, ravenous echo of the Harrowing rolled over me and I threw my hands up.

The closet door flew open.

I'd seen a lot of weird crap since I became a Magi—everything from mermaids to pixies to Elder Horrors—but seeing a two-and-a-half-foot tall dinosaur covered in black, white, and electric-blue feathers was right up there on the WTF meter. The dino-magpie came barreling out of my nephew's closet with a whistling shriek and threw itself half under his bed to clamp its jaws down on the arm that was clutching the covers.

The spindly arm tried to jerk back with a gurgling snarl, but the dinosaur was having none of it. It dug its clawed back feet into the carpet and put its entire body into trying to yank the Harrower out from under the bed.

Conner actually whooped and pumped his little fists in the air. "Get it, Spike!"

The Harrower bulged weirdly, its whole body rolling like a balloon full of water, and it knocked the dinosaur sprawling across the floor. Two more hands snaked out, and one lunged for the bed, nasty broken claws reaching. Conner yelped, hauling the blanket up in front of himself like a shield.

I caught the palm of the grabbing hand with my heel and smashed it back down to the floor.

The Harrower yowled, limbs flailing, trying to sweep my feet and knock me to the floor. I ground my heel down, twisting viciously.

The little dinosaur circled me, its golden eyes locked on the Harrower as it paced, its fore-claws working the air like it wanted something to grab.

"How dare you?" I almost didn't recognize my voice. I didn't think I'd ever been so mad. Not in the face of Cornelius's gentle condescension, not dealing with the bullshit of academia, not when my supposed friend and roommate stole years of my work. I felt like a volcano, rage rising through my body, ready to erupt into destruction.

Smoke curled out from under my foot and the Harrower wailed, flailing at my legs.

It didn't have a proper shape, too fluid and rolling through suggestions of limbs and eyes, and gaping, fanged mouths. The Fear of the Unknown clawed at my best pair of jeans, and I barely felt it when my skin broke. A fine tremor broke out over my body, and my breath was sawing in my throat, furnace hot.

"How dare you come here? How dare you try to touch him? How dare you!?"

That thing, that *monster*, crept into my nephew's bedroom, where he was supposed to be safe, all tucked in with his loving parents just downstairs.

He wasn't supposed to be scared in his own home.

The Harrower flailed frantically, trying to tear itself free. My lip peeled back off my teeth as I watched it thrash. It was pathetic. How had I ever been scared of something that survived by terrorizing children and feeding off people like a parasite?

Spike the dinosaur leapt up onto the bed with a surprising amount of grace and snuggled up beside Conner. It tilted its head to one side to keep a wary eye on the Harrower, though.

Conner started to lower his blanket. "Is it gone?" he asked in a trembling voice.

I forced my tone into something close to pleasant. "Not quite, buddy. Keep the blanket up another second, okay?"

I didn't need to tell him twice. The blanket bobbed as he nodded.

There were footsteps pounding on the stairs. I didn't have a lot of time, but I wanted that thing out of there and the hell away from my family.

The Harrower fought me as I reached down and grabbed a double handful. Arms, claws, a tentacle, I didn't care. With a twist of my hips, I hauled the whole-ass monster out from under the bed, and it squirmed and thrashed on the carpet like a salted slug.

It was weird how small it was once it was out in the open. It looked bigger under the bed.

There was probably a metaphor there.

I dragged the thrashing nightmare over to the hole in the outside wall, sand gritty under my boots. I'd have to figure out how to fix that, because November was making itself comfortable in Conner's bedroom, and no amount of robot sheets could deal with that.

I stuck my head out from where the window used to be, looking down at Bastian where he stood, waiting like a sliver of night in the moonlight. Claws dug into my hands, blood gliding in hot trails over my skin. I ignored it.

"Hey, can you hold something for me?"

Bastian cocked a brow, a small smile on his face. "This ought to be good."

With no other warning, I hauled the Harrower up and over the sill, and dumped it into the backyard.

Just in time. Conner's bedroom door flung open, Scott and Lindsey barrelling inside.

We all froze.

"Ash?"

I gave a little wave to my shocked sister. The blood streaking my hand probably wasn't very reassuring, but hey, I tried. "Hey, Lindsey."

Scott looked around, wide eyed, his chest heaving. "Aisling, what the hell?"

Conner popped his head up from under his comforter. "Mommy! Daddy! I told you!"

Lindsey dove forward and snatched Conner up into her arms. The look on her face wasn't exactly friendly as she glared at me, and suddenly, the Harrower was the second scariest thing I'd seen that night.

"Ash," she said, in that too-quiet, measured tone I knew from when we were young. It meant that I'd pushed her too far, and that revenge was imminent if I didn't tread very, very carefully. "What the hell is going on?"

I let out a shaky breath. Adrenaline stung along my veins, leaving my knees feeling like Jell-O. "Yeah. About that." I blinked. "Scott, is that an umbrella?"

My brother-in-law glanced at the heavy-duty umbrella he was clutching, like even he hadn't known he was holding it. "I grabbed the first thing in reach."

"Ash."

I had to tell her something. Lindsey was approaching nuclear meltdown mode, and I did not want to be on the wrong side of that. Especially not when I still had a Harrower to deal with. I needed to get out of there and figure out how the hell it even found Conner. He wasn't a Magi—not that I could tell, even if he leaned that way—so why would a Harrower go after him? Random chance? I didn't believe in coincidences.

Conner squirmed like he wanted to be put down, but Lindsey held him easily, like she wasn't carrying almost fifty pounds of motivated toddler.

"Mommy, I told you. There was a monster under my bed, but Aunt Ash and Spike got it."

Lindsey was clearly half-listening. She didn't even glance to the side when Conner flung a hand toward Spike, still nosing around on the bed. Her eyes never left me.

It was damn uncomfortable being looked at like that. Like she wasn't sure if I was a threat or not. *Ouch.* I couldn't blame her. Conner wasn't even my kid, and I would melt the world to glass if someone tried to hurt him.

Scott stumbled further into the room, still clutching the umbrella. He raked a hand back through his hair helplessly. "What the heck happened to the window?"

Yeah, I could see this all going very badly. Well, there wasn't any way out but through.

"Conner called me. He said he was scared."

That was the truth and… even if not the whole truth, it was a place to start.

Lindsey stared at me, still clutching Conner to her chest. "So, you broke in and destroyed a window instead of calling me or knocking?"

Well, when she put it like that, it sounded stupid.

"Is there a guy in our backyard?" Scott asked, sounding just a hair hysterical as he leaned out the hole in the wall.

I glanced back at him. "Oh, yeah, that's Bastian. It's okay, he's here with me."

Bastian's, "Hey," drifted up, and I had to fight the insane urge to laugh. Mostly because if I did, I was pretty sure Lindsey would murder me. I hated the way she was looking at me. Like I was a stranger. Or worse, like something dangerous.

Screw it.

"Okay, cards on the table. Monsters are real. There was one under Conner's bed. It was trying to scare him. He called me because you and Scott couldn't see it, so I came over and threw it out."

With Lindsey and Scott staring at me like that, all I could think of was the little whistle and hand motion Stefan had made earlier, with the crash at the end.

I inherited my gran's temper. It was a short fuse with a colossal explosion that was over quickly. But Lindsey got angry like Mom did. She didn't get hot and loud—she went icy and quiet. It snuck up on people like hypothermia, and usually by the time you noticed something was wrong, it was already too late.

"This isn't a joke, Ash," she said, her voice barely above a whisper. Her face was pale, the skin pulled tight over her bones. "This is my son. I don't know what the hell you're playing at, but—"

I could already feel the frost creeping. Scott was frowning. Conner looked like he might start crying again. Things were about to go spectacularly wrong.

So, I did the only thing I could think of.

I strode over to the bed and scooped Spike up into my arms before turning back around to face my sister.

The dinosaur was surprisingly heavy and squirmy in my arms. But he didn't bite me, so that was a plus. "What do you see, Lindsey?"

She glared at me, her patience gone.

Scott glanced between us, trying to play mediator like always. "A pillow?"

"No. Look again." I hoisted my arms a little higher, hoping Spike wasn't about to shred my face. His feathers smelled dusty, like dry desert heat. They rasped against the front of my coat with every twitch of movement. "This is Spike. He's a dinosaur. I think he was supposed to be a velociraptor, but there's been some creative license taken. He's covered in feathers, black, white, and blue. No sickle claw, but that's probably for the best. Conner made him as a protector to keep away bad dreams, and then just believed in him hard enough that he became real. That's how magic works, Lindsey."

She glared, icy and remote. "It's a pillow, Ash."

I took a step forward. "Look. Again."

Lindsey glanced down, and then away fast. Her eyes were too wide. I could see white all the way around the edges. Her chest was rising and falling like she'd just sprinted a mile. "It's just a pillow."

This part was so hard. I knew how hard it was. How scared I'd been.

I hadn't had any choice when the veil had been ripped from my eyes, but I would never choose to go back to being blind, unaware of the world around me. I had no idea if I was doing the right thing, but Lindsey couldn't protect Conner, couldn't protect herself, if she refused to see. She *had* to see.

I shifted Spike again and felt the prick of his claws poking through my jacket. He let out a trilling sound, and Lindsey flinched, her eyes darting around the room.

"It's okay. I know you're scared. But Lindsey, you can look. You can see it. You're safe. I'm here, and I'd never let anything hurt you. It's going to be okay."

She was clutching Conner so tightly it was probably uncomfortable, but he didn't make a sound. Her pulse was jumping in her throat, eyes darting. One second, she looked straight at me, the next anywhere else but me. Her brain was trying to shield her, to let her not see what was right in front of her face. She was probably feeling the same warning I had, the primal part of her telling her to look away before it was too late.

But it was already too late.

I took a deep breath and held it for a three-count. "Lindsey. Trust me."

I saw it, the second the last protection dropped. Her pupils flared wide, until there was only the thinnest ring of green around the edges, and she stumbled back with a shocked breath. She twisted, putting herself between Conner and Spike, trying to shield her son.

Scott swore, and I heard the clatter of him dropping the umbrella.

"What the hell, Ash?" Sweat stuck her hair to her face. Her eyes were so wide, it looked painful. "What the hell is that thing?"

"That's Spike, Mommy." Conner wriggled, asking to be put down, but he didn't kick up a fuss when Lindsey kept a tight grip on him. "It's okay, he's not mean."

Spike made a grumble, and, not wanting him to use any of those razor teeth in his snout, I put him down quickly. He shook himself vigorously like a dog before nosing around under Conner's bed, searching for any trace of the Harrower. Or maybe a lost sock. Who knew?

"He's an Aether-born. A bit of raw creation given form by human belief. Conner's, in this instance. He won't hurt Conner. I actually don't think he can. He was dreamed up as a protector."

Scott slowly dropped into a crouch, both of his hands pressed to his mouth as he watched the little dinosaur snuffle around. Lindsey stared at me, like she'd never seen me before.

I raked a hand back through my hair, for once not getting my fingers snagged. "Look, I get it. It's freaking weird. It scared the crap out of me when I first started seeing. But these things have always been here. Nothing's really changed."

There was another minute of silence, and Lindsey's eyes narrowed into slits. "Wait. How long ago did you start 'seeing'?"

Incredible that I heard the air quotations without her even

moving a hand. Feeling like I was picking my footing while moving across a frozen lake, I shifted my back foot. "Um... a couple of months."

A muscle ticked in Lindsey's jaw. "You knew about this, and you never said a word to me?"

The ice underfoot started to crack. "Okay, hold on there. You understand how freaky this stuff is, right? I was trying to keep you safe."

"All those times you joked about me believing in magic. In crystals, and Reiki, and you were dealing with all this," she jerked her chin toward Spike and the gaping hole where the window had been. "For months?"

Oh, boy. "Okay, back up a couple of steps there. You were talking about water having memory, and planets in Gatorade, and crap like that."

"Retrograde," she growled.

"Sure, whatever. The point is, this is just like a really weird branch of science."

"Did you just say it was shaped by human belief?" Scott pointed out, because of course he'd remember that.

I glared at him. "It's complicated. Whose side are you on, anyway?"

Scott waggled his left hand at me, the light from outside glinting off his wedding ring. "I mean, I thought that would be obvious."

Lindsey gave me a look that made me suddenly really glad that both her arms were occupied holding Conner. "What else is real? Who else knows about this? Why would something come after Conner?"

Scott straightened up, glancing toward the window. "Is he in danger?"

I held up my hands like that could shield me from all the questions hurtling my way. "Okay, I will totally explain every-thing, but first, I need to take care of something. Then we can all sit down, and I will answer questions. But for now, I need you to trust me, and all of you stay away from the windows."

That had Scott and Lindsey exchanging a concerned look, but they really did not need to see me dealing with a Harrower right off the bat.

"Oh, right. Speaking of windows." Before either of them could react, I picked my way through the shifting piles of sand to the hole in the wall.

It was a trick Cornelius taught me. I didn't know enough about the chemical process of making glass, and if someone had just handed me a box of tools and told me to get to it, the entire ordeal would probably have ended in an international incident and a three-alarm fire. Lucky for everyone involved, I had another option.

The wallpaper was smooth under my fingers as I laid my hand against the wall. Houses, or more accurately, homes, had an identity. Not enough to be alive in how I understood it, but enough to remember things were meant to be a certain way.

Walls, roofs, doors, and windows, vaguely understood their proper configuration. The house 'remembered' what it was supposed to look like, for a time, anyway, and just like healing a body, I only needed to provide the energy for it to make the repairs.

Golden light flared behind my eyelids, and I heard Lindsey gasp behind me as sand flowed in a reversed waterfall back up into the window frame. It flared white-hot, a glow I could see even with my eyes closed, before cooling again. And if the glass was maybe a little less even than it had been... well, sue me—I wasn't a contractor.

At least I hadn't made the hash of it that I had done with Cornelius's house. The shingles had grown over one of the upstairs windows when I tried to fix the roof.

Scott's jaw was hanging open when I turned back around. Lindsey was staring at me with something that was in the same neighborhood as awe. It was better than fear or distrust, but still uncomfortable.

Hello, awkwardness, my old friend. I scrubbed my hands against my pant leg and tried not to fidget. "I have to take care of something outside, but then I'll be back. I'll explain everything."

I was almost to the door when Lindsey finally found her voice. "You better. Or I'll sit on you."

When I was eight, she'd done exactly that to get me to help her figure out what our parents had gotten her for Christmas. The memory floated up to the surface of my mind and forced a small laugh out of me. Something in my shoulders relaxed.

If Lindsey was making jokes, we would be okay.

I held that warm feeling to me like a shield as I slipped out into the night to deal with the Harrower.

CHAPTER TEN

*S*now creaked under my boots as I picked my way across the backyard to where Bastian waited with a writhing mass of nightmares pinned under one foot. I could only hope that my sister would listen to me for once in her entire life and stay away from the windows. I didn't want them to see the monster that had crept into their house.

And I *really* didn't want her to see what I did to it.

Bastian waited where he was, as still as if he'd been carved out of ice and shadows, while I walked toward him. He'd fallen back into that place where the world seemed to warp around him like a gravity well. Everything pulled slowly and inexorably into his orbit.

Including me.

The only sign of movement was the wind ruffling the strands of his hair over his brow. His chin was tucked down toward his chest as he stared down at the Harrower with that terrible stillness, his eyes full of the darkness between the stars.

I thought he glanced up at me at one point, but with no pupils in his eyes, it was hard to tell. He just stood there... like a statue… like a sentinel keeping the Harrower pinned to the ground, because I asked him to.

It was unfairly hot. And so not the time for the slow heat easing through my veins like warm honey.

Fortunately, the Harrower was as sexy as a pile of maggots and killed any inappropriate interest. It thrashed against the ground, churning up dirty snow with limbs that couldn't seem to decide exactly what they wanted to look like. Its body shifted in a roiling that made my stomach flip over to watch. An eye poked through the surface, orange and with rectangular pupils like a goat. A lipless, fanged mouth parted with a hiss. Another eye, bloodshot and bulging, opened wide as I got close, and I had to resist the urge to step on it.

It was way different from the monster who tormented a little boy just a few moments ago. The Harrower looked small, and kind of pathetic, pinned under Bastian's foot. The Fear of the Unknown just wasn't scary when it was dragged out and confronted head-on.

I fixed it with a glare. "You. Talk."

It made a sound like a furious cat that ended in a series of clicks. Two bony, hairless arms lashed out, trying to drag itself backward.

Bastian didn't even shift his weight.

I'd swoon a little about it later.

The fury I tamped down with my sister bursting into the room flared back to life like banked coals prodded into a blaze. Smoke curled around my palms, twining between my fingers as the Aether came eagerly into my hands. Creation wasn't all fluffy duckies and rainbows, after all. If I burned something to the ground, then technically, hadn't I 'created' a smoldering ruin?

"I've never had a lot of patience," I told the Harrower. My voice was flat, as neutral as I could make it. Yelling would just upset the neighbors. "But you've officially used the last of it. If you can make a mouth, you can talk. Or do I have to figure out a more direct way to find out how the hell you even knew to come after my nephew?"

Whatever it could sense in me, the Harrower must have figured that I wasn't screwing around. Just when I worried that maybe it actually couldn't talk, a mouth rolled to the surface of the amorphous blob, thin and lipless with a hint of broken, yellowed teeth behind it.

"We watch." The words came out in a vicious whine, like a buzz saw carving through wood. "Since awakening."

Just the sound of its voice had disgust rolling through me. Then what it said sank in. The Harrowing had been watching me? Well, that was unwelcome. And creepy. I would have to ward everyone's houses and let them know exactly what to keep an eye out for.

Oh crap, I was going to have to talk to my parents.

"Maybe ye should worry about one problem at a time, ye daft girl."

My little inner voice had the double sin of being right as often as it was annoying. A Harrower in the yard was worth a thousand in the night, or something like that.

"Okay," I said, trying to organize my thoughts out of the chaotic mess rattling around in my skull. "Your boss made some kind of deal with Oliver, but he's dead, so what the hell?"

The Harrower laughed, its form churning against the ground, tendrils licking out like a fog bank. The horrible gurgle sounded like the last gasp of a drowning man. "Always more. Allies for the King."

The moon slipped behind the clouds, and the night got a little darker. Even the soft yellow glow of the lights in my sister's living room seemed very far away. An icy chill dribbled down my spine.

The King of Night.

That was what Cornelius called the leader of the Harrowing.

The oldest and most primal fear known to humanity—the

fear of the dark—was the only thing the rest of the nightmare horde came close to taking orders from. For some reason only the nightmare and the madman knew... the King of Night had struck up an alliance with Oliver.

The Harrowing had been dispatched to 'thin the herd', to terrorize newly awoken Magi until they burned up under the force of a power they hadn't even realized they could control. There was one waiting for me the night in the physics labs at Seaton.

If Cornelius hadn't come, I'd have died that night.

I had absolutely no doubt.

Then there had been that jackass, Gregory, and his multi-level murder cult. He hadn't come right out and said it, but he insinuated heavily that the Harrowing taught him how to torment Aether-Born to death to steal the power bound up in their existence, so they could hang around to glut themselves on the terror of their deaths.

It seemed like the Harrowing had their creepy little fingers in a lot of pies.

That wasn't good for anyone.

Especially because, as much as I hated to agree with the little monster, I could totally believe other Magi might've signed up to join forces. The people I hung out with aside, Magi were kind of a paranoid, power-hungry group at the best of times.

If I thought about it, wasn't magic just a direct application of hubris?

We willed things into being, because that was the way we wanted the world to be. And there was basically a never-ending supply of people dumb enough to think they could get one over on the Harrowing or control them somehow. People had tried to harness the Void in the past, too, even though they universally died in the attempt.

And the Void wasn't even malevolent like the Harrowing.

Still, there would always be someone who thought they were

the most special snowflake ever, and that they could do it when everyone else ended up a pile of reduced carbon atoms.

I could've asked why they came after Conner, but the answer seemed pretty simple—to scare me. Mission accomplished. And now, I would do my best to make them realize what a stupid idea that was.

My real question was, why me? I was probably the least impressive Magi out there. Everyone else had more training, more experience, just *more*. Sure, there was the possibility that somewhere out there a brand-new Magi was really good at making butter sculptures, or something, but the point stood.

I was a nobody in the magical community.

If people knew about me, it was because I wrecked stuff and did things wrong.

Although, on paper, I *had* stopped the Aether Storm. And I *had* busted up Greg's monster hunter LARP. If no one knew the specifics, and how both had been either a panicked, last-ditch effort, or a borderline accident, it could have looked notable.

My fingers drummed against the inside of my crossed arms. I had a lot of questions, but I wasn't sure how much I'd get out of my gross, oozing little friend—I had to make them count.

So, I went with what it all really boiled down to.

"Your king. Let's talk about him. What's he doing? What is he up to?"

I hadn't realized I'd stepped too close until a thick reptilian claw launched from the mass of the Harrower's body. My heart slammed up into my throat and I jerked backward, hands coming up to protect my face.

Apparently, I needn't have bothered. The claw crumbled into black dust before it came within a foot of me, and dropped to the ground, mixing with the snow drifting around the yard.

Bastian's voice echoed strangely, like it was coming from the bottom of a dark pit. "Don't do that again."

The Harrower pulsed, writhing in silent agony as it pulled itself back into a ball the size of a suitcase.

My pulse was still thick in my mouth. It throbbed in my tongue when I swallowed. "Thanks," I croaked out.

The corner of Bastian's mouth quirked up. It was a tiny secret smile, there and then gone.

After a couple deep breaths, when I was sure I could talk without my voice quaking, I turned back to the Harrower. "How about you try that again? Use your words this time."

Another mouth formed, one with an extra joint in the middle, the lips bending strangely when it snarled. "The Dark. Eternal. He has waited. Many plans for Magi. And their gifts."

The dry, sibilant hiss, full of creaking doors and musty tombs, sent a shudder down my spine. It sounded so eager. Almost gloating, like it was proud of what the dark was doing.

"Well, that's ominous." I wanted away from the thing. My skin felt dirty, like I walked face-first through a spiderweb just by being in its presence.

Still, some things weren't adding up.

My teeth worried at the corner of my lower lip, so many thoughts whirling through my skull. I didn't have much time. No way would Lindsey patiently wait for me inside for much longer. She was probably waiting for Conner to fall asleep before she came storming out.

I didn't want her anywhere near a Harrower.

The night pulled closer around us, the shadows draped over the lawn, until even the snow seemed dingy.

"Okay, so your King. He's old. He's eternal. Whatever. I get that he's in it for the long game, so why now?" That was part of what bothered me. From what the others mentioned, while the Harrowing wasn't rare, they didn't swarm in place, either.

Fears were deeply personal, after all. The fact that two extremely separate fears had teamed up to come after me had surprised Tessa.

"What's the catalyst? It couldn't have been the Aether Storm because that happened after your king teamed up with Oliver. And it couldn't have been me because Oliver was already aligned with him and killing Magi when I awoke."

The Harrower pulled tighter, the weirdly jointed mouth vanishing.

I wanted to poke it, but even with Bastian there, I couldn't bring myself to touch it. "Your king teamed up with Oliver. I get what Oliver wanted. His whole 'there can be only one' rant made that clear, but what did the King of Night get out of a partnership with a Magi? What did Oliver offer him?"

Silence. And a little more roiling. I would puke if that kept up.

There was something there. Something it didn't want to give me. That implied the Harrowers were more than just fear-eating monsters. There was reasoning, planning. And this horrible little monster knew there was something worth hiding.

Torture might have gotten it to spill its guts, but even against something that wanted to terrorize a little boy, I wasn't willing to cross that line. One monster in the backyard was plenty.

I crossed my arms and tried again. "Or maybe your king isn't all that smart. He saw a chance and went for it. Like a cat staking out a mouse hole. There's probably no 'grand design'. A Magi called, and he jumped, simple as that."

The Harrower thrashed, a weird, mottled tone passing over its shapeless body. "No," It growled, a low, thrumming sound.

I shrugged, trying to look disinterested. It wasn't hard. I simply channeled the last department meeting I went to at Seaton. "Then what? What could he possibly get out of working with Oliver?"

A tattered bat wing raked the air. "Magi."

I cocked my hip. "Yes?"

The Harrower made a series of guttural sounds that echoed like footsteps on the floor of an abandoned house. More mouths

115

popped up across its body, some human, some very much not. Each of them spoke in unison. "Got. Magi."

My eyes narrowed. What did that mean? "He got Magi? The King of Night got Magi? You mean the ones the Harrowing killed as they awoke?"

It went still, creepily so. All the mouths disappeared again, and the whole goopy body contracted like it was shrinking in on itself.

"Hey, hey, we're not done here, buddy. I want to know—"

It struck.

I jerked back as its fluid body lunged, the whole side of it wrenching open into a gaping mouth filled with jagged teeth. Ropes of saliva stretched across it as it snapped. It didn't have any hope of reaching me—not with Bastian's immovable foot pinning it to the dirt—but that hadn't been the point.

I realized why it attacked a second too late. "Wait!"

I barely got the syllable out, but it was too late. The second the monster lunged for me, it exploded into a fine dust that billowed over the top of the snow like charcoal dust.

Well, crap.

Bastian grimaced and rubbed the back of his neck. "Sorry about that."

"I mean, it's hard to get mad. Thank you for not letting it eat me." I hadn't gotten all the answers I wanted, but if the Harrower committed suicide by Void-Born rather than talk to me, then I probably wouldn't have gotten much more out of it, anyway.

What the hell had it meant, the Harrowing 'got Magi'? Oliver had alerted them to when new Magi were awakening, and led them to attack, but that didn't feel like a 'got Magi' to me. Unless it meant it got to feed off their deaths.

Ugh, I could not express in words how much I hated the Harrowing.

Unease slithered down my spine, coiling in my gut.

It wasn't possible, was it?

Oliver hadn't just set up the newcomers, trying to whittle down his competition. He'd also deliberately flawed the ritual that the Council had performed, trying to seal up the Akasha. The resulting backlash had torn across the world, culminating in the Aether Storm.

The backlash of the ritual also sent the Senior Council... somewhere. Somewhere where none of us could find them. Not with magic, not in dreams. Most people were convinced they were dead, because how else could some of the world's most powerful people just be lost?

Even the others who stuck it out with me were losing hope. They tried to hide it, to keep looking, but I could tell. It was in the wistful way they talked about their lost mentors. It sounded like a wake.

'Got Magi', the Harrower said.

What if the backlash hadn't been random? What if losing the Senior Council had been the plan all along? What if the whole reason we hadn't been able to track down Cornelius and the others wasn't because they were dead, but because they were trapped?

What if the Harrowing had them?

"Shit." My breath came out in a punched-out gasp.

Bastian's hand skimmed over my shoulder, barely a touch at all, but it jolted me back to the present.

"Ash?"

"I'm okay. I'm not hurt, I mean." I could barely wrap my head around the thought, though. The Council, trapped with the Harrowing. Holy shit, what would that mean?

And how could I even test that theory?

Maybe hunt down other Harrowers? They seemed to be popping out of the woodwork like termites lately, but I didn't trust them as far as I could throw them—and considering I had the upper body strength of a rutabaga, that wasn't very fucking far.

"Calm down. Breathe, ye daft girl."

As always, my inner voice was annoyingly right. I couldn't fly off the handle. Even if my hunch was right, I still had no proper way to get into the Akasha, assuming I could use Cornelius's memories to track him down.

I wished I had a pen with me. I wanted to jot down notes so badly, it was physically painful. The app on my phone just didn't cut it.

I raked my hair back and looked up into Bastian's worried face. His eyes had gone back to normal, or as normal as they got. No more echoing Void from lid to lid.

"Sorry. Thank you for your help. I mean it. I had a thought which I need to chase down, but I had a really nice time tonight. Like, the best time I've had in months. Before all the horror, I mean. So, thank you."

That slow smile curled his lips, and he took a half step closer. I had to crane my head back to look up at him. My eyes caught on his mouth, and it took effort to wrench them away, especially with the gritty dust that used to be a monster still blowing around the yard.

Bastian leaned forward, bringing our faces closer together. "Me too."

I wanted to sway forward, to lean into him… but there were horrors to be dealt with, and I didn't usually have that much trouble concentrating on a problem in front of me. I wanted to slap my own face to snap out of it. But another part of me wanted to sink into it, to see what would've happened under the glow of the fairy lights if we hadn't been interrupted.

Dangerous thoughts.

I shifted back, not fully stepping away but getting some space. "Well, after monsters and a mad dash to the rescue, the real terror begins."

Bastian tilted his head a little to the side, looking me over carefully. "What do you mean?"

I shuddered, and it had nothing to do with the winter air trying to snake down the back of my coat. "Now I have to explain all this to my sister."

CHAPTER ELEVEN

*a*fter a lot of yelling, a lot of finger-pointing, and a lot of unbearable smugness, I really thought Lindsey might make good on her threat to sit on me. You'd think fifteen years and motherhood would change a person, but no.

I filled her and Scott in the best I could, downplaying the shittiness of the magical world, but not so much that they'd be caught unprepared. Seeing the brief glimmers of golden light flickering around Conner's sleeping body told me they'd have to know about a lot of stuff, and sooner than I would've liked.

The only thing that got me through the ordeal was watching Scott and Bastian making awkward conversation in the background. Bastian didn't look uncomfortable, exactly. More like he was trying to get a good grade in acting human and might be tested on it.

It took hours before Lindsey finally let me slink off, and after saying goodnight to Bastian, I dragged myself home to fall into bed, barely remembering to shut my door. At least Lindsey hadn't busted my chops too much, and she let me put up some protections on her house before we left, so that was something.

My dreams were unfortunately absent that night. If there

had ever been a time when I could've used Cornelius' advice, it was then. But there was nothing except darkness until someone started poking me incessantly in the cheek sometime way too early.

"What?" I growled, trying to tunnel further under my blanket.

Percy, the little shit, just pecked at my fingers instead. "Hey. Statue's gone."

What fresh hell? I hadn't even had a coffee yet. "What statue? Context, please."

Feathers rasped against my comforter as Percy flipped her wings. "The important one of the guy on a horse."

I poked my head up, glaring blearily through eyes that really did not want to open. "Percy, this is Boston. Do you have any idea how little that narrows it down?"

Crows couldn't roll their eyes, but the way Percy arched her head back meant the same thing. She clicked her beak in annoyance before spitting out a surprisingly good impression of a man's voice. "The British are coming."

It took a second to land in my sleep-addled brain, but when it did, I sat up straight like I'd been electrocuted. "Are you telling me the statue of Paul Revere is *missing*?"

The statue of Paul Revere was missing.

"Shit, shit, shit," I hissed, raking a hand back through my hair. Percy cawed in irritation, flapping her wings to keep her balance on my shoulder.

I *so* did not need this.

I had a million theories to check out, people to talk to, Magi to find, a Harrowing conspiracy… but instead, I was standing ankle-deep in snow at the Paul Revere Mall in the blue light before dawn, staring at a huge, empty, marble stand.

Because the statue of Paul Revere, the enormous bronze casting of him sitting astride his horse—possibly the most photographed statue in the entire city and smack dab in the middle of the bloody Freedom Trail—was *missing*.

The thing had to weigh a thousand pounds. Who could just make off with it? People would notice it was gone. There wasn't any way around that. The only reason the place wasn't swarming with cops already was the fact that it was before dawn, and the area wasn't as crowded in November as it was any other time of year. They'd even turned the fountain off farther back in the park, the whole thing covered in a blanket of fluffy white snow.

And of course it couldn't have been a normal theft, someone living out their comic book supervillain dream—oh no. Because then it would've been a problem for someone else, probably the F.B.I. But no, there was magical nonsense afoot, which meant it fell squarely into the *me* problem pile since no one else would handle it.

I hadn't seen or heard from Mason since the night I kicked a Harrower out of his house. Not that I was holding my breath for a thank-you gift basket or anything.

But how did I know that the missing statue was a Magi problem?

Because of the huge hoofprints leading away from the base where the statue once stood. It looked like it had stepped down off the platform and trotted away.

My fingers curled into a fist in my hair, and I resisted the urge to pull only because the beast could get dangerous when provoked. "What the hell? Why is this my life?"

I hadn't even had a chance to write my thoughts down after all the nonsense last night. I had so many calls to make, and instead, I was trailing along after hoofprints in the snow like the world's most inept Sherlock Homes.

Percy squished a little tighter to the side of my neck, nestling down into the collar of my jacket. "You said watch for weird stuff. This is weird."

"Yeah, no argument." I huffed out a sigh, the air pluming into a white cloud. "Just rotten timing."

The sense of urgency to find Cornelius and the Senior Council had ramped right back up to where it had been in the first days they'd gone missing. I couldn't just go racing off with a vague warning and a half-assed direction, but man, was it tempting.

If there was even a chance that the Harrowing had their nasty, fear-loving claws on them... I shuddered. There was no way I could leave them to that.

The air was icy in the early morning light. It was also damp and smelled like more snow on the horizon. I trudged through the drifts, trying not to slip on the spots where dozens of feet had trampled the snow down to a slick, mirror finish. The red brick buildings were all tight together in that area, forming narrow roads that could barely fit a man on a bronze horse.

I just hoped he hadn't wandered far.

The hoofprints turned down another narrow alley, and up ahead, I could feel a prickle in the air. It wasn't so much a rip in the Akasha as it was a slow leak. To me, it looked like a crack between the bricks that made up the side of the building, golden light leaking out where the mortar should have been.

Well, that explained a few things, at least. And it was a quick fix, smoothing the edges of reality back together, if not seamlessly, then well enough that no other bits of the park should go on a walkabout.

Most of the alley was full of a huge metal dumpster that, even in the cold, reeked of garlic and over-ripe tomatoes from the Italian place next door. It wasn't the worst smell, but I wouldn't have wanted to be hugging it at the height of summer.

One of the only good things about winter—less rot.

I held my hand up toward the little fissure in the world,

letting the crackle of power play over my skin. It felt different than it used to. More like intense sunlight than electricity that was liable to bite. I couldn't help but compare it to my first days as a Magi, when holding any amount of power for too long made me feel like I had a sunburn on the inside of my skin. I was paranoid about holding any kind of magic for too long, especially after seeing people burst with it.

The fight with the sea serpent had been long and hard. I should've felt aftereffects from that. But other than being tired and super nauseous, there hadn't been anything. Maybe Magi magic was like physical endurance, something that could be built up over time.

Not that I knew anything about physical endurance.

The last time I tried to run a mile, I almost had a heart attack.

Then again, maybe it was something else.

I let the power seep through the crack, into my hand, flowing down my body in lines of warmth. The little Void seed in my belly was like a sliver of ice, drawing the heat toward itself.

That made sense. It was diffusion—high concentrations of anything tended to flow to areas of low concentration.

And, despite the dogma, everyone kept trying to stuff down my throat... the Void wasn't the evil enemy of the Aether. It was just the other side of the coin.

A counterweight.

The power flowed, draining away into that little fleck of nothingness I'd taken into myself, and the cold throbbed through my body in a wave. I jerked back, breaking the connection. Sweat coated my face and my breath burned in my lungs, the air outside my body suddenly scorching warm in comparison.

Well. That was interesting.

Percy's feathers were plastered to her body, and she

hunkered down as small as she could make herself. A little unhappy click sounded in her throat. "What was that?"

"I'm not sure." My hand came up, and I hesitated before stroking her head gently. She leaned into it, needing the comfort as much as I did. "Sorry. I didn't mean to scare you."

Her derisive little caw was way quieter than usual. "You didn't."

My lips twitched. "Good."

"Enough playing around, ye daft git."

I shook my head and finished yanking the edges of reality back together before plastering over the fissure with enough energy to make sure another one didn't form. The glow died away, and brick and mortar and early morning sky became just that again.

Plastic shifted behind me, and I spun fast enough that Percy's bad foot slid, and she whacked me in the side of the head with one wing while trying to keep her balance.

The dumpster was open, just a bit, the lid propped up by what looked like a chunk of wood to make it easier for the kitchen staff to get into it. A pair of huge, pale eyes like moonstones stared out at me from that little strip of darkness.

My heart seized in my chest like it was in a vise. "Um, so, what are the odds that a revolutionary hero on a horse is hanging out in the dumpster?"

Percy didn't answer, which, fair, it was a stupid question.

The lid of the dumpster slammed open, the crash of metal on brick echoing through the narrow space between buildings like a gunshot.

I jumped, my breath stuttering in my chest as something long, pale, and hairless oozed out of the steel box. Its face—if I could call it that when it had absolutely no features other than those staring eyes and a line that could have been a lipless mouth, was weirdly elongated, like a gourd. A bulbous head narrowed down into something that could have been a muzzle, but just wasn't. It was almost human-shaped—in that it had a head, two arms and two legs—but after that, things took a hard swerve into the uncanny valley.

The creature was skeletally thin. I could've counted each of its ribs if I wanted to, which I did not. Its limbs were all too long for its short trunk, looking like they should have extra joints in them as it padded toward me on mostly human-looking feet. Each of its fingers were twice the length that they should have been, and looking at them, all I could imagine were those pale, wormy digits wrapping around my throat and squeezing.

The Aether-born slunk toward me, its head tilted at a strange angle like it was trying to figure out what I was. The stupid crack had hidden it from me, but I could feel the power bound up in it now, pulsing like a little sun. It wasn't anywhere near Stefan's level of power, the weight of the entire vampire mythos fueling him, but it was still potent.

The worst thing was, I recognized it once it had oozed its way out of the dumpster. I'd seen that same shape on countless T-shirts and crap peddled to tourists, not to mention websites that celebrated Massachusetts local weirdness.

"It's the Dover Demon." The laugh that slipped out of me as I took a step back was edged with hysteria. "Of course it is. Hey, little guy. We're cool, right?"

For something that had its first sighting in the seventies, the Aether-born had a surprising amount of mojo. It usually took a long time for a myth to build up that kind of metaphysical weight to it.

But it was fine. The Dover Demon wasn't particularly harmful in pop culture. I mean, I didn't think it was...

Right until the thing dropped to all fours and bolted toward me.

"Oh, screw this." I scrambled backward, trying to keep the distance between us. Percy gave a startled caw and launched herself off my shoulder. For a second, I couldn't see anything but black feathers and long, icy fingers wrapped around my ankle.

The kick was reflexive, but it tore my leg free from the Dover Demon's hands before its grip could tighten. That didn't stop it from lunging for me again.

My shoulders slammed against the brick wall as I scrambled to get out of the way. One foot slid in the snow, and I twisted to keep it from going out from under me while trying to stay out of reach of those horrible, grasping little hands.

"Oh, what the hell?"

The alley was too narrow, there was nowhere for me to go, and however I was going to deal with the little monster, I didn't want it on top of me while I was doing it.

I bolted back for the park, trying to keep some distance. Percy cawed overhead, either telling me to move or trying to warn the critter off. I couldn't tell which. My heart slammed against the inside of my ribs, chills running over my skin.

It wasn't even that big, maybe a little larger than Conner, but the wrongness of it was creeping me out. The way it moved, so close to human and then not at all.

I didn't want it anywhere near me.

As soon as I was back in the open, I whipped around, and my hand snapped out. The easiest way to release energy was through heat and light, which was why fire had been my go-to for as long as I'd known magic was real. And while it might've been instinct and fear in the beginning, it was actually deliberate these days.

Flames shot through the air between us, but the Dover Demon was wickedly fast, twisting around the gout of fire and letting it hit the ground in a fountain of hissing snow. I danced backward, cursing, trying to stay out of reach, but that horrible little hand wrapped around my ankle again and *yanked*.

My heel skidded in the slush and snow, and I went down with a thin yelp. My skull bounced off the pavement and pain shot through my head, stars bursting across my vision. For a horrifying moment, my limbs went slack... like they weren't even attached to my body.

Cold hands and feet pressed against my knee, off my hip, claws dug into my ribcage as the Dover Demon raced up my body toward my head. I flinched back, wildly twisting my face out of the way while my stunned brain tried to come up with something, *anything*, that wasn't staring up at the slowly lightening sky.

A shadow passed overhead.

There was a huffing squall, and the demon's weight was gone.

I blinked against my swimming vision and scrabbled onto my elbows to see what happened. The man made of bronze calmly pulled himself back straight into the saddle of his bronze horse from where he'd dipped down to kick the Dover Demon off my chest.

Something made entirely out of metal shouldn't have been able to move so smoothly, but the horse spun on a dime. Its carved ears flattened against the smooth arch of its beautiful neck, and it charged back toward where the Dover Demon was picking itself up from where it was thrown.

The horse reared back on its hind legs, stretching to its full impressive height, before the entire weight of that solid bronze body came crashing down directly on top of the Dover Demon, and it vanished beneath the trampling hooves.

I winced, looking away. By the time I braced myself to look back, the Dover Demon was crumbling apart into motes of golden light that merged into the first streaks of dawn sunlight angling over the nearby buildings.

Whoa.

I wasn't often literally stunned into silence, but watching Paul Revere turn his horse to amble back in my direction was enough to send anyone for a bit of a trip.

Prove me wrong.

The man himself leaned down in the saddle and stretched a hand toward me. It took me an embarrassingly long moment to realize he was offering to help me up from where I was still half-sprawled in the snow. His fingers were chilly, and his grip was surprisingly careful as he hauled me back to my feet.

I dusted myself off, not having a clue what to say, but finally stuttered out an awkward, "Thank you."

And then immediately flushed, feeling like an idiot.

Okay, yes, in my head I knew that wasn't the actual Paul Revere, the silversmith who warned people of the British army's approach during the Revolutionary War. That didn't help at all when someone out of the history books was suddenly right in front of me, not exactly in the flesh.

Two hundred years of being hailed as a hero was a lot of power for the Aether to bring to his commemorative statue. Lucky for me, because I'd been about a second and a half from getting my face eaten.

Paul Revere tipped his hat to me, and I couldn't stop the stupid smile that stretched across my face. It was so much worse than meeting a celebrity. I was fangirling over someone who'd been dead over two centuries before I was born.

I watched with something uncomfortably close to awe as the horse and its rider picked their way across the snowy expanse of the park before leaping with supernatural grace back onto the enormous stone slab of their original position. One leg curled high, one arm outstretched, and then the pose froze in place.

The golden potential of the Aether ebbed from that cast bronze surface, waiting.

Percy hopped down from the tree she fled to, her bad foot slipping on the material of my coat before she caught herself. "Are you okay?"

Weirdly enough, I was. I double-checked though, patting

down all the places that the Dover Demon grabbed me, just in case. "Yeah, I'm not hurt."

At least there were no puncture wounds or scratches or anything. My shoulders ached, and my head was pounding, but that was ibuprofen stuff. Nothing I needed a doctor for, which was close enough to 'not hurt' for me.

Percy flipped her wings, her feathers easing down into something more relaxed than the puffball she'd been a second earlier. She jerked her beak toward the waiting statue. "So, what are you gonna do with that?"

"I think," I said slowly, feeling out the words. "Nothing."

One black button eye gave me a curious look as Percy cocked her head toward me. "Nothing? You're just leaving this one?"

"I think I am." There wasn't any playbook for this sort of thing. Cornelius would have either drained the magic from the statue or banished it to the Akasha. Who knew what Mason would do if he ever got up off his butt to play magical sanitation worker?

But neither of them was there—*I was.*

The statue wasn't hurting anyone—the opposite. He saved me from bloody injury. And I got the impression he was content to stay put, waiting for the next time he might be needed.

In the middle of the horror and uncertainty, it was a pleasant reminder that the Aether could make wonders, too.

And Boston could use having another person watching out for her and her people.

So, I gave the statue a brief salute and left well enough alone.

CHAPTER TWELVE

"*And* that's why I need your help to punch a hole in the Akasha so I can find the Senior Council and bring them home." I clicked over to the last slide and ended the presentation. The ringing silence wasn't exactly encouraging.

I had asked the other apprentices to forgo the mirror shards and do a video call with me. I didn't want things messed up by the cruddy enchantment I'd done on my piece of the mirror, and the PowerPoint I put together for my proposal would be a lot easier and a lot clearer if I shared it online instead of through a foggy piece of glass.

Everyone managed to meet me. Will looked like he was on a laptop in a library, if the wall of books behind him was any indication, but the signal was stable for all of them, so I probably couldn't blame lag for the way everyone was staring at me.

Silently. Wearing expressions of varying degrees of disbelief and alarm.

I fought the urge to squirm. Tough crowd.

It was Koji who finally broke the awkward tableau everyone had fallen into, leaning forward until his face took up most of his little window on my laptop screen. "You want us," he started carefully, sounding like he was carrying a too-full glass of something he didn't want to spill, "to help you rip a hole in reality, to go spelunking through the Akasha, on the off chance that the Senior Council is in there. Somewhere."

Annnd we were off to a great start.

I cleared my throat. "It sounds ridiculous when you put it that way... but essentially."

Sean made a sound that might have been a laugh if it were full of humor instead of disbelief. "Are ye out of yer bloody mind?"

"Okay, maybe I didn't explain the PowerPoint well enough." I clicked back a few screens. "Let me go over the last slides again."

"Ash, it's not the presentation." Will did that thing where his face was all gentle concern, like he was worried I was a second away from some kind of emotional breakdown. "This is actually nuts. I'm not trying to be judgmental, but are you okay?"

"That sounds pretty judgmental," I muttered. "But yes... I am okay. And this isn't nuts. I've been thinking about this for weeks now. Think about it; where else could the entire Senior-freak-ing-Council of the Seven Spheres have ended up that they couldn't just teleport their butts home? If anyone else has a theory, I'm willing to hear it."

And there it was. I could see it in the lines of their faces, the way they wouldn't meet my eyes. They thought the Council was dead. Even across thousands of miles of cable and through a screen, I could feel their grief like a suffocating blanket.

A muscle ticked in my jaw as I ground my teeth. They weren't dead. I didn't know how I knew it, but I did. I wouldn't accept any other possibility.

Koji sighed, slumping in his chair. The bruises on his face had faded to sickly yellow and green, and the only dark shadows left were the ones underneath his eyes. "I admire your loyalty, Aisling, I do. But they wouldn't thank you for throwing yourself onto their pyre."

I scowled, ready to snap back that they weren't dead and I didn't appreciate him saying it like it was a foregone conclusion, but Tessa jumped in before I could say anything.

"Ash, I understand why you want to do this, but it's not possible." Her big, dark eyes were so full of sorrow, her lips turned down. "This isn't like going off-road into the backwoods. The Akasha is literally another world, and not a friendly one. There's no GPS, no way to navigate to a certain place. So, what? Say you pull it off without ripping a hole in the world. What then? Do you just wander? Forever?"

This was the part I really hadn't been looking forward to, which was a big deal, because I hadn't been looking forward to any of the other parts, either. I crossed my fingers that this talk wasn't about to go sideways in a terrible way. "Yeah, so about that. I kind of have something of Cornelius' that I could use to link to his energy and track him."

"Oh, bloody brilliant." Sean leaned back in his chair, an unlit cigarette dangling from between his lips. "Yer going to risk yer life, hoping what? That a favorite bathrobe will lead ye to the old man? Feckin' hell."

I glared, ramping it up to an eight on my scale. By all rights, it should have burned a hole in the screen. "No, it's not a bathrobe, but thank you for assuming that I'm an idiot."

Getting angry wasn't going to win them over, so I used Sean's second of chastised silence to take a breath and get it together. "So, here's the thing. Cornelius had a premonition when he took me on as an apprentice. He knew something was going to happen that would keep him from having the time to do things the traditional way. It was all vague and stupid."

What good was information bouncing backward through the Aether—which Cornelius assured me had no real concept of time being linear—if it was so ambiguous that no one could do anything with it?

I waved it off. "The point is, he did something where he gathered together all his memories of working with the Aether from his life, and he kind of implanted them in my head. Like software that was supposed to integrate."

"He feckin' *what?*" Sean screeched, nearly falling out of his chair when he tried to yank his feet down off of the table.

Tessa blinked, shocked. Koji looked concerned, in his way, leaning forward to examine my face through the screen. It was intense enough that part of me wished for my crappily enchanted mirror shard back.

Will just looked stunned. "He... that's so dangerous. He could have overwritten your personality. He could have given you a stroke. He could have fried something in your memory center."

Well, wasn't that good to know months after the fact? When I saw that old man again, I was going to strangle him with his tie until his stupid little glasses popped off.

"Well, luckily for me, none of those things happened."

Koji's intense gaze flicked over my face again. I didn't know what he saw in my expression, but the muscles around his eyes relaxed a little when he found it. "So, it actually worked?"

I made a waggling motion with my hand. "At first, it was more like a trauma dump directly into my brain. It worked a bit, but then all the memories faded and we assumed the whole thing had bombed. Then, once he pulled his vanishing act, I started having dreams."

Why did telling them feel so personal? But I had to put my cards on the table. I couldn't very well ask them to take a leap of faith with me if I was holding back big chunks of information. Still, my palms itched, and I scrubbed them against the legs of my jeans.

"In the dreams, I could meet with Cornelius. Like a dream

copy of him. He didn't have any information past the point of when he gave the memories to me, but he could still teach me things, share information."

I glanced up, wanting to see their reactions. Mostly, they seemed surprised, but there was a flicker of something very much like jealousy in a few faces, and I instantly felt bad. They lost their mentors, too. People they had known for years, not just a few weeks like me. But I was the one who got to keep a piece of Cornelius, because of a stray bit of a warning from the Aether.

My old nemesis, self-consciousness, reared its ugly head, and I cleared my throat. "Anyway, the memories started fading again a few weeks ago, and I haven't been able to reach dream Cornelius since then. But I'm pretty sure they've just been..." I made a rolling gesture with my hands. "Absorbed by my subconscious. The memories are still in there, somewhere. They've just merged with the rest of me. But what better way to track Cornelius than with a copy of himself?"

"It... it could work. Couldn't it?" Sean leaned forward, gripping the edges of his screen. The naked hope on his face was hard to look at. It made him look younger than he was. "Guys? This could actually feckin' work."

The others all started to talk at once, and my speakers struggled to catch it all. It was Tessa holding up her hand that brought silence to the channel again.

She took a breath, visibly calming herself. "Ash, I know you mean well, but the Akasha... It's not like anywhere in the world. It's the thing that keeps reality safe from the Aether. Think of it like a lead wall protecting us from intense radiation. If you went there, you'd be bombarded, constantly, by the power of the Aether."

Her face twisted with grief for a moment, her eyes too bright with tears she wasn't letting fall. "You remember what happened to Jamie? That could happen to you just by being there. It's not a place humans can go, no matter how determined."

"She's right," Will jumped in, his drawl thicker than normal. "Aether-born can set up camp in there because they're more magic than anything else. And even they shield themselves, I'm sure."

He took a breath and shook his shaggy dark head. "You wouldn't even have that, just wandering around."

A warning about wandering coming from the closest thing to a knight errant I'd ever met felt a hair too ironic for me, but his point was valid.

I chewed my bottom lip. Below the desk where none of them could see, my hand crept to the cold spot around my belly button where the Void seed waited. "About that. I think I have a way to shield myself. Or at least ground out some of the energy."

I saw the barrage coming and cut them off before they could get started. "And no, I won't be answering any follow-up questions on that one."

Trust was one thing, but with how squirrely they all got at any mention of the Void, no way was I getting into that one. Even I didn't understand how I hadn't imploded around it, and it wasn't anything I wanted people poking at.

"Well, that isn't concerning at all," Koji said, with the kind of dry sarcasm that almost circled back into sincerity.

Tessa folded her arms across her chest tightly enough that it looked like she was hugging herself. "Look, we all want them back. I'd give anything just to see Imani again."

Her voice broke, and we all waited while she took a couple of deep breaths. Will's hands flexed on the table and he half-rose from his seat like he could step into the other room to comfort her instead of being hundreds of miles away.

Though, he was really good at the doorway thing he did, so maybe he could.

Tessa cleared her throat and wiped carefully at her eyes, somehow not smudging her liner. "The fact is, no matter how you spin it, this is wildly, stupidly dangerous. What you're proposing... can't be done. And none of us can ask you to do it. I'm not sending you on a suicide mission, not even to get them back. If they're even there to be found."

The others reluctantly nodded, looking down at their laps. Sean tapped his cigarette against the table over and over until it fell apart.

Since Stefan had started going out in the evenings again, I'd set up in the main room of the apartment, with my laptop on the table, and all my notes strewn around it like a corona of ink and equations. I ran my fingers over the pages, sliding them against each other. With everyone on the video call so busy looking down silently like mourners at a funeral, the soft hiss of paper on paper was the loudest thing in the room.

Their heads jerked up when I laughed.

"I'm sorry." I dabbed at my eyes, trying to rein it in. "I know that's not appropriate. I just..." I trailed off into a wheeze, weeks of stress bleeding out of me in hiccupping giggles. "Look, you seem to be operating under a fallacy here. Let me explain."

I sucked in a breath and forced the rest of the giggles down when they tried to escape through my nose. Seriously, Ash. It was time to pretend I was presenting a paper.

I met their gazes on the screen, all of them still looking shocked.

"You seem to think that I'm asking your permission, and that it's your responsibility to give or deny it. In fact, you have three choices in front of you. One." I held up a finger. "Help me set this up so it's done as safely as possible and with the highest chance of success. Two: refuse to help me, and I'll do it anyway, but with a bigger chance that something will go breathtakingly wrong."

I lifted a third finger, still making as much eye contact as possible—this was the trickiest one. "And three: try to actively stop me, and potentially abandon the Senior Council, your friends and mentors, to the Harrowing and their plans."

My words landed like a sucker punch.

If the room had been silent before, it was ringing now.

It was a cheap shot, I knew it. Emotional jabs usually were. But I wasn't kidding when I said that I'd need their help if there was going to be even a chance for things to work out. It wasn't just getting into the Akasha that had me worried—it was making sure nothing took advantage of my passage to sneak out.

Boston had been through enough during the past months, it didn't need another disaster.

But I'd go, anyway. I had to. I didn't know what the Harrowing was up to, but I wasn't going to let it slide, regardless.

It was Will who spoke first. "Ash, think about this. There's a chance you could die, and not a small one."

I was trying hard not to think about that, so it was kind of rude to labor the point. I shook my head. "Guys, I'm going. You can't talk me out of it. I've been through the science. I'm smart. Like *really* smart. So, you can either help me, or stay out of the way and see what happens."

The guys started muttering again, but Tessa was silent. She just sat there, watching me. I wasn't sure how much she could do magically-speaking from over the internet, but the intensity of the look was uncomfortable.

After what felt like an hour but was probably less than a minute, she let out a shaky breath. "When and where?"

Relief blossomed in my chest, making my arms tingle. I had really hoped they would help, but if they'd dug in and refused to let me make the attempt, they could've thrown serious issues my way. And that wasn't even taking into consideration that

Will could step through a door and instantly be in my apartment whenever he wanted.

"Three days," I told her. "Same place as the first ritual."

I figured that going in through the same spot that Cornelius did couldn't hurt my chances of finding him and might actually help.

The others followed Tessa's lead, like usual, and we sketched out a hasty plan to get things set up. It was with a mixture of excitement, relief, and panic that I closed the lid of my laptop an hour later. I was really doing it. I was going to go where no Magi had before.

And I was possibly about to die in the stupidest way imaginable.

A laugh dragged its way out of my throat, and I tunneled my fingers into my hair, gripping hard enough to tug on the roots. Well, one trial finished—a million more to go. I just wished I was as confident as I'd made myself sound.

The truth was, I was scared as hell. I didn't know what I was walking into, and there weren't many people I could talk to who could tell me what to expect.

I wasn't an idiot. While physics wasn't a big one for field studies, I wouldn't throw myself into an alternate dimension without a backup plan. I planned to be very careful about how I went about this. I had three days to figure it out.

Piece of cake.

The front door opened, startling me out of my thoughts, and the front legs of my chair thumped back against the floor when I rocked forward.

Stefan came in, glanced around at the mess of paper, notebooks, and the whiteboard covered in frantic scribbles I had propped in front of the stove, and rolled his eyes. "Nesting, are we?"

I realized the mess had gotten away from me a little, as I

looked over the drifts of paper piling up like snow. "Yeah, sorry. I'll clean it all up."

He shrugged out of his coat and absently picked up a torn piece of printer paper, flipping it around to get it right side up before giving up and tossing it back onto the couch. "What are you trying to figure out this time? Building a death ray? Time travel?"

I snorted. "Don't be stupid. Time travel isn't even possible."

Or was it? I stopped to think about it for a second. If there was no time in the Aether, then wasn't all time technically happening at once? Would the energy only flow in one direction?

I shook it off. One problem at a time, and I already had half a dozen of them on my plate. I shelved that one for future consideration when I was seized with the need to inflict pain on myself.

My back cracked as I stood, and I groaned with the pain-edged relief. I twisted a little, trying to work out muscles that had been hunched for too long. "I'm trying to figure out how to track something through the Akasha. It feels a bit like I'm traveling to Mars, honestly. There are a lot of variables to consider."

I glanced at Stefan, one arm locked in the opposite elbow, trying to work out a stubborn kink in my shoulder, and froze at the wide-eyed look he was giving me. "What? What's wrong?"

"You're actually going there? Not to a demesne, but traveling through it? Do you have any idea how dangerous that is?"

"No," I said shortly, not loving his tone. "Do you?"

Stefan took a short, angry stride forward. His hands flailed as he gestured with each word. "No, I don't. I've never been crazy enough to try, but when Magi shove Aether-born out of the world, where do you think they end up? And let me tell you, a lot of them are probably homicidal about not being able to hunt in the real world anymore."

I knew logically that Stefan was a vampire—it was hard to miss—but easy to forget exactly what that meant.

I couldn't ignore it then, listening to him rant. Not when his skin was pulled tight over the stark bones of his face, his citron-colored eyes practically glowing. Fangs flashed between his lips as he spat the words at me.

"You're signing up to take a stroll through a prison where you, and people just like you, sent all the inmates. Does that seem like a good idea to you, genius?" He swiped a hand through a pile of papers, sending them fluttering to the floor like wounded birds.

"What the hell, Stefan?" Mess with me, whatever. Don't touch my notes. I crossed my arms, giving him a glare that was a solid six out of ten. "What is your problem?"

He didn't even notice the glare, too busy giving me one of his own. "Why do you always do this? Risk your life for people who don't even give a shit about you?"

That rocked me back on my heels. Was he angry or worried? I didn't have the social skills to navigate around feelings like this, but I did my best to de-escalate. Stefan wouldn't hurt me, but picking a fight with an angry vampire still seemed like a stupid thing to do.

"So, what would you rather I do? Nothing? Should I sit around and let bad things happen, knowing I could have done something about it?"

Shit needed to get done... and no one else was lining up to deal with it. If the Harrowing didn't want me gatecrashing their plans, they should've stayed the hell away from my family.

His jaw worked like he was chewing his words. Stefan curled his lip up off his teeth, putting one fang on display. "You're going to get yourself killed, Magi, and I don't want to watch."

Before I even processed that, he was moving. Not toward his bedroom, but toward the front door, grabbing his coat as he went.

I sputtered, feeling like the conversation was giving me whiplash. "Where are you going?"

"Out," he snapped.

"Stefan, it's *your* apartment! Why are you—"

The door slammed, cutting me off. The floor rattled with the force of it, sending another cascade of paper sliding to the floor. I dropped my head into my hands.

Well, that went well.

CHAPTER THIRTEEN

With everyone so damn convinced I would croak the instant I set foot in the Akasha, I got a wee bit nervous. I thought maybe a test run might've been in order, so to speak. I mean, they weren't wrong. It was dangerous. I once sent a pencil through a tear and it had fallen into two pieces like someone cut it with a laser.

Passage had to be possible or the Aether-born wouldn't be able to do it.

Of course, they were pure energy when they entered the world, I assumed, only taking on physical form once they got shaped by a particular bit of belief.

The point was, it might be trickier than I hoped.

That meant it was time to get my mad scientist on.

Normally, I'd never do an experiment outside of a lab setting. The more random variables that were in place, the more skewed your results could get. But it was too cold and snowy out to find someplace outside and away from people, and anywhere inside had the chance of random people stumbling across me. So... the middle of the apartment, it was.

I just hoped whatever bug Stefan had up his butt kept him elsewhere for a few hours.

I didn't want to imagine how he'd react if he came home to find me making portals in the living room. Which, honestly, was unfair, considering the things I'd walked in to find *him* doing in the living room.

It took me a few minutes to get ready, moving the furniture out of the way and rolling back the rug. I didn't know if the Akasha stained, but the less evidence left behind the better.

Once that was done, I sat crossed-legged on the floor, and pulled out both the box I picked up at the electronics store earlier, and a knife.

It wasn't just *any* knife. This was the knife that Bastian gave me when he got the crazy notion that I got into dangerous situations often. It looked like someone had forged the whole thing out of obsidian, except that its surface was matte black without a hint of shine.

The light didn't glint off the blade—it got sucked into it.

The whole thing looked like a splinter of darkness.

It was made from the Void, and I had no guess about how it was stable enough to take on physical form. The only time I'd seen the Void in the real world in action, it had been through Cornelius' memories, and it had been horrifying.

A gaping maw, crumbling the edges of reality. Everything fading away to nothingness.

Worse than nothingness—oblivion.

Which meant that I wasn't super comfy with carrying the thing around on my body. It seemed like it could cut through anything—like those kitchen shears they advertised on TV when I was a kid—so it stayed at home most of the time.

Which defeated the entire purpose of him giving it to me, but oh well.

The box was my compromise with my sense of self-preservation about sticking my head into an unknown and unknowable pseudo-dimension. That was what we in physics would call a 'bad idea'. So, I'd popped down to the hobby store and picked up one of those drones that had a camera, hoping to get some kind of useable footage.

It only took a few minutes to get the software set up, and a few more than that to figure out the controls on the stupid thing. Eventually, my little method of scientific inquiry was up and hovering, and I only took out one lamp.

The knife was cold enough in my hand that my skin stuck to it if I wasn't careful. It was a good thing my hands were steady, so I could reach out with intent and carve a small slit through the fabric of reality itself. The tear was just big enough for the drone to buzz through. No way was I making anything bigger, not after the tentacle incident.

When that was done, I carefully laid the knife back down and scrubbed my palms on my thighs to get rid of the feeling that clung to them. Then the drone was up and moving, buzzing toward the place where light bent into a glorious rainbow circle, colors bleeding around the edges.

"This is either really stupid or really brilliant, I muttered to myself as I concentrated on steering the drone."

"Yer sitting on the floor in yer jim-jams and talking to yerself. Which do ye think it is?"

"Shut it."

A flicker of light, the whine of the propeller, and the drone was gone.

I craned my head around to watch the screen, fumbling with the controls now that I was flying blind.

My eyes went wide. My jaw dropped.

For a split second, I thought I was looking out into the vastness of space. Velvety darkness stretched out in front of my eyes, with dazzling pinpricks of light breaking it up. Colors warped at the edge of the screen, like the aurora borealis, but in brilliant reds and pinks and purples and blues. There were rocks floating out in the darkness, just hovering there. Was there no gravity? Or were they floating in something, some kind of superfluid?

"Holy shit."

The drone dipped, and I struggled to keep it flying on course, taking in everything I was seeing on the screen.

Something huge rocketed by overhead. The shadows and gusting wake of its passage sent the drone spiraling. Static flickered across the screen and I swore, fighting to get it back under control.

The camera lens twisted, distorting the picture. Static fluttered again, and the feed died.

Grumbling, I hit the switch for the drone to return to starting position. With any luck, I could get it back through the tear. Thanks to Cornelius' control freak tendencies, I wasn't exactly hurting for money. That didn't mean I enjoyed wasting it.

Luck was with me for once because after another eye-watering flare of light, the drone popped back into my living room.

At least *something* popped in.

I caught the movement of spiny little legs, the clatter of metal wings turned into something insectoid, and the great glass eyeball where a camera lens should have been, and I was already kicking my foot out to knock it back through the tear.

"Nope, nope, nope."

The second it was through, I tossed in the remote for good measure and slammed the edges of the tear closed back together so hard, the air itself rippled.

I sat there frozen for a long second, before letting myself collapse backward onto the floor, not even caring when my bruised shoulders stung at the impact.

I lay on the floor for a long minute, my heart skipping along at double time, and waited for my fingers to stop tingling with the last surge of adrenaline. Despite everything, a grin stretched its way across my face. "I'd call that a success."

The echo of my grandmother's derisive snort rang through my head, but even my mean little inner voice couldn't get me down.

Sure, the drone hadn't been reusable, but I'd proven material things could pass through a tear. How successfully seemed dependent on where things went in, though.

I tapped my fingers on my chin.

The Fae were my best bet to ask more about traveling the Akasha, but they felt they'd repaid whatever debt they owed me. I wasn't thrilled at the idea of making a bargain with them for the information. My gran would have dragged herself out of the grave to box my ears if she knew I was out dealing with the 'fair folk', and for a tiny old woman, she had really strong hands.

There was one other option, but that one was almost as scary as the looming specter of Gran's disapproval. Almost.

I didn't have many choices... and what was the saying? Better the devil you know.

I dragged myself off the floor and went looking for some nice paper.

I'd never been much of a fan of tea, but taking a sip of the bright, sweet, floral drink in my hands, I thought maybe I could have been convinced. The man sitting across the low black lacquer table from me watched over the rim of his own cup of tea before setting it down so lightly it didn't click against the surface.

Even after hanging out with Faeries and vampires and all manner of magical types, somehow, the Dragon was the one who made me feel the most like I was a six-year-old with messy hair and peanut butter smeared on my face.

It wasn't anything he did or said. Considering he was one of the most scarily powerful people on the planet, he was a surprisingly gracious and considerate host. Though I felt a brief surge of pity for anyone who disrespected that hospitality. The problem was more his general air of grace and competence that left me scrambling to catch up.

I had fired off the letter—that I took the time to write out longhand, like a Luddite—and had been surprised at how quickly I received a reply, inviting me to meet him for tea. The strip of paper with beautiful calligraphy inked on it meant that I hadn't needed to call Will to awkwardly ask him for a ride.

I hoped Stefan didn't try to go into my bedroom while I was gone, or he'd end up crashing our little tea party, and I didn't think that would make him any happier with me.

I had run around the apartment in a panic, trying to make myself presentable. The last time I faced him, Caitriona worked me over for hours, and something very close to divine intervention was used to get my hair to behave. Tonight, I did the best I could and crossed my fingers.

Being late for a meeting I requested seemed like a bad idea.

Apparently, I hadn't needed to worry.

While his hair was still pulled back into a braid that draped over his shoulder and pooled into his lap, the Dragon had foregone his formal suit that made him look like he should strut the runway, and went for something that seemed even more formal, but also more casual at the same time.

Sitting across from me, he carefully arranged the fabric of his flowing robes around himself. They were black and gold, with hints of red in the intricate embroidery. The sleeves alone looked like they should've been framed and hung on the wall of a museum.

There were some awkward pleasantries, and it felt a bit like trying to stumble my way through a dance that I didn't know the steps to. I wasn't trying to be rude, but I didn't really understand why he asked how my journey was. I stuck a strip of paper on a door and then walked through it.

He made me the talisman. He knew how it was better than I did.

Maybe he was asking about how well it had worked? So, I told him it worked perfectly, and the trip was a smooth one. That seemed to make him happy... or at least he didn't turn my intestines into scorpions, so I *assumed* he was happy.

It wasn't empty flattery. The transition was the smoothest I'd ever felt. Even Cornelius' Way between Marblehead and Cambridge felt like an elevator dropping a floor suddenly.

Eventually some mysterious social threshold must have been passed, because the Dragon swept his elaborate sleeve out of the way as he refilled my tea from a beautiful, glazed teapot with dragonflies painted on its surface, and smiled. "So, Aisling O'Reily. What brings you to me today?"

"I had some questions I was hoping you could answer," I said, tearing my eyes away from the delicately embroidered cranes taking flight on his sleeves. I wasn't a textile craft kind of gal, but Lindsey tried embroidery in high school. A lot of tears and bloodshed later and she had given up, but it gave me an idea of how much work had gone into that piece of clothing.

The Dragon noticed my attention and smoothed the fabric with his fingertips. "You like it?"

"It's beautiful," I told him honestly. I'd never seen anything quite like it.

He preened a little, lowering his arm in a way that made the trailing sleeve flare. "This one is a favorite of mine. It reminds me of my youth."

The man didn't look a day over thirty. He had no lines on his face, and the only thing that might have been considered a blemish, a small scar on his upper lip, just made him look real and alive and still stupidly handsome.

"Uh-huh."

His smile grew more genuine, little crinkles appearing at the corners of his eyes. "Well, I'm sure you didn't come here to discuss fashion."

There was a hopeful lilt to the statement, turning it into a question. Part of me almost wished that was what I was there for, so I didn't have to disappoint him... but all I knew about clothing was how to wear it. Mostly.

"Sorry, no."

He waved a hand. "No, no, think nothing of it. What can I do for you?"

He was being shockingly agreeable for a man who'd once sent me an invitation to an interrogation that was basically 'show up or else', but I decided to not overthink it and hoped for the best. I doubted very much there was anything he could want from me he couldn't get for himself.

"I wanted to ask you about how you built this place." I waved my hand around to indicate the pavilion we were sitting in, the lake surrounding it filled with water lilies and frogs, with dragonflies humming across the water's surface. "And about traveling through the Akasha safely."

The Dragon gave me a look and slowly lowered his teacup to the table. "Whatever are you up to, little Magi?"

Always with the follow-up questions. Could no one just spill the information I needed without knowing the specifics?

"Do you need to know that to answer?"

If anything, he looked more intrigued. "Possibly. But building a domain is something your own Senior Council members could teach you easily. So, why come to me?"

I froze, searching his face. His too-knowing eyes.

Some of the humor drained away, replaced by something very close to pity. "When a Magi lives long enough, we become attuned to the Aether to a degree. We notice when things change. When you know the parts of a symphony by heart, it makes it easy to notice when fresh notes are added. Or when instruments are taken away."

A cold lump formed in my throat, and I couldn't have forced a word past it if I tried. He knew. He knew the Senior Council was gone. Was allowing me to come here a trap? Part of a game? How badly had I just screwed up?

The Dragon watched me for a moment and then sighed. He nudged a little tray of nuts across the table toward me. "Here, try them. Careful though, they're spicy."

I took one automatically, because it meant I didn't have to try to talk for a second. He wasn't kidding about the spicy part, though. Fire tore through my mouth, hitting the back of my throat, and burned straight up into my sinuses. I had to blink away tears and pray my nose didn't start running, because that would've made the moment extra special.

The Dragon smirked, the jerk. "There we are. Back with me? Don't panic. I haven't shared my observations with anyone, and I don't intend to."

He sure looked like he was telling the truth, but all good liars did. I was not built for social games—not in academics, and not in magic circles. There was a reason I ended up doing more marking, and for worse classes than the rest of my fellow TAs.

"Why bring it up, then?" I finally asked when the burn in my mouth died down to more of a campfire than a towering inferno.

The Dragon tilted his head to one side, examining the bottom of his cup like he'd find some answers there. "I hoped it would prompt you to ask what you truly want to know, instead of stumbling through a lot of unnecessary information."

My fingers curled into fists in my lap under the table. What it really came down to was, did I trust him? The answer was hell no. I didn't know him. I didn't know what he wanted, or why he was doing any of this. But ultimately, I needed to ask what I wanted to know, otherwise why had I bothered to ask him for a meeting?

"I need to find something in the Akasha, but I don't have any proof that it's in there, or where it might be. I want to know how to do it safely without being bombarded with magical radiation or turned inside out or anything."

The Dragon blinked at me. "Turned inside out?"

"Or into some weird creature." I waved my hand. "Insert bad thing of your choice. I'd really rather skip it."

"You're not going to turn inside out."

"Tell that to the drone I sent through," I muttered into my tea before taking a gulp. I had no idea where the critter it had become had gone off to, but part of me expected to hear the clatter of its little metal wings at any second.

With a very put-upon sigh, the Dragon shook his head at me. "Of course a drone could be changed. It's a machine. It has no sense of self to protect it, no identity to cling to."

I paused, my cup halfway to my mouth. "So, people don't change, because we understand who we're supposed to be?"

"A simplified way of saying it, but yes. Your belief of self will keep you from being warped by the Aether."

A brief flare of something too small to be called hope guttered to life in my chest. I put my cup down a little too loudly, clumsy with the idea that I might actually pull this off. "So, it is possible to travel through the Akasha?"

"Anything is possible. You simply need to be sure you're willing to deal with the consequences."

Well, that was ominous. "Is that a warning?"

He gave me a slight smile, looking up through his lashes in a move that on someone one ounce less masculine and a lot less scary would have been coquettish. "You didn't come here for warnings."

And there I was, right back to feeling wrong-footed.

Communication was hard enough when everyone was making an effort. I didn't need cryptic, thanks.

"Maybe not... but that doesn't mean I wouldn't listen to them." I huffed out a breath, shaking my head. "The Council gives me nothing *but* warnings."

That made him laugh, wide and open. It wasn't mocking or threatening. It was a genuine laugh, like he genuinely found what I said funny. Still chuckling, he shook his head. "Well, you need to see where they're coming from. The Council has a rather long history, and their roots come from a place, ultimately, of fear. So, they seek control to minimize threats to themselves, and to others."

I wanted to lean forward, but the idea of resting my elbows on the pretty lacquer table made my atrophied social graces clutching their pearls, so I folded my hands in my lap instead. "Is that wrong?"

The Dragon waved his hand, golden rings glinting in the false sunlight trickling into the pavilion. "Right or wrong is irrelevant. It just is. What matters is whether it is effective or not. Things change, the Aether is nothing but change, but they cling to their ways that were established a millennium ago. What was once a shield may become a prison."

He smoothed out the fabric of one of his sleeves carefully. "Sometimes, change is necessary. The world needs something to shake up the status quo, to break up the old, dried and dead shell, so that something new can quicken. Sometimes, someone needs to break the rules."

For some reason, that made me blush. I cursed my pasty skin, knowing I was turning scarlet and unable to stop it. The grin that stretched across the Dragon's face absolutely didn't help.

I went to take another drink, but my cup was empty. Before I could put it down on the table, the Dragon was already refiling it from the teapot on the table. I watched him for a moment, watched his long fingers as he held his sleeve out of the way with a practiced gesture.

"Is that why you're helping me? Because you think I'm breaking rules?"

His head tilted from side to side as he carefully set the teapot down again. "Perhaps. Perhaps I'm curious as to what you'll do. Perhaps I was bored, and your letter arrived at just the opportune time for you. Or perhaps I'm interested to see if the ripples of your choices will affect other troubling things."

That got my interest, and I zeroed in on the last words. "Troubling things? What kind of troubling things?"

The Dragon didn't answer for a long moment. He just sipped his tea, holding it in his mouth to savor it before finally swallowing. The only thing that kept me from getting impatient was that it was exactly the same crap Cornelius used to do to stall for time while he decided how to answer me.

Who was I kidding? I still got impatient.

"Baba Yaga has been courting unfortunate friends. And she has been attempting to convince Ceridwyn to do the same."

At first, I thought he was changing the subject, and then I caught on to exactly what he was so casually hinting at.

"Allies for the King." That was what the Harrower had told me. Was that what the Dragon was trying to tell me? The old woman had sent some of her circle to kill the Council and had almost succeeded with me. She'd also come to the summit, only to hover over the room like a malevolent toad. Could I see her willingly teaming up with some fear-eating monsters?

That was a big old yes.

And holy crap, that would be bad news for everyone. I didn't even want to think about what she could unleash if backed by the Harrowing.

The Dragon gave me a knowing look. "There are dark things prowling the night near her territory. Their presence is... offensive."

"I wouldn't think something like that would bother you."

He looked at me. It was such a simple thing, but having the full weight of the Dragon's attention was a bit like having the full force of the sun directed at me. The power in him was immense, and without the teasing, flippant mask in place, that one look was enough to have me struggling to breathe.

He glanced down at his tea, breaking eye contact and letting me suck in a full breath. "We're all afraid of something, Aisling O'Reily. And the more you fear it, the more power it has over you."

Something about that tickled at the back of my brain, but I was too busy trying to convince my adrenal system that, no, we were fine, no need to freak out or try to tease through the thought.

I tried to laugh, but it came out as a cough. "I'm surprised you even let her into your domain, honestly. You don't seem to like her much."

That got a smile out of him, and some of the tension broke. He made a wide motion with the arm holding his teacup, somehow not spilling a single drop. "Oh, I just enjoy the drama. All those powerful people in one place, constantly trying to get one over on each other. It's fun."

That had not been what I was expecting, and the giggle slipped out of me before I could smother it behind my hand.

The Dragon outright grinned and rose to his feet in a single move that was honestly more impressive than magic. I needed to grab the table to get up, and one of my feet had fallen asleep, but at least he didn't comment on my little stumble sideways.

"You asked about domains. This is how I hold mine."

The Dragon raised a hand and golden light flared, bright enough to have spots dancing across my vision. On every pillar, on the roof, on the floor, on the zig-zag bridge that led over the pond to the grassy shore, there were calligraphy characters painstakingly written in pure sunlight. I couldn't read any of them, but by reaching out with the part of me that touched the Aether, I could get a sense of them. How they directed the energy, made it flow around the space, and protected his fabricated world from unwanted intruders.

It reminded me a bit of the warding that I'd done at the apartment and my sister's house. Of course, I used messily scrawled chemistry formulas, but to each their own.

I could feel the Dragon's will, how he'd coaxed everything around him into being. The whole little world was his, right down to the frogs singing in the long grass. He shaped it all.

I wrenched my gaze away from staring out over the water, fascinated by the way the Aether flowed through the roots of the water lilies. "But what was it like before? Before you made all this?"

I turned, my arms outstretched as I took in everything. Every dazzling color, every graceful arch and pitch, all formed from nothing but one man's will. "What did you see when you first set foot here?"

He didn't say anything. Instead, he raised his arm and swept it to the side.

The world rolled back like a curtain being swept aside, and beyond it...

I stared.

It took a few minutes to really comprehend. My brain tried to throw the brakes on, to find some pattern I could recognize, some way to see the full force of the Akasha without my mind turning into a lump of soggy bacon. But there was nothing like it, no comparison I could've made to anything I'd seen or felt before.

My gaze swam, dizziness rolling through me. It was too much.

"Just breathe, ye daft girl. You took the full force of Creation and lived. Dinnae choke now."

Focus was what I needed. To just look at one patch and stop

trying to take in the entire picture. The ground—if it could be called ground when I was pretty sure there were no directions —was made of little chips of reflective material. If a beach could be made of crumbled mirror, that was the closest I could come to describing it.

Rainbow hues rolled through it, super-saturated and dazzling. There were shadows of other colors I didn't have names for, that I'd never seen in the real world. My chest ached, and I realized I'd stopped breathing. The gasp I pulled in brought the taste of ripe citrus and petrichor, and the smell of the sea had my head swimming.

It wasn't a breeze as I knew it, more like a solar wind that brushed over my face, tickling like the faint bite of electricity, something gentle that could turn into agony really fast, if I wasn't careful. I swayed, overwhelmed. My head felt like it could detach and float away like a balloon.

Focus. Control. That was what being a Magi was about.

It wasn't any different from learning how not to set everything around me on fire.

Besides, I had a theory I wanted to test, and this was the closest to a scientific control I would get when it came to the Akasha.

Energy bombarded me, passed through my cells, and returned to the unformed places of reality. I let them sink through my body. It was warm—too warm. Too much energy for a body made of flesh and bone and blood. Humans needed a pretty strict homeostasis to survive as we did in the heart of a slow explosion, and I was rapidly approaching the point of no return.

I reached down, down to that little place that wasn't actually a place, where a shard of black ice had nestled into my soul, and coaxed it awake.

The power drained away, drawn somewhere else, and left

me feeling a bit scraped hollow inside, but clearheaded and not on fire.

I risked a glance at the Dragon where he stood framed against the stunning color of the Akasha, the lights flowing and spiraling like an animated Monet painting. He didn't look surprised or disgusted. He looked *delighted*.

"Little rule breaker," he murmured, shaking his head. With a flare of his arm, sleeve trailing behind like a pennant, he gestured to the Akasha. "It is potential in its purest form, and like all potential, it is up to us what it will be used for. You are the one in control. Not it."

And if the last comment felt a little pointed, he was polite enough not to gloat.

CHAPTER FOURTEEN

or the next trial I had to face, there was no spell, no alliance, and no miracle that could save me. I scrubbed a hand through my hair, feeling like someone being escorted to the gallows, with about as much hope. The text message was still up on my phone, glaring like an accusing eye.

Five damning little words that had ruined the entire day.

Family meeting tonight. Be there.

I was screwed.

When Lindsey wasn't using gifs or emojis, the bodily waste had well and truly hit the rotating blades.

Maybe I should've flung myself into the Akasha right then and there. If I got lost, or trapped, or died horribly, I could avoid what was sure to be an emotional and awkward conversation.

I probably should've been worried that the idea was so tempting.

"Ugh." I slapped my cheeks, trying to spark some neurons into working.

After meeting with the Dragon the night before, I had staggered home to a still worryingly empty apartment and collapsed into bed. I'd been so tired I barely noticed Percy letting herself in once the sun went down. She was still sleeping on the little perch I set up for her in the corner, her beak tucked down on her chest, feathers looking easy and relaxed.

Must be nice.

Two and a half cups of coffee later, and my brain was finally coming to life. Too bad it didn't have any ideas about what the hell I would say to my parents that night.

"Have ye ever considered the truth?"

I stopped, my mug hovering just below my chin, feeling stunned.

I could do that, couldn't I? I hadn't told them what was going on at first, mostly because I was still struggling to find my footing, and then it seemed cruel to worry them about things that they couldn't do anything about. But how would I have felt if someone I cared about locked me out of a huge portion of their life because they thought I wouldn't get it?

Pretty crappy, actually. And maybe a bit patronized.

And while I understood running down the streets hollering that magic was real would be a terrible idea, why shouldn't I tell my family what was going on? If there was a rule against it, no one had ever told me about it. Lindsey already knew, and while she could actually be pretty ride or die for secrets, it didn't seem fair to make her try to keep that one.

Besides, if my suspicions about Conner were correct, it would be better for everyone to be forewarned.

Might as well rip the bandage off.

There was food, because of course there was food. I wasn't complaining... The last thing I remembered eating since the hellfire-coated peanuts the Dragon offered me was the microwave burrito I inhaled directly over the garbage can, so I didn't have to wash a plate.

Don't judge. I had a lot going on.

Dad had been baking, and his stress response was my gain. I snatched a blondie off a plate on my way through the kitchen and pressed a crumbly kiss to his cheek as I carried on toward the living room.

Scott and Lindsey were already sitting on the couch, with Mom perched in her usual wingback chair. Conner had been set up in the den, playing some kind of handheld video game that he was glued to. He barely noticed when I ruffled his hair before I sat on the padded footstool of Dad's favorite chair, my hand under my chin to catch any crumbs while I ate.

After a moment, Dad shuffled into the room, flour in his graying hair, with a plate of sausage rolls, of all things. Whatever... I wasn't picky.

I glanced at Lindsey, who looked like she usually did, in her yoga pants and a pretty peach sweater that hung off of one shoulder. She was clinging to Scott's hand a little tight, but I had nuked her entire worldview, so I couldn't blame her.

Everyone got settled while I worked my way through the blondie, trying to figure out exactly what I was going to say to cause the least amount of trauma.

Mom took a breath, smoothing her hands over the legs of her dress slacks. "Aisling, we're your family, and we love you. You know that."

My chewing slowed. Stopped. I swallowed. "Yes. I know that."

"Good, good," Mom said, her voice soothing.

Was that her professional voice? Why was she using it on me?

"And we're here because we're worried about you."

"Worried? About me?" I darted a look at Lindsey, but she looked as confused as I was. "Why?"

Mom reached toward Dad, and he took her hand. They faced me with the same careful, calm smiles.

"It's just that it's been months since that little b–" Mom visibly reined herself back in, falling back into the pleasant mask of her work face. "Since that unfortunate trouble with that… girl and your research. It's not the end of the world, sweetheart. I know it's hard when your life takes a direction you didn't expect, but there's still so much more you can do. Even taking on a teaching position would be something."

"Where, at Hogwarts?" Lindsey muttered, not quite under her breath.

I glared.

"Your mom's right, kitten," Dad chimed in, his blue eyes twinkling. "There are other universities. Or even research positions, places that would be thrilled to have you."

"Wait, wait." I made a T with my hands. "Time out. Is this an intervention? Is that what we're doing here?"

Scott made a sound like a deflating balloon.

"We're just worried about you, kitten." Dad reached out with his free hand to give my shoulder a squeeze. "I know it hurt. I can't blame you for taking some time."

"But you're hardly ever here, and you're not in school or working, and you're living with strange men." The words kept coming faster and faster, like a dam had burst and Mom just couldn't hold the torrent back any longer.

Lindsey started laughing. Full-blown from the belly. The wench. "I'm sorry," she wheezed, clearly not sorry at all. "Can I just take some pictures? I want to remember this moment forever. I need it framed. Visualizing just won't be enough."

"Lindsey," Mom scolded.

I dropped my head into the hand that wasn't holding my precious, precious blondie. Baked goods had never betrayed me this way. I saved the world. That made me a good person, right?

What had I ever done to deserve this? Excluding my entire childhood and teen years, of course.

Dad gave Lindsey a look full of paternal disappointment and moved the plate of little baked cheeses away from her. "No brie bites for you."

All traces of humor vanished. "Wait, no, I'm sorry. Really. Come on, Daddy."

The contrition was mildly vindicating, even though I knew it had everything to do with melty cheese and nothing to do with my suffering. I'd faced down monsters and the closest thing to a supervillain I'd ever seen outside of a comic book. Why was it so hard to talk to my parents?

I dug my thumb into the space between my eyebrows, trying to ward off the headache blooming there. "Mom, Dad, I'm not depressed or anything. You don't need to worry."

Mom leaned closer. "We don't even know what you do with your days, sweetheart. You barely answer texts or calls. There's no shame in asking for help."

"There isn't, but it's not because I'm sleeping or hiding away."

What I wouldn't give to sleep all day.

Dad squeezed my shoulder, his fingers warm through my sweatshirt. "Then what?"

I glanced at Lindsey, but she just shrugged. Absolutely no help at all. Scott was staring into space like a man desperately trying to astral project out of his body.

Better to get it over with. I could always toss myself bodily out of reality if it went badly.

"Mom, Dad..." I braced myself. "I'm a Magi."

They both blinked at me, waiting, all concerned and patient.

Right, why would they know what that even meant? I scrambled for a better explanation. "Um, like a wizard? I had a bit of a breakdown, and realized I could manipulate reality, and these people found me and helped me, and taught me how to do magic."

My voice trailed off. Every word made them look more and more concerned.

"Kitten," Dad started, worry in every line on his face. "Are you in a cult?"

Mom gripped the neck of her blouse. "Lindsey, how could you let your sister join a cult?"

Lindsey sputtered. "How is this suddenly *my* fault?"

There was no fighting off this headache. It was pounding away merrily in the front of my skull like a jackhammer. "I'm not in a cult."

Dad patted me awkwardly. "I know they can seem very convincing, and they deliberately target people who are lost or confused in their lives. It's not your fault you got taken in."

The surrounding voices surged, each word louder and more strident than the last. My head throbbed, my skull feeling too tight, squeezing my brain.

Practical over theory, then.

I reached inward, looking for the place where the possibilities of the world pressed against the inside of my skin. A quick equation of conversion of matter, and the coffee table went from oak to rose quartz.

Everyone went quiet.

Mom and Dad stared.

"Not a cult," I told them firmly.

Mom reached out with fingers that shook a little, pressing them against the table. As soon as she felt cool stone instead of room-temperature wood, she yanked it back.

My throat was tight. Tears prickled at the corner of my eyes, and I had no idea why. What was there to cry about? My voice sounded weird to my own ears, hoarse and thin. "I, uh... they taught me how to use it to help people. And I try to. To keep them safe. I do my best."

And then Dad pulled me into a hug, and it was everything I could do to not sob into his shoulder like an infant. Emotions were so stupid.

"Oh, sweetheart." Mom smoothed my hair back from my face and tucked it behind my ear. "Of course you do. You always do."

They let me breathe for a minute, and I got myself back under control without bursting into tears, but I was sure my face was red and blotchy, anyway. I sank back down onto the footrest and gave them a short rundown of all the things that had happened.

"Wait." Mom shook her head, her brow creasing. "That night you came here and you were so upset. It was because there was a magic storm about to hit?"

Telling them everything felt a bit like putting down a heavy rock I'd been hauling around for months, and having the crushing weight gone had left me feeling a little giddy. "Oh, yeah," I laughed. "There was a good chance the world was going to end, and I wanted to see you."

"You thought the *world* was going to end," Lindsey screeched loud. "And you didn't say anything?"

I twisted around just enough that she could see my face. "What could I have said?" I asked, incredulous. "*Bye?*"

She threw a mini quiche at my head.

Mini food fight aside, they took it way better than I expected. It might have been the shock of it. But it might also have been the fact that both of my parents were scientists, and the explanations had quickly devolved into them getting me to shift mass and turn things into other things, and abuse the laws of thermodynamics to heat and cool things until my body was throbbing from using more Aether in an evening than I had in weeks.

But there was still no pain, no too-tight feeling of being sunburned on the inside of my skin. I made a mental note of that.

Before the end of the night, I tugged Lindsey aside. "Hey."

She shook her head. "I still can't believe it. Years of aura readings, palmistry, yoga, meditation, and *you're* the one who ends up with magic. I bet that pisses you off. A universe that doesn't follow the scientific method."

I crossed my arms, her smirk making me regret ever telling her anything. "It does, mostly. If you take the idea of science to its widest possible definition. Anyway! I didn't want to talk about me. I wanted to talk about Conner."

All the gloating drained out of Lindsey's face, her shoulders going tight. "What about him?"

I picked at my thumb nail, not sure how to start. "How are you handling Spike?"

"What's to handle?" Lindsey rolled her eyes, but her face was still tight. "He doesn't eat, he doesn't poop. He just hangs out in Conner's closet, and I occasionally see him prowling around the house."

"Good. Good." Just diving in was my usual tactic, but this felt like something I needed a bit of grace for. And not just because Lindsey had taken a couple of kickboxing classes back in the day. "You know Conner is special, right?"

She gave me the look I deserved. "I'm his mom. Duh."

"Yeah, that's fair. What I mean is, I see a lot of energy pooling around him, kind of hovering. I think that in a few years, he might be like me."

Wonder flickered across her face, followed closely by terror, and Lindsey wrapped her arms around herself and nodded.

I let her work through the feelings before pushing forward. "I'm telling you this, because if I can see it, other people like me might see it too. And... other things. Just keep an eye out, and if anything that makes you uncomfortable happens, call me and we'll deal with it. Okay?"

After a long moment, she nodded again, more firmly. "I'm not worried."

"Oh," I said, surprised. "Well, good. I'm glad." I was also confused. A bit of worry would be natural. Even sensible.

Lindsey's lip quirked up into something that was almost a smile. "Yeah. I'm not worried, because I know he'll always have his Auntie Ash in his corner."

Well, crap. It looked like I would cry after all.

CHAPTER FIFTEEN

J had taken a personal vow against cardio, but nothing got the feet moving quite like someone screaming, high and terrified. Percy banked around the corner of a building just ahead of me, screeching a crow warning. I wanted to tell her to wait, but all my breath was occupied with keeping me from passing out right there on the street.

I turned the corner, slipped in slush, and narrowly avoided face-planting by going to one knee and scrabbling forward on my hands while the screams turned into terrified sobs.

Ahead of me, a teenage girl was doing her best to press herself backward into the brick wall behind her. She clutched her arms tight to her chest, tears streaming down her cheeks, her shoes sliding in the snow as she tried to back away.

There was nowhere for her to go.

A huge black dog crept toward her, slinking low to the ground. Ropes of saliva dripped from between barred fangs. Its ears were pinned to its skull, and a low, bass growl echoed in the street, so deep I could feel it in my sternum.

The proportions were all wrong. It was almost cartoonish how deep the chest was, how long the fangs. But while it might've looked like a cartoon, there wasn't anything funny about it. If someone had taken the most threatening physical traits from *Canis familiaris*, squashed them all together, and then stripped them of all loyalty or domestication, that might've come close to the dog in the street.

Only it *wasn't* a dog. Even from the corner, I could read its starving pit of hunger and its horrible, greasy aura.

Harrower.

People should have been coming to help. A screaming girl... in that neighborhood? They should have been streaming out of the nearby restaurants and stores, ready to help. But the smothering aura of the Harrower kept her alone. Isolated. No one was coming.

Like hell.

She tried to duck sideways to reach a store or some kind of safety, but the dog bounded in front of her, herding her back, and she choked out another panicked cry.

Percy circled overhead, screaming abuse down on the Harrower. Her wings pummeled the sky as she dove, trying to distract it. The dog never took its horrible, scarlet-tinted eyes off its prey. It slunk another step closer, bloody saliva flecking its muzzle.

The girl whimpered and brought her arms up to shield her face.

I planted my feet and reached for the Aether. Golden light surged through my body, into my hands, ready and eager to be given form.

"Hey, Hound of the Baskervilles! Eat the second law of motion, asshole!"

Numbers blazed through the air, mass, downward force, and velocity. I concentrated all the gravity on the street into an area of about three feet across, right on top of the Harrower.

Everything else lurched up for a terrifying second. Cars

rocked on their wheels, a planter box flew up and tumbled back down to the ground. A shop's awning tore.

And the Harrower went from a huge, snarling mass of Cujo-based nightmares, into a fleshy pancake about a quarter of an inch thick.

A horrible wheeze and whine leaked out of the pile of former Harrower, which... gross.

The girl staggered, yanking her arms down as she tried to figure out what was going on, and I stepped between her and what was left of her attacker.

"Hey," I panted, still embarrassingly out of breath from my run. "Come on, I think I scared it off for now. Let's go."

Normally, I would have warned her to maybe not instantly agree to go to a secondary location with a stranger, but even I had to agree that a curvy redhead in a puffy blue jacket was less threatening than two hundred pounds of apex predator.

And she was shaking so badly, I wasn't sure she could've walked under her own power.

Luckily, less than a block up the road, there was a coffee shop, so I could whisk her inside somewhere warm and behind a door, even if it was glass. The lady behind the counter looked alarmed as we came in—crying teen, me half soaked from my fall, and Percy perched on my shoulder.

"She got attacked by a dog," I explained as I got the girl sitting down. "And don't mind the crow. She's mine and she won't poop on anything."

Percy flapped her wings. "You don't tell me what to do."

Luckily, I was the only one who understood her, so the woman behind the register mostly just looked bemused as she gave me the hot chocolate and cookies I ordered. She kept glancing at the girl. "Does she need an ambulance? Should I call the cops?"

Oh, how I longed for the days when I could have called the

cops for any of my problems. "It didn't get her. She's just shaken up."

The woman nodded but didn't look convinced.

The girl startled when I set the cup in front of her. "Here. Something sweet will help with the shock... and it's warm."

She wrapped her hands around the white ceramic mug but shook her head at the peanut butter cookies I set on the table. "I don't think I can eat anything," she whispered, her voice thick with the remnants of tears.

"Well, that's probably for the best, since these are for her." I set the cookies in front of Percy, who happily hopped forward to dig in.

The wonder of a crow inside at a little café table, happily bolting down cookies, was enough of a distraction for the women that I could slip out the door unnoticed. Backtracking to where I left the Harrower smashed in the street, I studied my options.

It was still just as grotesque, but one good thing about magically created nightmare creatures was that they didn't have much of a smell. Because that mass of pulped meat and organs should have been absolutely rank. Talk about counting your blessings.

It was already crumbling away into flickers of light and gray ash when I got there, and I kicked what little was left of the thing into the snow, doing a half-assed job of covering it up. I might have cared more earlier in the day, but it was the third damn Harrower I'd taken care of that day alone.

The things were swarming. They were worse than roaches.

Kill one, and a dozen more pop up to take their place.

Wasn't it funny, I started making plans to go rescue my potentially trapped mentor, and suddenly Boston is wall-to-wall Harrowing? I didn't believe in coincidences at the best of times, and this wasn't anywhere close to the best of times. The things had kept me hoping so much that I was struggling to get my act together for my foray into the Akasha.

Which was the point of it, I was sure.

One last half-hearted pass with my boot, and I trudged back toward the café. At least the Fear of Dogs had gone down easily enough. The Fear of Ridicule had been a stone bitch, and it did not stop laughing the entire time.

I shuddered just thinking about it.

The Dragon's words popped into my head as I walked, and I turned them over and over, examining them from every angle. Of course, everyone was afraid of something, and that fear had power over them.

Harrowers consumed fear—*were* fear, in their twisted-up way.

The easiest time I'd had fighting the Harrowing, was when I was too angry, or too burnt-out to be frightened. Wasn't that interesting? Like the other Aether-born were transformed by their mythos, it was a double-edged sword. The more power gained from belief, the more they were bound to that particular weakness.

Percy had just finished up her second cookie when I stepped back into the coffee shop, and the girl looked better than she had. There were some drying tear tracks on the curve of her cheek, but she didn't look so haunted. She clutched her mug and let out a shaky breath when I stepped inside.

"It's gone now." I gestured over my shoulder in case she was confused by what I meant. "Will you be okay?"

Her breath hitched, but she nodded. "Thank you. I'm so sorry. It's so stupid." Her eyes were glassy, and she blinked rapidly, her voice thickening. "I got bit once when I was little, and now they just freak me out. It's dumb, I know."

"Yeah, no." I drummed my fingers against the table while I tried desperately to find something comforting to say and came up empty. "It's not stupid. Dogs can be dangerous, even if people like to forget that they're living with, what is essentially, a lazy wolf."

She stared at me, and the lady behind the counter gave me a judging expression. So, of course I opened my mouth and let the words spill out.

"Fear is important, too. It keeps us alive. Tells us when to run away from stuff. Don't feel bad just because something twinged on your very specific survival urge."

In hindsight, I should've pulled a Batman and vanished without a word. That would have been less painfully awkward, even if I didn't have a cape to make it look cool.

But she smiled a little, and even huffed out a laugh, so took I it as a win.

"Anyway, I should go. Take care." I held out a hand. "Come on, Percy."

She took her time catching the last crumb before bypassing my hand and flying straight up to my shoulder instead. I heard the click of a photo being taken as we headed out and just barely resisted the urge to sigh.

We'd probably end up trending again.

I just hoped Lindsey didn't see it.

CHAPTER SIXTEEN

*T*he Back Bay was one of the nicer neighborhoods in Boston. It was no Beacon Hill, but it was nestled on the edge of the Charles River, and full of a bunch of old Victorian-style brownstone houses and shady tree-lined streets.

I would've enjoyed looking around at the shops and trendy restaurants since I wasn't in the area very much—if ever—but was too busy scowling down at my phone as I walked.

Stefan still hadn't come home, as far as I could tell, which was ridiculous.

I didn't understand what he'd been angry about in the first place, and the silent treatment was annoying. I finally just fired off a text. *You'd better not be kidnapped again.*

There wasn't any response, but then, if he *had* been kidnapped… there wouldn't be.

"Ugh." I stuffed the phone in my pocket, determined not to worry about stupid Stefan vampire-face. He was five hundred frigging years old. He kept himself alive for most of that without ever having met me. He could manage another couple of days.

Though, if I got myself killed, it would suck having the last words he ever spoke to me being an angry rant. Wouldn't he feel stupid then?

Ugh.

I finally reached the six-story brown-bricked building I'd been aiming for, and double-checked the address before heading inside.

I wasn't planning on getting myself killed. Actually, I was trying really hard to plan *not* to.

That didn't mean it wasn't a strong possibility... and if, for some reason I didn't come back from my little rescue mission, there were people I wanted to say a few words to.

Just in case.

Too bad one of them had forgotten how his stupid phone worked.

I shook off my irritation.

The apartment was nice. Nothing like the places where I lived as a student. It was an older building than Stefan's but had clearly been renovated with the times. The few holdover pieces of antiquity were deliberate choices, instead of neglect.

One of them being the brass cage on the elevator, which took me a couple of minutes to figure out how to close. No wonder they had attendants who took care of that kind of thing.

There were only five apartments in the entire building, so other than some privacy doors, the elevator opened right up into their living rooms. The apartment on the fifth floor had been left open, so when the ancient elevator finally creaked its way to the top floor, Bastian was waiting to spring me from my literal cage.

A slow smile crept across his face. "You made it."

I eyed the brass grill between us, feeling a bit like a zoo animal. "Let's not get ahead of ourselves."

With an insulting amount of ease, Bastian flipped the locks imprisoning me and slid the gate open so I could step into his apartment for the first time. I didn't even pretend *not* to gawk.

I wasn't big on interior design. I had really lucked out in living with Stefan, because other than my bedroom furniture, everything was taken care of, right down to the throw pillows and the jar of glass beads he kept in the kitchen for a 'pop of color'.

Before that, I mostly picked things that were cheap, or were vibrant enough for me to find easily if it was something small and misplaced.

But from the tips I'd picked up through osmosis, and mostly against my will, decorating all followed the same procedure. People picked a color or a theme, and then they worked around that. Paint, wallpaper, little knickknacks to put on the shelves. Bam. Simple.

Bastian's place was so very different from all of that. It was obvious he'd chosen things because he liked them, not because they 'looked good' together. Not that things were ugly, but it was very busy in a bizarre way.

There was no theme—unless the theme was a comfortable garage sale.

The main wall, which was dominated by an enormous fire-place, was covered in what I suspected were hand-painted tiles. None of them matched, but each of them was a work of art all on their own. Colors, patterns, one had a swallow in flight on it, another almost looked like a mandala in shades of blue.

The floors were wood, probably original hardwood carefully restored, and it had been covered by several rugs that seemed to have been chosen for how they would feel underfoot instead of matching. That extended to the huge sectional couch, too. It was a deep plum color and covered in throw pillows that were all made from a different fabric.

Some had long furry pile, some were almost knitted, others were soft velvet, and one looked like embroidered burlap, but it was probably some fancy fabric I didn't know the name of, because who would ever make a pillow out of burlap?

It was like he decorated the entire place for texture and touch instead of color, and that was totally fascinating to me.

The bookshelves were crammed with everything from paperbacks grabbed from the bestsellers list, to leather-bound editions that were so old and worn they were cracked and falling apart. There were at least six Rubik's cubes hanging around, puzzles of metal and wood, Lego half constructed, and a partially put together puzzle on the coffee table, which was an ancient-looking steamer trunk that looked like it was a circle of entirely blue pieces.

I waved a hand at the half-done puzzle. "Okay, that seems masochistic."

He shrugged, unfazed. "I like a challenge."

I wasn't sure what to say to that, so I let it go. I had a plan walking in there, but it trickled out of my head like grains of sand now that I stood in front of him. The silence wasn't exactly awkward, but it was growing thicker by the second while he waited for me to say something.

A shiver went down my spine, my breath hitching.

Bastian was superb at waiting. At standing there, completely at ease, just waiting for me to deal with the tangled snarl of my thoughts as I picked through figuring out what I wanted to say. He felt like a stone at the edge of my senses. Something strong, enduring. Like he could stand there waiting until the building decayed around us and the sea reclaimed the land.

It was dizzying. It was intimidating.

But in some twisted-up way, it was also really comforting.

Stalling, I ran a hand over one of the pillows on the couch. It was soft, but the fabric had little raised dots on it, and I ran my palm back and forth. I had the insane urge to roll around on a pile of those pillows, feeling all the different textures. I wasn't usually what I would consider a hedonist, but the whole vibe of the apartment had me curious. Humans were such visually based creatures... it was neat to see a place that appealed to the other senses.

Bastian continued standing in the middle of his own living room, watching me move around his space, touching things, picking them up to examine them with a little smile. In his place, I would have probably been annoyed, and that had me putting down the little Lego boat I'd been looking at with a flush. "Sorry."

"You didn't do anything wrong."

He really thought that. It was in his voice, the way he watched me, enjoying my exploration. All the dumb things I'd done or said, and he still didn't think I had anything to apologize for. I ducked my head, letting my hair swing forward to cover my face, hoping it might make me feel less exposed.

Again, he didn't comment. He let me hide until I got annoyed at myself enough to straighten my spine and march over to the couch.

Then I froze, hovering awkwardly in the air. "Um, is it okay if I...?"

Bastian gave me an incredulous look, shaking his head. "Sit down, Ash. You're fine."

I did, letting the soft cushions pull me into the couch's depths. "Sorry. I swear my parents are good people. I really wasn't raised by wolves."

He folded himself down onto the couch, close enough to be distracting, but far enough away that we weren't touching. If he'd been anyone else, I would have felt the heat from his body, or been able to smell his cologne or something. But there was just the faint whiff of fabric softener from his clothing.

If I closed my eyes, I might not have known anyone was there with me at all.

Okay, that was a lie. There was a weight to Bastian, a presence. Even blindfolded in the dark, I would have known he was standing beside me. He was like an event horizon, holding his own gravity. Maybe that explained why I wanted so much to let myself slide into the depression he made on the couch, let our thighs press together all the way up to the hip.

"Or maybe ye could focus on why yer here, ye daft girl."

Right. I gave myself an internal slap, trying to jerk my thoughts back into order. I'd come there for a reason, and it wasn't to stare at my lap like a weirdo. I almost jumped out of my skin when Bastian reached over to put his hand over mine where I had it white-knuckled on my thigh. Huh... maybe I was more tense than I'd realized.

"Ash," he said, his voice a deep rumble. "Whatever you want to say, it's okay. Just tell me."

He was right. I was being stupid. Only... saying it all out loud made it more real. I'd been planning it for weeks, but it had been in theory—a problem for me to twist and poke at until the answer revealed itself. Now, I had one more day before the theoretical became, well, reality.

Holy shit, this was all so fucking dangerous... maybe Stefan had a point about me throwing myself into these situations. I was a researcher, for fuck's sake, not some magical secret agent.

Bastian's hand squeezed mine, solid and grounding. "Ash."

Right.

"I have to go somewhere. I'll be back in a few days. Hopefully." The laugh that slipped out of me was a shade too close to hysteria for my liking, and I bit down on it savagely, trying to keep it together. "Anyway, I wanted to let you know I won't be around. And if I don't come back, I didn't want you to think I up and disappeared."

Bastian looked more and more confused as I babbled, but as the last words squeaked out of me, his hand tightened on mine. "Go? Go where?"

Yeah, that was a fair question.

"I'm going into the Akasha on what may or may not be a

suicide run to rescue the Senior Council. I think. I'm pretty sure. I don't know where else they could have ended up."

And if I thought too long about how little proof I had about any of it, even if they were still alive, I was going to have a meltdown. So, that all got stuffed into the closet at the back of my brain, with a mental wardrobe shoved in front of it.

The words spilled out of me, like the first rocks bouncing down the mountainside to signal an avalanche. "Cornelius saved my life. He didn't have to, and I'm pretty sure helping me made a lot of problems for him, but he did it anyway. So, I can't just leave him wherever it is he's stuck. And if I'm right, the Harrowing might be all up in this, and fuck those guys, they get nothing as far as I'm concerned. And I'm pretty sure I'm the only one who has a chance of maybe pulling this off, and that sounds super egotistical now that I'm saying it out loud, but I still think it's true."

My chest felt tight. My eyes felt hot and achy, and I could not seem to shut the hell up.

"I'm pretty freaked out, though. I really think I need to do this, because who else will? But also, I don't know what I'm doing, and I'm worried I'll screw this up, and then everything will still be messed up and the only difference is I'll be too dead for it to be my problem anymore."

A firm hand cupped the side of my face, his thumb running across my bottom lip. "Ash." Bastian met my gaze. His eyes were so dark. "Breathe."

I sucked in a much-needed breath and managed not to choke on it. My chest hurt. My lungs burned. I held my breath until my ribs ached, then let it out slowly to calm my heart the hell down.

Bastian waited as patiently as only someone whose lifetime could involve the idea of eons could. And when I clawed back some semblance of control, he tipped his head down to make sure I was looking him in the eyes and spoke quietly into the minimal space between us.

"I'm coming with you."

I shook my head, sure I hadn't heard him right. "What?"

"I said, I'm coming with you, Red."

My anxiety surged full force back to the front of my skull, and I shot up from the couch, desperate to move. I paced three quick strides toward the wall before spinning back. "Are you not listening? Did you miss the part where this has a greater than zero chance of ending in death?"

"I always listen to you."

I faced him, suddenly furious and also sort of wanting to cry. Even my own emotions were totally confused. "Why would you do that? Why would you risk that? You could die. You could get trapped in the space between worlds. You could have some horrible thing happen to you I can't even guess at because I don't even know what can happen in the Akasha!"

He sat there, watching me quietly, like we were debating what kind of takeout to get and not a potentially messy death. "I know all that. I'm still going."

I wanted to yank on my hair. Maybe scream into a pillow. I wrapped the confusion and anger around myself so I could fight off the desperate gratitude, because boy, I did not want to go alone, and wasn't that the most selfish thing in the world? To let him risk his entire eternal existence because I made stupid decisions?

"You can't be serious. You don't even know me, and you can't bet your life on me knowing what I'm doing."

For a heartbeat, Bastian was still. I wasn't even sure he was breathing. Then he leaned forward, grabbed my hand, and *yanked*.

Totally caught off guard, I fell forward with something embarrassingly close to a squeak, and only barely kept from straddling him by catching myself on the back of the couch. I stared into his face from inches away, too shocked to be embarrassed.

"I don't *know* you?" He bit the question out, his voice closer to a growl than I'd ever heard it before. "Red, I've *been* you. You might have forgotten what it was like when the Aether pulled us together, wove us through each other, but I haven't."

I hadn't forgotten, exactly. It was more like I hadn't let myself remember.

It had been shockingly intimate in a way that was deeply uncomfortable. Forget seeing someone with their clothes off. We'd seen each other with our *skins* off. Just thinking of what it had been like to know someone like that, instinctively, entirely, had me biting my lip hard enough that I was surprised I didn't taste blood.

"Aisling, I know you're brilliant, and curious, and stubborn. The way you constantly move, even when you're thinking. I know your bright colors, and golden power, and I know how you look at me."

My mouth was bone dry. I had to peel my tongue off the roof of my mouth before I could answer. "How do I look at you?"

I knew how strong Bastian was. He was a pretty big guy, but it was more than that. There was a lot of power in his body. So, when his free hand came up to cup the side of my face like it was something delicate, I couldn't stop the shiver that raced through me.

"Like I'm a person," he said simply.

I blinked rapidly, a frown tugging at my lips. "Well, yeah. You *are* a person."

The ghost of a laugh huffed out of his mouth, and he leaned forward enough to bump our foreheads together. "That's not how people usually see me, Red. They see me as a monster in waiting. Or a weapon to be used."

My back went stiff, indignation pricking at my skin. "What

the hell? You're none of that. Who said that? Give me an address. I just want to talk to them."

I'd seen the way Mason and Cornelius acted around him, treating him like a mad dog foaming at the mouth. He hadn't even said a mean word, but they were ready to throw down right there in the street.

The unfairness of it had been a kick in the gut, and that wasn't even taking into consideration that the first time we'd sort of met, he saved my life, just because he could.

Bastian's lips twitched. "They want me gone... or they want me for my power... But you never have."

Guilt curdled in my belly like sour milk, and I sat back, pulling away from his hand. "I ask for your help all the time," I muttered. I suddenly wished we were having this conversation anywhere but half sprawled in his lap.

"Exactly. You *ask* for my help. You *ask* me to stand beside you, not to fight *for* you." He took a breath, deep enough that our chests brushed together, even with my hands still braced against the back of the couch to keep from falling on him entirely. "I haven't had many people in my life that cared about me, much less stuck up for me, especially when that wasn't the smartest option on the table."

I snorted.

"The point is," he kept talking like I hadn't made a sound. "If you're going into danger, you can be damn sure that I'll be right there beside you. You're stuck with me, Red."

My breath caught in my throat, and emotion started pounding at the gates of my fortress of logic and reason. It didn't take long for the stone to crack and give way, and all the warm, messy things I'd been holding back for so long came pouring out.

I stopped holding myself back and dropped forward onto Bastian. He didn't make a sound, just slid his hands up my back to hold me in place as I tunneled my hands into his hair and kissed him.

Half a second later, I jerked back. "Oh, sorry, I should have asked—"

He yanked me back down, hands clutching, and if the kiss before had been warm, now it was scorching. His mouth moved over mine like he was starving for it, and the warmth that had pooled in my belly since I walked through the door turned molten.

He tore away for a second, staying close enough that his warm breath made my lips tingle. "Don't ask me to stay behind when you go into danger. I can't do it."

It was hard to force the speech center of my brain to focus on something other than 'more please', but I scraped enough together to manage a coherent sentence. "I don't want you to get hurt. I couldn't bear it."

Bastian huffed a laugh. "I'm a lot tougher than you are, Red."

"That might be worse."

The idea of him lost, trapped somewhere terrible, but enduring. I couldn't face it, so I buried my face in his neck and pressed my lips to where the shadow of a pulse beat under his skin. Had it always been there? Was it new? Was it rude to ask?

One hand stroked up my spine, and my body went boneless. "Trust me."

"Of course." It came out a little waspish, because duh, I wouldn't even be there if I didn't trust him.

The tone didn't deter him, not by the rumble I felt way down deep in his chest. It dragged an answering shiver out of me, and the banked fire within me roared back to life.

A shocked sound slipped out of my mouth when Bastian lifted me up with no effort, and twisted to drop me back on the couch, sprawled out across the cushions. He followed me down, as close as he could get, and I wrapped my arms around him. The Void-seed was vibrating like a struck glass, the Aether singing through my body, and I could feel an echo of a darker melody in Bastian.

"Don't go, Aisling," he breathed against my lips like a plea. "Stay with me."

My eyes fluttered shut, my breath feeling punched out of me as I pulled him back down into another kiss, letting some of the light in me flow into him, and felt the darkness damn near purr in response.

And I did. I stayed.

CHAPTER SEVENTEEN

*P*ercy poked her head out of my bedroom to watch
me bustle around the kitchen with an air of suspi-
cion. "You didn't come home last night."

It wasn't a question, so I didn't bother to answer. Instead, I
cracked two eggs into a pan, humming quietly. "Do you like
eggs? What am I saying? Of course you do." I added a couple
more and scrambled them with a fork.

Percy landed on the edge of the kitchen island, eyeing me
warily. "You're in a good mood."

"Am I?" I smiled, adding a teaspoon of water to the pan. "I
hadn't noticed."

Pain shot through my arm, and I jumped, dropping my fork.
"Percy, what the hell?"

She hopped backward, wings flapping, and I slapped a hand
over the back of my arm where she'd pinched with her beak.
"You were scaring me," she cawed. "Smiling. Cooking. Talking
before coffee."

"Oh, for... It's not that weird, is it?" I started scraping the
eggs onto two plates, adding salt and pepper to mine, and
pushing the other one in front of Percy.

"Yes, it is," she said, picking up a bit of egg and eating it with surprising delicacy. "But if you keep making food, I don't care if you're an imposter."

"Gee, thanks," I said dryly.

My phone rang as I was getting my first coffee of the day, and I took a hasty slurp before answering. "Hey, Mom. Good morning. Thanks for calling me."

There was a pause on the line before she spoke. "Good morning, Aisling. You sound like you're in a good mood."

"That seems to be the running theory." I took another sip.

"Your text was vague. Is everything all right?"

"I'm fine. Listen, I know you're headed to work, but I hoped you could help me with something."

"Of course, sweetheart." I heard her car door close, and the brief tone that told me she'd switched the call over to her Bluetooth. "What do you need?"

I'd thought things over—where I was going, and exactly what I was trying to accomplish—and had a few ideas. The problem with magic was that the Aether responded to the will of the Magi. If the Magi didn't have any clue what they were trying to do, usually it resulted in fire and explosions.

I learned that the hard way.

And while I'd come to an uneasy truce with all things magic, putting my special brand of geek into my spells, there were still some things I didn't have a good enough grasp on for me to get the result I was aiming for.

Which was where Doctor Caroline O'Reily, the clinical psychiatrist, came into play.

I leaned back against the counter, watching Percy shamelessly pilfer eggs from my plate. "I need you to tell me about brains."

Biology had never been my strong suit, never mind medicine. Too many squishy parts, and oozy parts respectively. I knew the basics, of course, and had a vague understanding of how all the pieces went together and what jobs they did... but one thing I wasn't willing to muck around with was my brain.

Luckily enough, my mom had spent years not just in medical school, but specifically dealing with the brain and all its wonderful bits and bobs and various chemicals. So, while she couldn't exactly cram a doctorate degree worth of information into her morning commute, she could give me enough of a run down that I was confident I wouldn't accidentally spend the rest of my life thinking I was a hummingbird or something.

Trying to tease Cornelius' memories back out of my hippocampus was a bit like trying to catch minnows in a stream with my bare hands. Little silvery flashes, there and gone, slipping back into dark water. It was painstaking and extremely frustrating.

But bit by bit, minnow by minnow, I dragged them free.

The gleam of his glasses. The silver glint of the handle of his cane. His fussy suits, his little folded handkerchief, his roses. The way he'd arch an eyebrow at me when he thought I was missing the obvious that always had me ready to bite something.

Decades and more of him working the Aether, protecting people, his triumphs, his losses, his crushing grief, his pride... I dragged it all loose, condensing it into a little silver ball. Doing it felt like death... like I was losing him all over again... but if that was what I needed to do to bring him home, then so be it.

When I finally opened my eyes with a gasp, the sun was slanting through my window at an angle that told me it was close to setting, and my face was streaked with sweat and tears.

The little bubble of memories was so small in my hand, about the size of a walnut. It seemed too fragile for what I needed it to do.

My fingers closed around the bubble, squeezing it tight as it hardened under my hand, and after I scrambled around in my dresser and found an old necklace to use, I threaded the little silvery pendant onto the chain and clipped it around my neck, letting my fingers rest on it for a moment. "Hang on, Cornelius," I whispered. "I'm coming for you, you old goat."

The vertebrae in my back popped when I shifted, trying to work out stiff muscles. I'd been at it for more hours than I thought I'd need, but still wasn't done.

The Akasha was an unknown. I wasn't sure it even *could* be known.

I was walking in mostly blind, and while Bastian was one heck of a backup slash scorched earth plan, he would depend on me to lead the way. There wasn't a lot I could do in advance, but I had one plan in mind that would help us against the Harrowing—I hoped.

Fingers crossed, I could pull it off without liquifying my brain.

Snow blanketed the garden at the edge of the cliff, muffling everything in a thick, white silence. Below me, I could hear the roar of the surf as the Atlantic threw pewter gray waves up to be dashed against the rocks.

The gazebo still stood, but I was glad that the gardens were hidden. I still couldn't bear to see what had been done to the roses in the Aether Storm's wake. It was stupid to mourn for flowers—especially considering everything else that had happened—but that didn't make the feelings go away.

It seemed fitting to be back at Cornelius' house at the edge of the sea. That was where it all started, and that was where it would end... one way or another.

Bastian shifted behind me, his shoulder brushing my back,

and I shuffled out of the way so that he wasn't stuck in the doorway of the gentrified little shed in the corner of the yard. The Way still held, and if I didn't come back, I didn't want my car left in Marblehead. It would have been awkward for my parents to collect.

Plus, the area was too rich, it was probably illegal to park a fifteen-year-old car there.

I wanted to ask Percy to come along, but she hadn't been in the kitchen when I finally staggered out of my room, and I hadn't seen her since. Crows didn't have phones, and I didn't have the time to track her down the usual way by hanging around her favorite restaurants waving around baked goods.

Stefan hadn't been home either, as far as I could tell. So, I'd come alone with Bastian, and tried to ignore how my shoulder felt cold and a little bare.

"Come on. It's this way." I jerked my chin toward the back of the house, not willing to pull my hands out of my pockets long enough to point. Hopefully, the space between worlds would have the heat turned on.

The snow creaked underfoot as we picked our way across the yard, and the weak winter sun overhead left the drifts looking like they'd been covered in glitter. It was almost enough to hide what I had accidentally done to Cornelius's house while trying to fix it.

It was fine. All houses leaned a little to the side like that.

I hadn't realized how tense I was until Bastian's hand slipped into my pocket to wrap his fingers around mine and I almost jumped straight out of my coat.

"Easy there." He gave a gentle squeeze. "Save some of that for our trip."

I managed a smile, but I couldn't quite bring myself to laugh. It was good, though, to lean my head against his chest for a second and soak up the feeling of him being there. With a sigh, I pulled away and tugged him toward the house. "Come on. Let's get this over with."

After another couple of steps, he gave me a curious look. "Did you warn anyone I was coming?"

My brow puckered as I picked my way through a deep drift near the back door. "Nope."

"And you don't think that might cause problems?"

There were a lot of things I could have said, assurances, maybe even something witty. I said none of them. "Fuck 'em."

Bastian stumbled a step, and it threatened to drag me with him if he fell. When we were sure we would both stay upright, I studied his shocked face.

"No, really. If they want to make a stink because someone came to help bail us out of the mess we created for *ourselves*, then they can take a long walk off a short pier. Fuck 'em."

The kiss he brushed against the top of my head felt like a reward. Really, though, he probably shouldn't have encouraged me.

I let us in through the back door, unsure of what to expect. The house had been abandoned for a couple of months, and I didn't know much about home ownership, but I didn't think that was long enough for it to transform into a ruin, or something out of a haunted house movie.

Everything looked exactly like the day I left, the same spindly legged antique furniture, the same Victorian drawing room level of clutter on everything. Cornelius was a tried-and-true pack rat, and over a couple of centuries, that added up to a lot of stuff.

It still felt strange being there without him. That was why I stayed away... because the house felt hollow—lonely—without Cornelius.

I gave one of the walls a consoling pat, only feeling slightly like an idiot, as I made my way toward the basement stairs.

The staircase that descended to the bowels of the earth was the bane of my existence. I'd had to sprint up all one million of them when we thought the house would collapse in the wake of the backlash, and I had never forgiven them for it. Our steps echoed on the stone as we went deeper and deeper, and the smell of damp rock and sea salt filled the air with a mineral rich tang.

The stairs opened into what Cornelius had called his workroom.

I called it a naturally occurring sea cave.

The stone had been smoothed out by centuries of the dripping water and tidal pools, and the sea still flowed inside at the edge of the far wall, filling the air with thick moisture. It dripped from the ceiling and ran down the walls.

The floor of the cave was still totally messed up from my fight with Oliver. He had melted stone and tried to kill me with lava. Everything was a lumpy, pitted mess, including the circle of silver that used to sit in the center of the space.

Now it was uneven, charred, and bubbled up in places.

Luckily, I wasn't planning on using it, because I wasn't sure even magic and a dozen metal workers could have fixed it.

Will had collected the others already, and they were assembled and waiting. Every one of them turned at the sound of footsteps on stone, and they all froze for a second as Bastian came in at my heels.

He glanced over all the pale, strained faces, his expression carefully blank. "Maybe we should have arrived separately. I don't think I'm doing good things for your reputation."

"Right, because that would have made things better." I snorted. "And bold of you to assume I had a good reputation to begin with."

The Aether flared, rolling through the cave as the others drew from the possibilities at the edge of the world. To attack or defend, I didn't know, and I wasn't about to find out.

I waved my hands in the air, like I was trying to tell someone to turn down the radio. "Okay, no, we're not doing that. This is Bastian. Yes, he is Void-born. No, he is not a bad person. He's here to help us, and if you all do not fucking chill, I will seriously consider revisiting my pyromaniac days."

"Ash," Koji started, his voice strained.

I made a warning sound in the back of my throat. "No. Just don't. He's with me. He's not even doing anything, and he came to help. You want your mentors back? You want to thwart the Harrowing? Then deal with it."

I made eye contact with all of them, staring until they finally looked away. I stared double hard at Will, who had swept Tessa behind him like some kind of bodyguard, and he didn't even have the grace to look sheepish when Bastian didn't do anything more threatening than shuffle along behind me.

When the silence picked up a ringing quality, he finally tugged a hand out of his pocket and gave a little wave. "Hey."

I laughed. I couldn't help it.

Weirdly, it seemed to break the tension. Sean openly stared, and while the others kept casting wary glances, they at least started pulling out the equipment they brought with them.

It was Tessa who stepped over to me, and Bastian moved away, pretending to study an unremarkable piece of rock to give us the illusion of privacy.

"Ash, do you have any idea what you're doing?"

"Nope." I made the p sound pop. "Not really. But I have some good ideas, and some backup plans." I patted my hip where the knife Bastian gave me hung, carefully wrapped.

Tessa's eyes popped wide when she saw it, the blood draining out of her face, leaving her dark skin almost gray.

"Hey." I jostled our shoulders together. "I've got this. Don't worry."

Concerned brown eyes searched my face, and she must not have found what she was looking for, because the corners of her mouth pinched tight. "Are you okay? You seem way too calm about all this."

I shrugged. "Not much point in being worried. It'll work, or it won't.

Tessa's hand rose and her power, so like spring sunlight and growing things, brushed over my skin. "Maybe I should—"

"How do ye want us to do this?" Sean interrupted, sidling over to us, never taking his eyes off of Bastian, who'd apparently found the neatest bit of limestone ever.

I started to answer when another voice rang through the cave.

"Why don't you ask someone who *actually* knows what they're doing?"

CHAPTER EIGHTEEN

reat. As if the interdimensional rescue mission wasn't stressful enough. I scowled as Mason came down the stairs with Caitriona following tightly behind him. She kept glancing back, and I almost asked her why she'd bothered to come if she was so freaked out, but the thought was interrupted by a crow winging past them.

Caitriona yelped, shielding her hair as Percy soared across the room to land on my shoulder.

Feathers brushed the side of my face as Percy came in for a landing, and I turned just enough to not get them in my eyes. "Percy? What are you doing here? Did you bring them?"

"Yep," she croaked, completely unrepentant. "Stefan asked me to 'get them off their asses' to help for once."

There were so many parts of that sentence that didn't make sense that all I could do was shake my head. Like that would rearrange the words into an order I could understand. "I have *sooo* many follow-up questions."

Mason looked better than the last time I'd seen him, but considering the last time I'd seen him he looked like a guy coming off a week-long bender, that wasn't saying much. He still looked haggard, his hair in need of a trim, the edge of his jaw shadowed with golden stubble—but his expression was the usual resting snob-face, so let's hear it for narcissism being a defense to trauma, I guess.

Caitriona, as usual, looked like she should have been strutting down the runway. Her sleek dark hair was pulled back into an updo, the hovering magical lights casting blue and green highlights. Her heels weren't made for walking across the lumpy stone, though, so she clung to Mason's arm for balance.

"Okay, first question. Why are you here?"

Mason ignored me—because of course he did—and glared at Bastian, a muscle ticking in his jaw. "So, it finally seduced you completely. I guess we'll be sweeping up your ashes soon."

I felt a headache coming on, and Mason's overt hostility had the others on edge again, which I did not need. "What is it with your obsession with me being seduced? If anything, I seduced him."

Bastian huffed a laugh. "Is that what we're calling it?"

I glanced back far enough to give him a half smile. "Let's face it, you just can't resist the awkward charm that I bring to the table."

Mason made a sound of disgust, but Caitriona's eyes were calculating as she looked between me and Bastian.

I waved them off. "Less judgement, more explaining."

Mason glared, but tugged the front of his suit jacket down like he was smoothing invisible wrinkles. "Your pet," he began, ignoring Percy's outraged squawk. "Told us you were planning to kill yourself dramatically, and we didn't want to miss the show."

I ran that through my Mason translating program, and it spat out "if you actually pull it off and get Cornelius back, I don't want to miss it." So, maybe there actually was something loyalty-adjacent rolling around under the boater's tan and fancy watch collection.

"Yeah, all right." I bumped Percy with the side of my face. "Now, what was that about Stefan? Have you talked to him? Because I haven't seen him in days."

"Yeah, well, I've been busy." Footsteps clattered down the stone stairs, and I turned to face them. Part of me thought it was a bit funny how everyone got over their 'No Bastians allowed' rule and skittered to stand with us when a potential new threat showed up, but most of me was too busy staring at the crowd flowing into the room for anything else.

There was Stefan in the lead, clattering down the steps with a smirk on his face and his chin tipped back. Anyone who didn't know him wouldn't have been able to see how his eyes flicked from Magi to Magi, never able to hold still for long, or how tense his shoulders were in his gray wool overcoat.

Behind him came Thalian in sweeping robes and his crown of golden branches, flanked by two other Faeries whose names I couldn't have remembered for all the sticky buns in Boston.

Then came Hester and Abigail, the witch sisters from Salem. Abigail glared around the room like she was daring someone to say something, never straying from the shorter witch's side. Hester seemed cautious, but she smiled when she saw me, and that was a really nice change.

I watched as the Aether-born filed into the work room beneath Cornelius' house with something that wasn't quite bemusement but was in the same postal code. "Um, hi?"

Stefan glared. "I keep telling people you're smart. Maybe you could help me out by proving it once in a while."

I scoffed. "Sorry. The last time we talked, you stormed out in a huff. I seemed to have missed a few steps between tantrum and showing up with a backup band."

Someone behind me barked a laugh. Probably Sean.

Abigail wrapped an arm around herself, her other hand coming up to play with a pentacle charm hanging around her throat. "We've got a debt to pay. I don't like owing anyone."

"Indeed," Thalian said, folding his hands in front of him.

"And we've got a score to settle." Stefan's eyes glowed amber in the dim light of the mage lights. His lip peeled back enough that I could see one long fang. "Don't think I forgot that the Harrowing taught your idiot flunky how to harvest us like cattle. If you're out for screwing those fuckers over, we're in."

I curved my fingers against my chest into a heart. "Thanks, dude."

"I can't believe you're going along with this." Mason wasn't sniping at me. He was glaring at Tessa and the other Magi still hovering behind us. Mason flung a hand in my direction, so I guess he hadn't forgotten me entirely. "I expect this kind of idiocy from her, but you're just going to let it manipulate all of us? This is some colossal scheme it dragged her into."

"Okay, oh wise Magi Stanford," I said, because it was that or slap him in the face for his patronizing, dehumanizing bullshit, and I didn't have time for a brawl. "Explain his grand plan to me. Step one, he saves my life. Step two, he risks his entire existence to help me save the world. Step three, he comes out with me to dispatch monsters from our streets. Step four... profit?"

Bastian's hand smoothed up my spine gently, and it wasn't until he touched me that I realized I'd taken a step forward, my hands balled into fists.

"You just make friends everywhere you go, don't you?" Stefan rolled his eyes, still looking like he was seconds away from bolting.

I glared, crossing my arms. "You're one of them, asshole, so watch it."

Koji eyed everyone, his hands flexing at his side. "This isn't productive."

I pinched the bridge of my nose and took a deep breath. Percy's feathers rasped against my face, tickling gently. "You're right. Look, we're all here for the same reason."

Stefan shifted his weight, scowling.

"Well, partly the same reasons," I amended. "I'm going to find the Senior Council and stop whatever the hell the Harrowing is up to. Can we all agree on that?"

There was some mumbling and shifting around, but it sounded close enough to agreement that I let it go.

"Great. Let's do this."

It was inappropriate to be amused by watching the various groups circle each other like wary cats, and I could read the room well enough to know commenting on it would have things going nuclear in a hurry, so I pitched in where I could, helping people set up what they needed.

Thalian and one of his people stood near where the silver circle laid in a twisted wreck, his hands up, palms directed out. A frown twisted his handsome face. "The veil is badly damaged here. It's thin as moth wings. It would be very easy to tear it completely."

"Isn't that good?" Sean straightened up, his face a little red from bending down to scrawl chalk markings on the ground. "Makes it easier to get through, yeah?"

"I mean, yes, but also no." I dusted my hands off, making Percy shift with a grumble. "Easier to get through, harder to keep intact. It'll be up to you all to keep it from spreading too large."

Thalian gave me a look of approval, and Bastian bumped my shoulder with his.

"You were listening," he teased.

"I always listen to you."

The easy smile fell away from his face, replaced by something more intense that had my pulse picking up. The Void seed inside me hummed, and I could feel the echo of the Aether responding in Bastian.

"No." Stefan walked between us, careful not to touch. He shooed us with his hands, scowling. "No magic weirdness. We have enough of that, thanks. You can be freaky deaky on your own time."

I rolled my eyes, but he was right, so I let it drop. "Thanks for coming. I mean it."

"Yeah, well." He shoved his hands into his pockets, looking like the petulant teenager he wasn't. "If you die, I'm going to make fun of you for eternity."

"Fair enough."

The witches bullied the Magi into letting them set what looked like chunks of amethyst into the pattern that they were etching onto the ground. Abigail glared at Will, daring him to protest.

"Yes, it's New Agey," Abigail snapped. "And whose fault is that? That our magic has gone this way? Oh, right—humanity."

Will, being a wise man for his years, raised his hands in surrender, and backed away.

That reminded me of something else, though.

I stepped away from the crowd, to where I could turn my head to whisper to Percy with no one overhearing us—even the people with super hearing. She listened to my instructions, her feathers slicked down unhappily against her neck. She gave me a long look out of one black button eye when I was finished, and finally nodded.

"Thanks, Percy," I whispered, pressing a little daring kiss to the side of her head.

The feathers on her face fluffed, but she clicked her beak at me. "You owe me."

"Infinite sticky buns."

I took her up onto my hand and gave her the little toss she needed to fly across the room and land on Stefan's shoulder. She bent her head to whisper into the vampire's ear, and he rolled his eyes, but nodded when she was done.

When it was all done, chalk lines, crystals, and a few golden leaves and acorns covered nearly every inch of the floor. They swooped around bare circles where everyone was meant to stand. There were areas of pictographs, Kanji, and script that looked like something lifted from a Tolkien novel etched in flowing lines.

Stefan hadn't been much help with the magic part, and no one had taken his joke about him using their blood in the ritual very well.

The Aether hung thick in the air, the smell of ozone and sunlight and green growing things even thicker than the scent of the sea where it slipped in along the far wall. There was a shimmer hovering in the corner of my eye, light flickering around the room that had no source.

Just breathing it in was intoxicating.

"We're ready," Tessa said, her voice strained. "Aisling, are you *sure?*"

I stepped to the center of the circle, Bastian a wall of shadow at my back. My hair lifted off the back of my neck, tugged by the sourceless wind. "Yeah."

She didn't look convinced, but I was too focused on what was coming to reassure her. Everything I'd done in the past months was culminating in that moment. Everything I learned, everything I put in motion, all the possibilities were moving now, homed in on that one point.

It was now or never.

Never.

Now.

I opened myself up to the Akasha, and the roar of it nearly deafened me.

Everyone there was connected, part of one great working. I felt them, where they brushed against me. Tessa's worry was like a raindrop sliding over the knobs of my spine. Will's determination in the taste of iron and blood in my mouth. Koji's resolve glittered like diamond-bright fractals of light scattered through the air, and Sean's desperate hope was a brilliance that was almost enough to rival the Aether itself.

Mason and Caitriona were a little apart, their caution making them feel as gray as the stone, and just as stubborn. Next to them, Thalian's calm will felt like tree roots sinking down into the bedrock of the earth.

I felt Abigail's spicy defiance, Hester's kindness opening like cherry blossoms.

Stefan's nervous loyalty was like the plucked strings of an instrument—in the minor key. My lips tugged up into a smile. Sketchy, but dependable... the best roommate I ever had.

Percy's bravery beat into the room in ruby light, her heart more fit for a lion than her tiny, feathered body.

It was all drowning deep. My senses started shutting down, and I couldn't keep myself from reflexively flinching away from the overwhelming power.

Bastian's hands smoothed over my shoulders before gliding up my neck to cup the sides of my head. His touch drained the fight away, made everything feel a little distant, like a shield between me and the world.

I let out a breath that only shook a little as it slipped past my lips. I left the knife on my hip, even though it could have parted the fabric of reality like Percy's claws slid through my dry goods. I was trying for something a little gentler, a little less likely to cause absolute chaos in my wake.

You've got to try new things, occasionally.

With Bastian's touch anchoring me, I let my eyes drift out of focus, just a little, and sank into the sensation deeper.

The world's stately dance turned around me, energy flowing in careful choreography. Blobs of concentrated power illuminated the room, heat and breath flowing through the people. Will exhaled, atoms of carbon monoxide gusting into the air. Blood flowed through people's veins, carrying energy along the highways of the body. And high above our heads, the slow trickle of electricity made its way through dormant walls and appliances.

I drifted deeper.

And there, I could finally see it. Beneath everything else, the last layer, a tapestry of vibrating energy, all carefully woven together. It became the simplest thing to reach out, to sift my hands through the singing strands that made up the universe, and not so much part them, but slip between them.

My arm disappeared into the gap between worlds.

There was coolness against my palm, the hair along my forearm standing on end as I tried to document what I was sensing. Nothing grabbed me. There was no burning, no pain. I wouldn't know exactly what I was walking into until I stepped forward.

I waited a second for commentary, but the little voice in my head was suspiciously silent.

Despite everything, excitement curled through me.

With Bastian clinging to me like a suit of armor, I stepped through.

CHAPTER NINETEEN

*T*here are certain things that you get used to in life, like gravity, and three-dimensional existence. The Akasha took those rules and regarded them as quaint suggestions. The first few seconds were chaotic while my brain pulled in hundreds of different conflicting bits of information about our surroundings, threw up its hands in defeat, and finally settled on showing me something like a floating piece of onyx in a river made of starlight.

Overhead, curtains of light danced in the air, moving in serpentine paths as they dipped and swerved to their destinations. Something above us flared—like a star going nova—and then vanished, three more lights igniting to take its place.

I staggered, feeling oxygen drunk as I breathed in pure magic, my veins humming with it. "Well, that's a rush."

The words echoed back at me from all directions, in every tone or inflection I could have put on them. Every possibility of how I could have spoken, all at the same time.

That would get annoying fast.

So would the way my hair floated around my head like I was standing underwater.

I raked it back with impatient hands before securing it with the tie I wore around my wrist. I had to wait while it went through every iteration of what the plastics inside could have turned into before it settled into black elastic once more.

"Oh, boy."

"*Oh, boy,*" the universe whispered back to me, resigned, flatly, joyfully.

Bastian hadn't let go of me, and I was glad. It felt like I could float away at any second. As if I could pick my feet up off the ground and drift away, the only thing keeping me standing on the rock being my expectation that that was my reality.

I wanted to comment, but the echoes were sounding increasingly mocking to me, so I pressed my lips together and tugged the little silver pendant out of my shirt collar.

Here it went. With any luck, I could release Cornelius' memories and chase them back to the man himself, and we'd be out of there and home in time for tea.

The silver softened under my fingers, the molecules parting like taffy until the silver bubble of memories Cornelius gave me hovered over my open palm. I bent my will on it, Aether leaping eagerly to wrap around me like an overexcited puppy. Power twisted through my fingers—my desires made manifest.

Find him, I whispered to the possibilities. *Find your source. Find your home. Find the puzzle that you are a piece of.*

Things that were once one remained one.

The ball broke apart into mist, and I had the impression of fluttering wings as memories swirled around me, glowing brighter and brighter with each pass. I set it free, tensed to move, to chase after it, wherever it was going...

Hold on Cornelius, we're coming.

The light slowed, making one final lazy curve before it looped around my head and winked out. I stared, stunned. My mouth opened. Closed. Opened again.

"It... it didn't work."

"It didn't work," the universe whispered, roared, sobbed back at me. *"It didn't work."*

∽

There was no way to tell time inside the Akasha, assuming time existed there. It could have been minutes, hours, or days that I stood there, blinking down at my hands like some kid who couldn't understand why their balloon floated away when they let go of the string.

Really, what it boiled down to was that we were screwed.

I'd brought some things with me, sure. No one went into totally unfamiliar territory without a few things necessary to life, like water and food, but after what happened with my hair tie, I was extremely reluctant to put any of it into my mouth.

Other than that, and the black knife hanging at my hip, I had nothing.

I banked everything on Cornelius' memories being the tie we needed to find him, which, in retrospect, had been stupid. Because they weren't Cornelius' memories anymore, they were mine. He gave them to me, and they had woven themselves into my psyche.

They were corrupted with too much me to be him anymore.

I was just so desperate for it to work that I hadn't let myself doubt it.

That meant Bastian and I were standing in the space between worlds with nowhere to go. It was officially the worst rescue mission in history.

When it came down to it, we had two choices that I could see. One, go back with our tails between our legs and confess to everyone that I screwed up, and hope the Harrowing didn't kick off Armageddon while I came up with Plan B.

Or two, find something that worked.

I was almost literally swimming in possibilities. There had to be something that could be done. If anything was possible, then that had to be possible, too. I just had to think.

And my choice had absolutely nothing to do with refusing to give Mason the satisfaction. What could I say? Spite was a powerful motivator.

"Okay," I said, and groaned at the inevitable echoes. "Do you mind? I'm trying to think."

Silence.

Well, that was probably fine.

"The only way I know how to find a person is with something of theirs, a part of them, or their energy."

Bastian nodded, still gazing around. "So, how do we get that?"

It was mildly annoying that his voice didn't do the instant replay thing. It sounded echoing, but more like it was coming from the bottom of a well.

"That is an excellent question. I wish I had an equally excellent answer."

I needed Cornelius. But if I *had* Cornelius, I wouldn't need something of his to find him.

Ugh, paradoxes were the absolute worst.

I ran it through my head, turning the problem this way and that, and Bastian stood silently to let me think. Man, if I hadn't had so much going on, I would have kissed him for that.

A few seconds or an eon later, an idea sparked, and my head came up like a hunting hound spotting the white flash of a rabbit's tail.

I needed Cornelius, but I didn't have Cornelius, because he was missing.

But what about when he wasn't missing?

Cornelius had only known to give me his memories because he had a premonition about it, information rippling back to him through the Aether, which had no concept of past, present, or future. It was all times happening eternally. And if information could pass back like that, couldn't something else?

Like, say, a Magi who was one hundred percent done with all of it?

I sketched out my thoughts to Bastian as clearly as I could. He let me talk, never interrupting, and shrugged when I was done.

"I don't do magic. If you think it will work, it probably will. But can't messing with time cause one of those paradoxes?"

"Probably," I agreed, more excited than I should have been. "So, don't sneeze on anything or sleep with your grandmother."

That startled a laugh out of him. "Never had one of those."

"I had two," I said, my thoughts already miles away. "It was a mixed bag, to be honest."

The power flowing through the air was whipping up into a tempest, already reacting to my desires before I could even say them out loud. And, you know what? I got it.

I got why people like Oliver craved it, that feeling of the world moving, shaping itself around you to whatever it was you wanted. It was heady, intoxicating, the kind of rush I usually got for teasing some new hint of data out of an observation or batting a theory around with someone.

But really, what was the point?

Yes, the Akasha moving itself as I wanted was extremely useful, but only because I had a goal. Who wanted that control when there was nothing to do with it, nothing to protect? What a waste of time.

Power crackled, sparking in my whipping hair. Magic coalesced, feeling like a thunderstorm that was about to break overhead, beneath our feet, inside my chest cavity.

I held out my hand to Bastian, not even trying to keep the manic smile from stretching across my face. "Are you with me?"

He took my hand without hesitation. His eyes were as dark as the space between the stars as he said, "Always."

And then we were gone.

CHAPTER TWENTY

*D*espite my blasé reaction, paradoxes really were something to avoid, if at all possible. Showing up, scaring the heck out of myself or Cornelius would not end well. Out of twenty possibilities, I could foresee nineteen and a half, going absolutely tits up.

Plus, I wasn't sure that time travel as seen on sci-fi tv was actually possible. Sure, information and energy could do whatever it wanted in whatever direction, but I had a body I was attached to, and flinging myself to the chronal sea seemed like a great way to change that in a bad way.

So, no appearing to young Cornelius and being all, "Come with me if you want to live." No matter how funny it might have been.

Since I also didn't want to risk bumping into myself, I concentrated on late summer. I hadn't even met Cornelius until the school year was underway, so that seemed like a big enough window to avoid myself.

There weren't really words to describe what moving through the Akasha felt like. My brain struggled to perceive it, like an old computer trying to run new software, wheezing and chugging and glitching along.

The best way I could put it would be that the Akasha pulled us somewhere, hovering as close to the world as a pair of ghosts, separated from the streets of Boston by a gossamer sheen of energy.

I was seeing the veil from the wrong side, and oh, boy, it was trippy.

Everything was green and bright and the streets were full of people, the harbor full of cruise ships, and somewhere across town, a slightly younger Aisling was toiling away at Seaton, working in the labs on her internship while her mentor went overseas, never knowing how badly everything was going to come crashing down around her.

The world swam, and I saw the first hints of trees and the outlines of the buildings on Seaton's campus, and I had to wrench us away with a firm hold.

No, thank you. I didn't even like seeing pictures of myself, so seeing my past self was off the table.

"No peeks at baby Ash?" Bastian asked from where he was draped over my back, solid and comforting.

"It was less than three months ago. How much do you think people age in three months?"

He brushed his lips against the space where my neck met my shoulder, and let it drop.

"Okay. Go to Marblehead. Get what we need. Get out. The perfect crime."

Which was, of course, when something moved in the corner of my eye and dragged my attention away.

It wasn't Marblehead. It was a park... possibly even Franklin.

I didn't look closely enough to know for sure. Over by one of the trash cans—where some thoughtless dorks had let their garbage dump onto the ground—I saw a bundle of struggling black feathers.

A crow had gotten its leg tangled in something and was desperately trying to break free. Black wings raked the air, but it got no height, pinned down as it was.

Then I saw why it was struggling so badly, unable to grasp anything with its free foot because the toes were all clubbed together, and I realized it was a very familiar crow.

Normally, I have a pretty good head for consequences. But those were extremely extenuating circumstances, and, plugged almost directly into the Aether as I was, I was reaching out with just enough heat to snap the plastic tie binding her poor leg before I consciously considered it.

"You all right, Percy?"

The crow jolted, hopping a few feet away, her head craning all around, and I realized she probably couldn't see me at all.

"Yeah," she croaked hesitantly.

Bastian tugged my hand. "Isn't this one of those things we're maybe not supposed to do?"

"Oh, shit. You're right." Percy and I hadn't even met at that point. With a wrench, I pulled us away, aiming for where we were actually supposed to be.

As the world streaked around us like a smeared painting, I couldn't help but remember one of the first conversations I had with Percy, once I realized they were conversations. I told her Percy was usually a man's name, and she'd given me such a look of scorn before telling me she wasn't a man, she was a crow.

"How'd you get the name Percy?"

"How does anyone get a name? It was given to me."

Something told me I had found out who gave it to her.

The Akasha was filled with the ghost of buffeting black wings, and the world shifted around us.

~

Seeing the rose garden again felt a bit like the time I'd gotten kicked by a pony at a birthday party when I was six. I went from minding my own business looking at a cool bug to getting knocked ass over teakettle and not knowing what happened or why I couldn't breathe properly.

Riots of deep red, white and peach blossoms filled the garden, their heads nodding drowsily toward the ground as bees droned among them, their legs heavy with pollen. The sea roared below, waves crashing against the cliff, sending spray up into the air. Gulls cried in the distance, but the sound was muffled and further away than it should have been.

The gazebo was still pristine, none of the white-shingled roof caved in like when I'd seen it that morning. Two wicker chairs, their seats softened with thick cushions, and the table set between them were all so familiar that a lump swelled in my throat.

Slumped in one of the chairs, a book on his chest and his glasses slipping down his nose, was Cornelius.

I stared for a long time. Probably an inappropriately long time, if I was being honest. It was just that I hadn't seen him for months, and I knew that wasn't my Cornelius, not really. But he was alive, and right there, and real.

And if I stepped through the veil and woke him, he would have had absolutely no idea who I was. *Oh. Ouch.*

I was just as glad to skip that emotional wound, so maybe it was my first twist of luck that he was asleep.

It felt weird, seeing him vulnerable like that. He looked frail, the skin around his eyes creped with wrinkles, his hands boney, the knuckles swollen. Cornelius had lived for centuries, but he'd never looked *old* before. Watching him while he was asleep, without the full force of his personality animating him, making him that endearingly infuriating mix of frustrating and comforting, he looked like a stranger.

My hand pressed against the shining veil of the Akasha. It

would have taken no effort to sift through it, less to rip a hole. But I didn't.

Come to think of it, maybe that was why Magi weren't encouraged to mess around in there, because I was starting to think I could do some serious damage without ever meaning to.

I didn't push through. I didn't shake him awake. Barely daring to breathe, I let my eyes drift out of focus until I could see the wisps of that blue-white light wafting off him like bio energy, his essence reaching out to the world around him.

Carefully, delicately, I teased it away from his aura—a word I would never admit to using to my sister on the pain of death—gathering it in my hands. A little shred of Cornelius' life force. It wasn't enough to weaken or hurt him, but with any luck, it would be enough to take me where I needed to be.

With one last look back, I turned, and let the Akasha pull us away.

Cornelius' energy twined around my fingers, as quick and lively as the man it came from.

In the Akasha, will and reality were basically the same. It was the easiest thing in the world to turn to that little wisp that was part of the man who *would be*, *is*, and *was* my mentor, and whisper my desires to it.

"Take me to him."

The spell I perfected with Stefan shimmered into place, the calculations blazing through the air and echoing through more dimensions than I could count.

The wisp shivered, stilled, and went arrowing off into the beyond.

I was giving chase before I even realized we were moving.

CHAPTER TWENTY-ONE

*W*hen the wisp finally slowed, the world around us had changed. Instead of darkness, there was a golden light with phantom colors threading through it, and what I had thought at first was a field of diamonds strung from the heavens.

Each diamond was a fractal, a little prism hovering in the air, turning gently like someone had bumped a baby mobile around us. The one closest to me showed the ocean, but it wasn't any ocean on earth. The waters were violet, shading to deep purple, and the fin of some monstrous fish broke the surface, amethyst foam dripping over its scarlet and black hide.

Another held what looked like a city, but the skyscrapers were rounded instead of squared, and each story had balconies absolutely filled with greenery, until leaves spilled over the edges to drape down the side of the building.

They were worlds, I realized with a thrill. Each one of those billion lights hovering around us was an entire world. Somewhere new, and strange, and amazing.

Another fractal drifted by lazily, and I peered through to find a forest full of trees bigger than red woods. They didn't all grow straight up from the ground—no. The trees in that world grew in all directions, including down from the sky. Their roots twisted together into a strange canopy, some leaning sideways or at an angle that couldn't exist if gravity was a thing.

"That one feels like the world was designed to mess with me."

I hurried to the next one, enthralled, and found a world that was in a continuous supernova cycle, a star bursting and reforming only to flare and die again. I held my breath, watching black spots flow over a white dwarf's surface as it burned down to red, only to burn out and ignite anew. I reached for it, my fingers tingling with the need to touch that power, to hold it in my hands, to see what no one else in my world had up close.

Bastian caught my wrist, gently urging me away from the fractal. "Maybe don't touch it. If you got pulled in, that's a lot of force for a human body to take. Also, no oxygen."

"Oh." I considered. "Yeah, that wouldn't be very good. Thanks."

He smiled. His eyes were chips of onyx in his face, but it didn't look bad or wrong. It was just Bastian. His fingers were icy when he smoothed my hair back. "Don't mention it, Red. You warned me."

That was true. Hooray for foresight.

Standing there, buffeted by the Aether and surrounded by thousands—*millions* of other worlds, it was all I could do to keep my hands at my side. I wanted to see them all, to note how they were the same, how they were different. Were there people there? Could I pop out into Thalian's Faerie if I walked through enough of them?

I shook my head, trying to focus my brain. "Is this hubris? Is this what hubris feels like?"

Bastian laughed. His teeth were white and straight. Behind them lurked the Abyss. It probably said something worrying about me that I wanted to yank him down to my level, kiss him, and see if I could taste the Void on his tongue.

I shook myself, trying to wrench my focus back by the scruff. The whole place was disorienting. Too much power, too much sensation. Even thinking about Bastian, and I could feel the memory of his mouth against mine, the careful way his hands had run over my body, afraid of gripping too tightly.

And there I went again. What was this place... where all the worlds seemed to converge together?

The Infinity Nexus.

The worlds breathed through my head, and I knew them without knowing how I knew them. There were so many questions I wanted to ask, so many things I wanted to know, and all I had to do was think about them.

I slapped my own cheeks. "Holy crap, O'Reily, focus. This is going to be your supervillain origin story if you're not careful."

Bastian didn't argue, which was maybe a hint of how well he knew me. Instead, he pointed one bone-white finger toward a fractal drifting lazily in the cosmic wind. "There."

The wisp was circling, floating around one of the fractals like a moth buzzing around a lightbulb, and between one blink and the next, Bastian and I stood next to it.

"That is really disorienting," I grumbled. "I never thought I'd miss using my feet."

The wisp made another pass, and through the silvery-blue light I could see a dark forest, filled with old rotting trees and slabs of gray stone poking up through ashy soil like teeth on a jawbone. In the distance, mountains loomed over everything, dark and jagged. There was no moon, no stars, just enough ambient light peeking through the fog and the foxfire of rotting organic matter to fill the world with shadows.

Shadow's Reach.

Just like before, the information came before I could even ask a question. And just as quickly, I knew it was the home of the Harrowing—if home was the right word. It was their lair, a place hollowed out from the primordial dark by the King of Night himself.

I eyed it, not feeling much of anything except annoyed. Maybe hungry. It was hard to tell.

But that was where Cornelius was. And that meant I was going in.

I reached a hand back for Bastian, vaguely noting how the Infinity Nexus had stripped him down to monochrome. White skin, ink-black hair. The Void filled his eyes. The only spot of color on him were those lime green sneakers he loved so much, and my eyes kept drifting to them like I needed reassurance.

His fingers entwined with mine. The only solid thing in my universe.

I reached out my hand and let the shadows take us.

There was no actual way to describe Shadow's Reach without sounding like a smartass. It was a world of nightmares, carved out of the place in people's heads where genetic memory lurked. The place in everyone that remembered a world where we were small, and weak, and prey to everything around us. Primordial forests that threatened to swallow us whole, and deep shadows that hid monsters in their depths.

A chilled wind blew through the woods, rattling branches together and rustling leaves with a dry hiss. The sounds of faint howls, screams, and distant sobs filled the air.

Cheery.

I tried to summon some light before Bastian reminded me that maybe drawing attention to us right off the bat wasn't the best plan. It didn't matter, in the end. The light drained away faster than I could call it, the darkness of Shadow's Reach swallowing it before it was anything more than a flicker.

I was tempted to alter my eyes to see better in the dim light, but I could screw it up and end up blind, which would have been a real pain that far from anyone who could help me fix it, so I sighed and resigned myself to squinting.

The little wisp of Cornelius' essence had shrunken down to the barest pinprick, and I caught it in my hand before it could dissipate entirely. It fluttered against my skin, as light as butterfly wings, beating just a little faster in one direction than another.

I jerked my head to tell Bastian which way, and we set off through the trees.

Pushing through the woods was like all my worst nightmares combined. Thick roots tangled around our legs, slowing us down. Woody stems like cypress knees jutted out of the soil, promising a nasty fall for anyone who caught a foot. Movement was frustratingly slow, with the wind constantly moaning in my ears like a damned soul.

"Remind me to give them an absolutely *scathing* review online," I muttered as I slapped away a mass of dripping moss that clung like cobwebs. "Zero out of ten. Do not recommend."

Bastian gave a thin smile, his lips pressed together. He'd gotten quiet since we'd stepped through the fractal, pulling into himself.

It was odd that I only realized exactly how much effort Bastian put into acting human when he suddenly stopped. His movements flowed strangely, the way he swiveled his head to keep watch just slightly *wrong*. Gone was the easy amble. Instead, he prowled, shoulders squared, danger in the tense line of his spine.

He was never more than two steps away from me as I cursed and pushed my way through the trees. And no, it wasn't my imagination. They actually were moving, slipping closer together to make it even harder to get through. *Rude.*

Bastian had to help me squeeze through at one point, when

two gnarly old oak trees caught my hips and almost squished me between them. He slipped between them, no problem, the trunks crumbling to black ashes as he brushed past.

"Cheater, cheater." I wagged my finger at him. "Who was talking about keeping a low profile?"

He just looked at me, his eyes filled with that echoing darkness.

I slipped closer, caught his hand, and lifted it to my lips so I could drop a kiss into his palm. "Hey. Stay with me, okay?"

A shudder wracked him, like he'd forgotten to breathe for too long. His hair brushed against the side of my face as he leaned down to press soft lips to the crown of my head. "Always."

I let him go with a reluctant smile to follow the fluttering tug of the wisp in my other hand.

We made it about two more steps before the first Harrower found us.

CHAPTER TWENTY-TWO

I hadn't known what to expect when I'd made the dumbass decision to go into the Akasha after my missing mentor. But if someone had asked me what I thought it might be like, at no point would I have ever mentioned hiding in the bushes.

The instant I felt the brush of the starving hollow aura of the Harrowing, Bastian picked me up with one arm around my waist and dumped us both in a thick and brittle clump of shrubs.

I'd been too stunned to even make a sound, much less react, but three heartbeats later, the monster came prowling through the trees.

It rolled across the ground like fog, leaving only the impression of paws, jagged, shining claws glinting in the shadows. Its body was thick and gray, but hazy, with no head or neck that I could make out. Bigger than a frigging bus, it spat electricity as it moved, sparks arcing through its form as it growled low and deep, like thunder.

Well, the joke was on it. I'd never been afraid of thunderstorms. It had been a serious problem as a toddler, with my parents having to sit on me to keep me from running out into the storm like a demented little gremlin.

"I can take it," I whispered to Bastian, twisting in his hold. I just needed to reach for the Aether, to see how big a boom I could make.

Bastian's arm compressed, firmly squeezing all the air out of me. If I had the breath, I would have squeaked.

He pressed his lips to my ear, and I felt more than heard the words, my skin tingling with every brush. "Ash, no. We talked about this, remember?"

Since I didn't have any breath to answer with, I slumped back in his hold to show my surrender. He was right, probably. That was why I asked him to be my spotter in the first place.

Eventually, the Harrower went away, and the wisp in my hand started squirming more intently. Bastian was nice enough to haul me out of the bush he dropped us in. The branches clung to me, clawed my jacket, and tried to tug me back.

"Ugh. I hate this place."

Bastian nodded, brushing bits of wood off my back. "Agreed."

There was no way to tell how long we walked, but we dodged two more Harrowers before the wisp in my hand gave an insistent little wriggle and squeezed between my knuckles before darting off between the trees.

"Shit." The curse hissed between my teeth, and I took off at the closest thing to a run that I dared in the strangling forest. A broken ankle would not be helpful.

I jumped sideways between two trees and dodged a branch that tried to grab my jacket. My feet skidded on damp, moldy leaves as the forest gave way suddenly, and I stumbled into a clearing full of standing stones.

Slabs of some foggy crystal stood arranged in the clearing, each one threaded with thin veins of pulsing red. There were shadows trapped inside each one, fluttering like a heartbeat.

Each one had to be over six feet, at least three feet wide, and just as deep. My stomach flipped at the sight of them. I did not want to touch one. They looked greasy somehow.

But it looked like I wasn't going to have a choice, because the wisp was buffering at one of the slabs, battering itself against the crystal.

"Okay, okay, I'm coming."

Getting closer to the slab didn't make it any more tolerable. The stones felt draining, somehow. Like just standing in their presence, they were trying to pull something from me, but they couldn't get a grip. I brushed against one and recoiled. It was warm. More than room temperature. Warm as blood.

I suddenly had a bad feeling about this.

The wisp bounced up, silvery-blue light illuminating the crystal, and I got a glimpse of a face inside. I knew that chin. I knew that curve of a wrinkled cheek. I knew those silver-rimmed spectacles.

Cornelius' eyes were only partially open, his face twisted into a rictus, teeth bared, but he didn't seem to be awake, or aware of what was going on around him. His pupils didn't react at all when I slapped my hand against the crystal. I didn't know if that was a blessing or not.

The veins in the crystal throbbed, pulling something, and I realized with a queasy lurch that they were feeding.

The other slabs were the same. Those pulsing, horrible veins were pulling something from them, like a Venus flytrap slowly digesting a meal.

There had been twenty-seven Magi in the inner circle when it vanished. There were less than a dozen slabs in the clearing. The piles of shattered and melted crystal littering the spaces between the standing stones didn't give me a good feeling about the ones that were missing.

I had to get him out. He'd been there, maybe for months, maybe forever. I didn't even understand how time worked in that place. But I knew I wasn't leaving Cornelius trapped in that waking nightmare for even one more moment.

I didn't want to use a spell, not with those little warning piles studding the ground. The knife at my hip was made from the Void itself, a piece of Bastian's power made solid. It could cut through anything, even fear.

It was the fastest, safest way I could think of to cut him free, and so I drew it from its protective sheath and got to work.

Minutes later, the crystal broke apart, spilling Cornelius into my arms. He was shaking, choking, clutching at me like a drowning man, but he was alive, and that was all that mattered. My heart squeezed in my chest, and it was a fight not to crush him in a hug. He was having enough trouble breathing already.

It took him a minute, watery blue eyes studying my face, before recognition flickered over his features.

"Aisling?" His breath caught, hands shaking where they dug into the folds of my jacket. "Aisling, is that you?"

"Yeah." Maybe my smile was a little watery, but I didn't care. "You're late, old man."

His head craned around, trying to look everywhere at once. "The others. We need to get them out. We can't..."

His eyes landed on Bastian, and his whole body went rigid.

"Nope. No, we're not doing that." I half dragged, half carried him over to one of the bigger chunks of rock that looked like it wouldn't cut him, and I sat him down on it. "Bastian is here to help. There will be no weirdness directed at him. I am going to spring the other Council members, and then we are all getting the fuck out of here."

Cornelius reluctantly tore his gaze from Bastian. He looked worn down, almost gray with exhaustion. The lines on his face had been worn into grooves. "Aisling, how are you here? What were you thinking? You have no idea—"

"I don't suppose you could shelve the lecture until the rescue is over? Is that a thing we could do?" I grunted as I caught another Council member as she tumbled out of her beautiful coffin, shaking uncontrollably. "Is there Magi therapy? You guys are going to need so much therapy."

Between Bastian and me, we got everyone out of their prisons and dragged them over to where Cornelius was sitting. They all had the same look in their eyes as they stared into the distance, very few of them managing even a couple of words.

Haunted. They looked haunted.

I looked over at my flock of little lost ducklings and tried to keep the fury bubbling in my veins out of my voice. "Okay, I don't mean to rush, but as soon as everyone thinks that they're capable, we need to get out of here."

And maybe, if I did a little felony arson on my way out, it might actually make me feel better about seeing people trapped and used like food.

I mean, it couldn't hurt.

"What is this place?" one person asked in a hoarse whisper.

"Shadow's Reach," Cornelius said in a clipped voice.

"Exactly. So, we should not be here for any longer than we absolutely have to." I drummed my fingers on the small pack I brought with me. Everyone looked rough, but I really wasn't sure how safe the food I brought was anymore.

Could it be worse than being trapped and fed from for months? Well, we'd see.

I broke out the water and supplies, making sure everyone got something. It helped with the trembling hands, if not the far-away staring. When I pressed a little package of cookies into Cornelius's hands, he finally really looked at me.

And blanched.

"You're not a hallucination."

"No." I paused. "Sorry?"

A flush crept up his neck. But honestly, it was so much better than gray that I couldn't even get worked up about it.

"What... how are...what were you *thinking–*"

AVA L BISHOP & AUBURN TEMPEST

"Again. Time and place. Wait, were you really going to lecture me when you thought I was a hallucination?" Figures.

The color drained back out of Cornelius' face, leaving him looking paper-frail. "You must go. Leave, now. You've no idea, Aisling. *Go*, before they find you. Before *he* finds you."

Like it had been summoned, the mountain in the distance parted with a sharp crack, its sides unfurling into monstrous wings that spread over the forest, blotting out what little light there was. The world was swallowed by shadow, but I could hear the luff like sails, enormous wings catching the breeze, carrying it toward us.

The world went dark.

And cold.

One of the Magi swallowed hard enough that I could hear the click of it.

"Too late."

CHAPTER TWENTY-THREE

*D*arkness was the first and oldest fear of mankind. We'd done our best to appease it, we'd barred our doors against it, and tried to keep it at bay with fire and lanterns and light pollution. But even in the modern world of neon and electricity, there was nothing that could get hearts pounding and palms sweating like shadows in places they shouldn't have been.

The Dark fell over us, sitting in the center of the ancient forest, and the other Magi cringed from its touch.

The voice came from everywhere and nowhere, sighing through the branches of the trees like a stiff wind. *"What do we have here?"*

The darkness pulled tighter, forcing us all to scuttle closer together. Weak flickers of Aether thrummed to life inside the exhausted, drained Magi as they attempted a defense.

The Night chuckled, a hollow, dead thing. *"Where did you think you were going, Magi? This is your home now. You belong to me."*

The wind rose to a shriek, shadows writhing at the edges of the clearing, thick and smothering. The others pressed together, and the way light flickered under their skin had me gripping their arms tight.

"Don't," I warned them sharply. "You're going to hurt yourself. Don't give him what he wants."

"*And what's this?*" The shadows wrapped around me, brushing over my skin like cobwebs. I caught sight of Cornelius' terrified face before the rest of the world vanished. "*Another Magi? New and fresh. Little thing, did you come here to free them? Did you think you were a hero?*"

I grimaced, batting away the bits of clinging dark. They stuck, as stubborn as an overly familiar shower curtain.

"No," I said bluntly. "I'm a researcher."

The voice laughed again, the sound dragging up my spine like icy fingers. Something screamed out in the darkness, high and terrified. Prey being brought down. "*What a gift you are, little one. So young. So strong.*"

It was all giving me bad first date flashbacks from undergrad. I dragged on the Aether, flaring light from my skin, trying to get some breathing room, but there was barely a flicker before it was snuffed out entirely.

"*You can't fight the Dark, little Magi. You were mine the instant you entered my realm. Your fear will feed an army of new Harrowers.*"

My face screwed up in disgust. "So, you were feeding off them? Using the Magi to make new Harrowers? I didn't think you'd want so much competition."

Shadows brushed over my face, and I tried to bat them away. I wasn't super touchy with people I knew, never mind amorphous nightmare creatures from beyond reality.

Something growled, low and liquid. A predator prowling the darkness.

"*There is no competition for me. There will be more fear. More death. My Harrowing will spread over the world and blanket it in terror, ushering in a new age. All worlds.*"

An army of Harrowers. The nightmares that hunted me,

ambushed me, crept into my nephew's room to terrorize him and feed. The ugly, bloated things that hung from the ceiling in a room where they waited to glut themselves on my friend's murder. They hunted people. Hurt people. And they wanted to use the Magi to do it.

"Yeah, no. That's not going to happen."

I reached for the Aether, hovering so close it felt like a second skin. Forget light, I went with my first magic. Flames erupted in the surrounding air, threading through my hair, blazing over my skin. Fuel plus combustion. The first people used fire to keep the night at bay.

A primeval weapon for a primeval monster.

The Dark snarled, jerking back and giving me room. It wasn't much... but enough to see the others. Bastian stood between the Magi and the threat, but there wasn't anything he could do.

The Dark had no form to destroy—it was already an absence.

There wasn't anything for entropy to bite into.

Shadows lashed through the air, rising and falling, reaching for me. One of them tried to slither over my throat, and the flames flared hotter, burning brighter. My hair was a shining thing in the corner of my eye, buffeted by a sourceless wind.

In a chemical reaction, energy was released most easily as heat or light. The point being, I could do this just about forever if I had to. Not that I wanted to. I needed to get my people home, stat, before one of their hearts gave out.

The shadows paused, but it didn't have anything to do with the fire. I felt the darkness loom, the night pulling in tight.

"*There is no fear in you,*" the wind hissed, outraged and baffled at the same time.

"Nope," I agreed brightly. I tapped my temple with one still-burning finger. "Do you know what the amygdala is? It's the part of the human brain that controls emotions, including fear. I didn't want any of you guys to feed on me, so before I came here, a very smart lady talked me through effectively nerfing my amygdala."

I grinned, remembering how confused Mom had been when I asked. "It took a forty-minute phone call and a mirror, but the result is, I am physically incapable of feeling fear right now."

The Dark pulled back. I think I confused it.

I propped my hands on my hips while the fire twined through my hair in a glorious halo of destruction. "I'm actually really hoping I can reverse it when I get home. It's causing some problems. As it turned out, my sense of self-preservation is directly tied to my fear of consequences. It's a good thing I arranged for a spotter."

With a low roar, the Dark rushed forward in a smothering wave, and buried me.

I couldn't see, but I didn't need to. I couldn't breathe, but without the instinctive panic, it was just annoying. Shadows coiled tighter, trying to snuff me out, like it had so many others before me.

I dropped all my defenses. Every shield, every protection I held in place, I let them go, and let the Aether consume me.

Light poured from every pore in my skin. The power filled me, every cell jammed to bursting with creation and potential. I burned with it, but it was a willing burn, and I couldn't be afraid, so there was a certain sense of peace to it.

The King of Night jerked back with a howl of nighttime predators hunting. The Dark tried to retreat, but I didn't let it.

I wrapped myself in shadows, pulling it closer, winding tighter. "No, no, this was what you wanted, wasn't it? A Magi to feed on? Well, come on then. Yummy, yummy, you prick. You can have all of it."

There was a frantic tone to the struggle, holes burning into shadow. After all, the dark was just the absence of light. Add light to the equation, and what was left?

Nothing.

My hair danced on a wind that didn't exist. Each strand was carved from sunlight and flame. My eyes were hot and swollen, any tears evaporated away. Breath came out of my mouth like a rush from a furnace. It was too much—way too much—for a mortal body to withstand. The deafening symphony of the Aether bore down on me, so much closer than I'd ever felt before.

Cracks formed, fissures snaking between my atoms as light forced the gaps wider and wider.

I'd made it so that I couldn't be afraid. But I was still sad. There were so many cool things I was going to miss out on. I wanted to see Conner grow up. To hang out with Percy and Stefan, to talk shop with the other Magi, and to have Christmas dinner with my family.

And Bastian...

But if it was the only way that they could be safe, then so be it.

The Harrowing was the worst thing the Aether ever spit out. Horrible, hope-sucking nightmares, whose only purpose was to feed on humanity at our weakest moments. To make us small and afraid. To make us prey.

Never again would a Magi die, their terror consuming them from the inside out. Never again would someone run from a monster through a crowd, surrounded by others but feeling entirely alone. And never again would someone listen to a child sob over the phone about a nightmare hiding under their bed, desperate to be believed.

No more.

Power layered on top of power, heat and light and possibility hammered down, like the Aether Storm had ricocheted back at me across time and space. Except this time, it wasn't my enemy, but my weapon.

Ice spread through my body, radiating out from my belly.

The Void seed was vibrating, shrieking like shattered glass as it drained away some of the power ripping through me. But it wasn't enough, it was just a seed, it couldn't keep up with the torrent.

The shadows ripped themselves away, the Dark itself trying to flee from the storm it felt growing under my skin. I twirled, wrapping myself more firmly in it, like a fly trapping a spider in its own web.

The Aether pulsed, cracks spreading.

A hand clamped down on my ankle.

I hadn't even realized I had levitated off the ground until then. I hung there, buffeted on a solar wind, just like that star going nova I'd seen trapped in the fractal in the Infinity Nexus. The one forever poised between life, death, and rebirth.

Bastian's hand tightened. His eyes were windows to the Void, a starless blackness. His face was set, almost savagely determined. I felt something fluttering in his chest, small, but strong. And the seed of entropy in my belly cracked open, sending ebony shoots through my body.

I sucked in a breath, shocked. Ice flowed into me, driving back the flames. Heat and cold, creation and destruction, life, and entropy—they raged through me... and the human body caught in between them suffered.

My mouth opened, but nothing came out. There was no room left for my voice. I couldn't even scream as I was torn apart on the inside. For an endless moment, I hung there, feeling nothing but pain, and that icy grip on my ankle.

Power flowed into nothingness, and the flames receded. Heat beat back the cold, and the spikes of ice melted out of my flesh. My whole body became a strange no man's land, power hanging in a balance instead of threatening to split me apart at the seams.

The Void pulled, and the Aether pushed.

Creation flowed through me and drained away instead of

building, and I took my first full breath in what felt like way too long.

Bastian didn't flinch, didn't cry out at all, but I knew the fires had roared through him. Between us, we reached a weird homeostasis, the Aether and the Void singing through us in an endless feedback loop.

That was a problem for future Ash, though, and I dragged my focus back to the King of Night—the Darkness might have been wounded, but it hadn't been destroyed.

Golden light swirled around me, a tame maelstrom, and I looked at the tattered wings of the Night and hesitated.

Was destroyed what I wanted? I definitely wanted the Harrowing stopped. But the Harrowing weren't just fear-eaters. They *were* fear. And if that little jaunt past reality's event horizon had taught me anything, it was that a world with no fear would be a problem.

Fear wasn't evil. It was a warning. It taught us when to keep ourselves safe, and how to recognize patterns, and encouraged us to run away from danger. It pulled us back when the brakes were off on our curiosity.

So, no. No preying on people, hurting them, *killing* them. But something else.

The little swell of nothingness in my belly rippled, pulling gently on the power running through my veins, and it gave me an idea.

The Void wasn't evil. It just was. It had a job to do, a balance to strike. Fear could be the same. It could be a tool, a teacher, instead of a hungry thing demanding to be fed. Nightmares that could show us how to fight back and overcome, and not just wake shaking and clutching a pillow to smother any cries.

The Dark thrashed, crying out in a thousand different voices as I caught it in a net of shining threads of light. The Aether sang through me, a melody that every act of creation was inherently an act of destruction.

Nothing could be made without unmaking something else.

The power swelled, fire to burn away the icy hate. Soothing blackness to drain away malice. This was creation as it was meant to be, glorious and vicious in equal measure. Matter and anti-matter. They coiled around the Harrowing, yanking as tight as a noose. She wouldn't destroy fear and darkness and nightmares, but she could soften them and ensure they weren't starving.

Something to overcome instead of being consumed by.

The power erupted. A star gone nova.

Things got a little hazy at that moment. The human body was essentially made of Spam, and it wasn't meant to handle one cosmic force, never mind two. No matter how nicely they tried to play with each other.

One moment, the King of Night's screaming filled my head like the wind blowing across a desolate plain, and the next, I was lying on my back staring up at the bare branches of some really ugly and probably dead trees.

A root was digging into my back, and I felt like I'd been hit by a garbage truck.

My head and shoulders were propped up in Bastian's lap, which was nice, because whatever it was on the ground there, I really didn't want to have to spend the next three months trying to dig it out of my hair.

"Hi," I croaked. "We've got to stop meeting like this."

His hand was cool when he cupped my face, and I had to force myself not to curl into it like a cat. My skin felt tight and too sensitive.

"Just so long as we keep meeting, Red."

I pressed my cheek against his palm and tried to put the apology I owed him into my eyes.

Someone shuffled off to the side, rudely pulling me out of what had been a very comfortable moment.

Cornelius staggered forward, his silver-handled cane long

gone. The remains of what had once been a very nice suit not far behind it. "Aisling," he said, far too calmly. "Would you mind terribly telling us all just what the *hell* is going on?"

I sighed and pouted until Bastian helped boost me into a sitting position. This was going to be fun. What was the saying? No rest for the wicked.

~

It was an uncomfortable walk back to where I left the gate to Cornelius' workroom, if 'walk' was even the right word for it, since half of it involved me willing myself through space. What was left of the Senior Council didn't seem to appreciate the Coles Notes version of events I told them. Too bad. I was tired, I was sore, and I'd literally given myself brain damage to save their sorry butts. They could wait until I slept and had breakfast if they wanted to know what happened over the last couple of months.

I kept myself between Bastian and the rest of the group, just in case anyone tried something. But they seemed just as eager to keep space from me as they were from him, which was fine.

Rude, but fine.

At long last, we made it back to the space in that river of stars where the veil hung like gauzy curtains, and it was hard not to knock them apart with an exhausted hand. Instead, I teased them apart as delicately as I could, and there, just on the other side, was the stone cavern I both loved and hated.

"Last stop, reality. All aboard." I held the way open while the battered and exhausted Senior Council started spilling through.

The joyful greetings and happy tears I could hear through the wavering veil were enough to drag a tired smile onto my face.

Right until Bastian and I took a step forward to step through, and Cornelius blocked the way.

"Come on, Aisling," he said, beckoning with a hand. He wasn't looking at me, though. His glare was all for Bastian. "Hurry, so we can close the gate."

I blinked, my exhausted, partially-fried brain struggling to catch up. "Excuse me?"

"That *thing* cannot be allowed back into our world," he spat. "It's already infected you. Don't fear, my girl. We will help you. You won't need to suffer it much longer."

I just stared. The words weren't even making any sense. He wanted Bastian to stay banished to the Akasha? After he'd come all that way, helped me, saved me, to find their ungrateful asses? What the hell?

But the worst part, the very worst part, was how Bastian— caring, protective, unshakably loyal Bastian—flicked his gaze to me... a twinge of uncertainty in his expression.

He thought I might actually leave him there.

I was burnt out, exhausted, and about nine miles past done. But I also didn't have enough gas in the tank to take on the Senior Council, no matter how roughed-up they were, and especially not with their apprentices backing them up.

So, I let my shoulders slump, like I was giving in, seeing reason, while resentment pricked at me with poison claws. And Cornelius relaxed.

I swayed toward my former mentor, not having to act really. I felt like I was a gust of wind away from toppling like a tree, and his hands came up like he was ready to catch me if I swooned. It brought me just close enough to the gate to call through.

"Hey, Percy?"

"Yeah?" she croaked back.

"Operation Sticky Bun."

Cornelius just had time to frown, his brow creasing, when Percy dove forward to grab one of the crystals anchoring the spell on the other side. With a flick of her beak, she tossed the amethyst through the portal, and miraculously, I caught it without fumbling. Her wing caught Cornelius in the face as she barreled through the collapsing hole in reality, and he took a half step back with a startled shout.

Just as the spell collapsed, the edges of the gate sweeping back together, I stiff-armed Cornelius through it, wincing as he sprawled back onto the chalk marked floor.

I heard Stefan bark, "Scatter!" and throw something on the ground as the Aether-born used whatever supernatural tricks they had to beat feet out of the ritual room.

And then the gate was closed, and it was just me, Percy, Bastian, and an ocean of starlight.

"Red," he whispered, his voice hoarse as his big hand cupped my cheek. "You didn't have to do that."

I let myself turn into the touch now that we didn't have an audience of old biddies anymore. "Of course I did."

He leaned in, our foreheads bumping together. Percy gave a disgruntled little grumble as she shifted over on my shoulder, but she didn't comment.

I watched the bob of his throat as he swallowed. "I hate the idea of you trapped here. You should have just let them leave me. You know I'd be fine."

"Trapped?" I leaned back, my brow furrowed. "We're not trapped. I can make a gate to literally anywhere from here. Possibly any*when* too, but that has some potential problems."

His mouth was hanging open just a little. I'd never seen him so stunned before. Percy cawed a laugh before turning and smugly preening her primary feathers. I couldn't resist leaning forward for a kiss from Bastian, just the barest brushing of our lips.

Something that looked very much like wonderment crept over his face like dawn breaking. "You planned for this."

"I figured someone would try something. I just wasn't sure who or what." I shrugged. "I wanted to be prepared, just in case."

237

His arms were around me then, crushing me to his chest, lifting and spinning, and I'd never heard laughter so full of joy. I wanted to catch it in my hands and hold it, but I settled for cupping his face instead.

"Hey, watch it!" Percy abandoned my shoulder, landing heavily on whatever it was masquerading as the ground. She gave a little mutter, shaking herself.

Bastian grinned up at me, looking so young and happy that I felt like my ribs were too small to contain all the feeling welling up in my chest.

"Where to then, Red? Where are we headed?"

"Oh, I don't know." I ran my fingers through his hair, playing with the strands while he shivered and leaned into every touch. "There's a great big universe to explore out there."

I tapped his shoulders, and he let me slide down his chest until I was back on my feet.

"I've just got to make one stop first."

CHAPTER TWENTY-FOUR

*T*wo months after his return from the Shadow's Reach, Cornelius Abernathy, Magi of the Council of the Seven Spheres, leaned back in the comfortable wingback chair he was seated in. He had been invited, among others, to the family home of his wayward apprentice, and felt a sizable headache coming on.

Months of memories—not his own—rolled through his mind.

And while they certainly answered some questions that had been nagging him, they brought new, more troubling questions to light.

His remaining fellow Senior Council members fanned out behind him in the living room of the comfortable home in Cambridge they'd found themselves invited to. He could feel their impatience like a drone of wasps on the back of his neck as they waited for him to tell them what he learned by accessing the little package that Aisling had left for him.

It was almost amusing how she had used the same memory spell he created to grant her his knowledge of the arcane to leave as both a set of instructions and her rather succinct notice of resignation.

She had improved the spell, too. It was wiser to anchor such a thing to an inanimate object. Less chance of decay that way. If he'd been thinking more rationally at the time, he'd have done the same. But then, she'd always been a precocious student.

Worry kept the proud smile from twitching his lips up like they wanted to.

"Can I have Trip back, please?"

Pulled out of his thoughts, Cornelius smiled at the young boy sitting across from him on the couch between his parents. The young boy was Aisling's nephew, and as he watched him, flickers of golden light ran through the boy's aura. It told him that Aisling's estimations were correct. If he made it to puberty before awakening, Cornelius would be shocked.

"Of course. Thank you," Cornelius said with as much dignity as he could muster when passing a crayon-blue stuffed triceratops back to the boy.

He immediately pulled it into his chest, wrapping both his arms around the toy while his gaze flicked from Cornelius to the other Magi with poorly hidden curiosity.

His parents and grandparents made no attempt to hide their hostility.

"Well, there you have it," Mr. O'Reily said with false joviality. "Right from the horse's mouth, so to speak. Ash is fine. There's nothing to be concerned about."

Cornelius sighed and pinched the bridge of his nose. "Mr. O'Reily, do you not understand that your daughter is missing? After vanishing into the space between worlds with a creature that is made of pure destruction? Fine is in *no* way the word I would use to describe this situation."

He'd already chased down every other possible avenue. The Aether-born of the city had gone to ground, and while he'd gotten the impression the remaining apprentices knew more than they were letting on, not one of them would breathe a word about Aisling.

Not even Mason, who seemed to take some kind of perverse pleasure in Cornelius' worry.

In desperation, he'd even reached out to the Dragon when Sean let it slip that he and Aisling had formed an odd friendship, but all he received for his troubles was a book of poetry with a passage about diverging streams marked with red and green ribbons.

Certainly, it was meant as a clever dig, but Cornelius couldn't bring himself to rise to the bait, not when Aisling was still lost.

"Nonsense," Mrs. O'Reily said with a sniff. "Bastian is a lovely boy. He came by with Ash for Christmas dinner. Very polite. And he loved the sweater we got for him."

Cornelius stared, not sure if he was hearing what he was hearing or if his wayward apprentice had finally driven him to a stroke. "She was here? She came here?"

"That's when she gave me Trip," the boy carolled, bouncing in his seat.

Conner, he reminded himself belatedly. The boy's name was Conner.

Cornelius sat forward, trying to impart his urgency when he spoke. "Where is she now?"

Mr. O'Reily lifted his mug and took an absent sip of coffee. "Oh, here and there. She comes and goes."

Corbin, never a patient man, snarled as he took a step out from behind Cornelius's chair. "Do you think this is a game? Do you have any idea what your child has done? The laws of magic she's broken?"

"You mean while she was saving all of your butts," the younger woman on the couch said as she bit into a mincemeat tart.

Lindsey, Aisling's memories supplied. Her sister.

241

Corbin glowered, and Cornelius' head shot up in alarm as he felt the first swell of the Aether moving in the room.

"We are the Council of Magi of the Seven Spheres," Corbin sneered down his nose at Aisling's parents and sister. "Do the smart thing and don't try to cross us. Things will go easier on you that way."

Mrs. O'Reily raised a scathing brow at that, and Cornelius flinched back from the movement. Aisling's memories were fresh enough in his mind that he knew what that particular expression heralded.

"Let me see if I understand," Caroline O'Reily said pleasantly. She smoothed her skirt over her legs as her lips curled into something that wasn't close to a smile. "My daughter defied the laws of magic as well as time and space, travelled between worlds, fought an ancient primordial predator that has hunted humanity since we first crawled out of the trees, and *won*, before escorting you all home. Do I have that right?"

There were some uneasy mutterings behind him, and Cornelius managed a weak nod.

He tried not to think of the shining, burning thing Aisling had transformed herself into, there in the heart of Night's domain. He still wasn't entirely clear about how she kept herself from burning up, burning out. She *should* have.

Thank heavens she didn't.

The smile got a hair sharper as Caroline continued. "And she did all of that on your behalf. A group of people she barely knew, and a man who mentored her for a few short weeks. Tell me, ladies, gentlemen. If Aisling would do all of that to protect you, a group of virtual strangers, just what do you think she'd be willing to do to protect her *family*?"

As if on cue, the Aether rippled, and for an instant Cornelius and the others could see that every inch of the walls, the floors, and the ceiling were covered in what looked like equations. All of them pulsed with a dangerous light. Aisling's family too.

They were warded more thoroughly than anything he'd ever seen in all his years.

Cornelius blanched. Behind him, he felt Corbin recoil.

"Perhaps we've been a little hasty," someone muttered.

"I'm certain the girl has it handled," someone else chimed in.

One by one, the others slipped away, and Cornelius could only feel relieved when they were gone. At least without an audience, he had the chance for one last plea.

"Please." He met all their eyes, tried to hold them. "I only wish to speak with her."

There were things he needed to know. Apologies that had to be made.

Caroline O'Reily must have heard some of the desperation in his voice because her face softened. "She's still around. And I have a feeling that if you ever need her, she'll find *you*."

He must have been getting fanciful in his old age, because the thinly-veiled threat actually brought him some comfort.

He bowed his head, gathered his new cane, and saw himself out.

Endnote

Thank you for reading Arcane Felonies, book 3 in the Boston Magi Chronicles.

While the story is fresh in your mind, click HERE and tell other readers what you thought.

A star rating and/or even one sentence can mean so much to readers who are deciding whether or not to try out a book or new author.

And if you loved it, continue with book 4, Veiled Threats. This series was planned to end as a trilogy, but your reviews and comments encouraged us to continue to follow Aisling in the Boston Magi Chronicles.

Bonus content: If you're curious to see how Bastian's Christmas in the O'Reily household went, we have a fun novella with that story for you. It's for sale on Amazon, but it's FREE for fans who follow the Dauntless Publishing newsletter. If you want to grab a copy and also opt in for new release news, click HERE.

ABOUT THE AUTHOR - AVA L. BISHOP

Author Notes

Ava L. Bishop

And there you have it, book three of the Boston Magi Chronicles. I've been absolutely blown away by the response to my little STEM Magi who could, and I'm so grateful to everyone for reading and joining me in my slice of weird Boston. It's been a really fun ride, with magic, and sass, and the occasional existential crisis over the proper use of a semi colon.

I'm currently sitting among empty coffee cups, and cracker boxes, with my ever-patient dog politely suggesting that it's walkies time, but I'm looking forward to sharing all the trouble Ash and the gang are getting into next. Thank you for everyone who took a chance picking up book one and followed all the way so far.

I hope you're having as much fun as I am.

Until then,

Ava

ABOUT THE AUTHOR - AUBURN TEMPEST

Auburn Tempest

What fun! Being the author who takes the second pass on this series, I have the privilege of learning what's happening in the Boston Chronicles as much as a reader as a contributing author. I was wondering how Ash would pull it off along with the rest of you, and I wasn't disappointed.

Well done, Ava!

And to the readers and fans, I'm excited to tell you, I talked Ava into giving us another trilogy. Yay! I wasn't ready to say goodbye to these characters and since several of you mentioned that in the reviews—I knew I wasn't the only one.

The first three are Aisling coming to terms with her new world order, and the next three will be about what she can do with that knowledge. I'm super excited to find out what she and Bastian will encounter next.

Looking forward to more.

Auburn Tempest

ALSO BY AUBURN TEMPEST

Find Auburn Tempest (JL Madore)

Facebook, Twitter, Instagram

Web page – www.auburntempest.com

Email – auburntempestwrites@gmail.com

Newsletter

Boston Magi Chronicles

Book 1 - Supernatural Disasters

Book 2 - Occult Misdemeanors

Book 3 - Arcane Felonies

Book 4 - Veiled Threats

Christmas Novella (or claim for FREE with a Newsletter signup)

Chronicles of an Urban Druid (15 book series)

Case Files of an Urban Druid (7 book series)

Chronicles of an Urban Elemental (6 book series)

Made in United States
North Haven, CT
22 July 2024

55274335R00157